BLACK HORN

A Creasy Novel

BLACK HORN

A. J. Quinnell

CHAPMANS

Copyright © 1994 A. J. Quinnell

All rights reserved

The right of A. J. Quinnell to be identified
as the author of this work has been asserted by him
in accordance with the Copyright, Designs
and Patents Act 1988.

First published in Great Britain in 1994 by
Chapmans Publishers
An imprint of Orion Books Ltd
Orion House, 5 Upper St Martin's Lane,
London WC2H 9EA

A CIP catalogue record for this book is avaiable
from the British Library

ISBN 1 85592 815 9

Typeset By Deltatype Ltd, Ellesmere Port, S. Wirral
Printed in Great Britain by Clays Ltd, St Ives plc

To Elsebeth

Author's Note

My thanks to Claire Potter and Maxie MacDonald
for their invaluable help with this book.

I would like to wish a long and well deserved
retirement to Marjory Chapman. Her advice
and encouragement will be missed by
this writer; and many others.

PROLOGUE

The hunter had no interest in the animals. He rested on his haunches within a small outcrop of rocks about five hundred metres from the Zambezi River. To his left, a herd of impala moved down to drink before sunset, the young bounding and leaping in circles around their elders. To his right, a pair of zebra moved in the same direction and, beyond them, a single male kudu, statuesque beneath his spiraling horns.

The hunter's eyes were fixed on the large khaki tent nestling in the shade of a giant baobab tree. The hunter glanced again to his right at the red sinking sun, and offered up a hope that he would not have to wait another night. The hunter was not a man to pray. He acknowledged no God.

The rifle was propped against the rock beside him. It was an old Enfield Envoy L4A1, much loved by World War Two snipers. It had the original number 32 telescopic sight. The hunter had grown up with it.

He stiffened as he saw a movement at the entrance of the tent. A big white man emerged. He had a shock of red hair. He wore only green shorts. He moved to the curling smoke of the fire and kicked more logs on to it.

The hunter reached for his rifle. Through the scope he could clearly identify the man's face from the photograph in his back pocket. Identification was positive, even though the red hair had been covered by a hat.

The hunter positioned himself. He sat back against a rock and rested his elbows on his knees, forming a natural tripod. Abruptly he stiffened again to the faint sound of a voice. He took his eye away from the scope. A woman had emerged from the tent. She was also wearing green shorts and nothing else. The hunter put his eye against the scope and studied her. She had long blonde hair, accented by a deeply tanned face, a narrow waist below high young breasts. She was smiling at the man.

The hunter cursed quietly. He had been told that the man would be alone. He glanced again at the lowering sun. There was no time to trek to his hidden Land-rover and radio for instructions.

The hunter took his decision.

The man was squatting by the fire, prodding life into it with a stick. The woman stood beside him, watching the herd of impala with a gentle smile on her face. The hunter shot her first, between the breasts. The second shot followed immediately. The man had half-risen. The bullet took him in the pit of his stomach. The woman lay still. The man was rolling around, clutching his belly. The hunter shot him again through the back. He did not shoot the woman again. The hunter was not a man to waste a bullet.

She drove fast, her black hair blowing in the wind. It was as black as the MG roadster which she loved as much as anything else in her life, even though it was almost as old as she was. Like her, it had been well maintained. At twenty-eight years old, her body was kept svelte by a good diet and plenty of aerobics. Kwok Ling Fong, known to her friends as Lucy, was eager to get home. The flight from Tokyo had been delayed and she did not want to be too late for her father's birthday party. Not a big party, just her parents and brother. Like most Chinese families, they were close and preferred to celebrate privately.

She sped through the Kowloon-Hong Kong tunnel, only slightly over the speed limit, and then wound up the steep roads of the Peak. She was looking forward to having a few days off. After three years, she still enjoyed being an air hostess and liked to travel, but lately the days off had seemed more welcome.

She parked next to her father's Honda, grabbed her overnight bag and ran into the house.

She could smell smoke, and as she ran past her father's study, she saw it; curling out from under the door. She ran on, shouting her father's name.

They were in the sitting room. They were hanging in a row by their necks from a ceiling beam. They were naked, their faces contorted in death. Blood dripped from her father's chest. Before she passed out, Lucy Kwok Ling Fong subconsciously noted that a symbol had been carved on it: 14K.

BOOK ONE

CHAPTER 1

She was old. Her once-beautiful face radiated pain and grief. Her talon-like fingers gripped the arms of the wheelchair as she gazed up across the desk at Senator James S. Grainger. They were in the study of his Denver home.

He gazed back at her and said quietly, 'I know how you feel, Gloria. It's been five years since Harriet's death, but I know what you're feeling.'

She nodded her grey, bird-like face vigorously.

'Sure you do Jim. And you damned well did something about it . . . if the rumours are true.'

He inclined his head to acknowledge a point, and then tapped the file in front of him and said softly and persuasively, 'Yes, I had my revenge . . . but I knew where to look.' He tapped the file again. 'But Carole's case is a dead-end. I used all my influence with State. I even spoke personally to our Ambassador in Harare. He's a good guy . . . a career officer. We give a lot of aid to Zimbabwe and he was able to get co-operation from the very top, including Mugabe himself. As you know, their police drew a complete blank. There was no apparent motive. No robbery or rape. Carole and her friend had been camped at that site by the Zambezi for three days, so they didn't just stumble across a bunch of poachers. Unfortunately, there was a rain storm that night and all tracks were washed away. As you know, Gloria, since the War of Independence tens of thousands of guns have landed up in that country . . . I'm afraid it really is a dead-end. I can't express how bad I feel. I watched Carole grow up. She was a fine girl . . . a credit to you.' Jim Grainger was a hard man, successful in both business and politics. His grey eyes softened as he looked at the old woman. 'You've had some hard knocks, Gloria. Harry, just a couple of years ago, and now your only child.'

Her fingers gripped the wheelchair more tightly. She spoke harshly. 'I don't give up, Jim. I'm sixty years old and I never give up on anything. If I wasn't stuck in this goddamned chair with this useless body I'd be down there myself, looking for the bastard or bastards that did it.'

The Senator shrugged sympathetically but said nothing.

The woman drew a breath and said, 'As you know, Harry left me more than well-off . . . Not that all those millions do me any good, while I'm stuck in this goddamned wheelchair.'

Grainger shrugged and said, 'Gloria, I'm helping you for two reasons. First, because it's my duty to do so, as the senior Senator for Colorado . . . and you are one of my constituents. Second, because although Harry and I often head-butted each other over some business deals, I respected him and counted him as a friend . . . I count my friends on the fingers of one hand.'

She gave him a thin smile.

'I guess I'm not one of those fingers, Jim.'

He nodded and said, 'You've always been a straight talker, Gloria, and so have I. I'd be less than honest if I said that we've got on over the years. You can be damned abrasive – and don't pretend that you ever voted for me at any election in these past twenty years.'

She shook her head.

'I sure didn't, and I won't in future. I think you're too far to the left for a republican, and always have been.'

He shrugged.

'I am what I am, Gloria, and thank God there are enough voters out there who do believe in me.' He waved a hand as though to dismiss the subject. 'Anyway, if Harry were alive, I know that he would leave no stone unturned or no dollar unspent to find Carole's killer or killers, and I guess you will do the same.'

'You're right, Jim. When our Ambassador in Harare came up with a dead-end, I decided to hire some people to go out there and find out who killed my girl.'

Grainger leaned forward and asked, 'What kind of people?'

She lifted her right hand and coughed into it. It was a sound like thick paper being torn. She looked up at him and said, almost defiantly, 'Tough people, Jim. Harry's brother-in-law was a Green Beret in Vietnam. He knows some guys.'

The Senator sighed. 'Mercenaries, I guess?'

She shrugged.

'I guess so . . . For sure they don't come cheap.'

He sighed again and his voice took on an edge of authority. 'Listen to me, Gloria – and listen good because I know about these things. It cost me a lot of money to learn the hard way. First of all, American mercenaries know very little about Africa, especially that part of Africa. You'll be wasting your money.'

Very coldly, the old woman answered, 'So I do nothing? Is that your advice?'

Her eyes narrowed as she watched his face. He was slowly shaking his head. He was deep in thought. She waited impatiently. Then she saw him nodding and, as though to himself, he said, 'There is a man. He is American. He is a mercenary.'

'He knows Africa?' she asked.

He continued nodding. 'Oh, yes. He knows Africa like you know your backyard.'

'His name?'

A single word rolled pleasantly from the Senator's lips: 'Creasy.'

They went out to the garden and moved slowly around the large, oval pool, the Senator pushing the wheelchair. A black Doberman bitch ambled alongside.

Grainger quietly explained. 'I first met Creasy in this house. It was a couple of months after Harriet had been killed in Pan Am 103 over Lockerbie. I came home late one night from a government dinner. I was a bit drunk. I found this big guy dressed in black sitting at the bar, drinking my best vodka.'

The old woman twisted her head to look up at him. She asked, 'How did he get past the dog and the alarms and your man-servant?'

Grainger chuckled quietly. 'He put a tranquillising dart into Jess here and then another one into my man-servant. Before he left, he advised me on how to make my alarm system more efficient.'

'What did he want?'

The Senator took some paces in silence and then answered. 'His

wife and daughter had also been on Pan Am 103. He wanted
vengeance. He came to me for half the money necessary and for
my contacts with the FBI and the government departments. Like
you, I had already decided to hire some mercenaries . . . I had
already paid a lot of seed money to one guy in particular. Creasy
fingered him for a con man and got most of my money back . . .
and later on killed the guy.'

'Tell me more,' she said with an urgency in her voice.

Grainger said, 'Well, the first thing I did was check with the FBI.
As you know, I sit on the relevant House Committee, and the
Director tends to kiss my ass. They had a file on Creasy. He joined
the Marines at seventeen and was kicked out two years later for
striking a senior officer. He then went to Europe and joined the
French Foreign Legion and became a paratrooper. He fought and
was captured in Vietnam and had a damn bad time. He survived to
go and fight in the Algerian War of Independence. After that, his unit
was disbanded and he was kicked out. Together with a close friend,
he became a mercenary, first in Africa, then the Middle East, then
Asia. He ended his mercenary career in what was then Rhodesia and
is now Zimbabwe. Like I said, he knows that country well.'

He stopped abruptly as she flicked on the hand-brake to the
wheelchair. Opposite them was a wooden bench. The Doberman
flopped down alongside it. She gestured at the bench and said,
'Please, Jim . . . I want to look at you while you talk.'

He moved around the chair and sat down a few feet away from
her.

'Do you want a drink?' he asked. 'Something cool . . . or a
scotch?'

Her smile was more of a grimace.

'I save the scotch until late evening . . . then I drink at least half a
bottle. It helps the pain and it helps me to sleep. What did Creasy
do after Rhodesia became Zimbabwe?'

'I don't know the whole story, but apparently he drank a lot,
and kind of wandered around aimlessly. Then he got a job in Italy
as a bodyguard to the daughter of an industrialist. Something
went badly wrong and he ended up having a full-scale war with a
Mafia family. After that he married, settled down with his wife
and had a daughter . . . until they were both killed over
Lockerbie.' The Senator's face had turned very sombre. He was
looking down at the grass between his knees. Slowly he raised his

head and looked at the old woman and went on, 'Gloria, I understand you and how you feel even though Harriet and I had no children. Because when Harriet died, I had nothing left at all. But Creasy came along and satisfied my vengeance and somehow after that I felt better.'

She was abruptly all business. 'He works alone?'

He shook his head.

'Creasy is now in his early fifties and as fit as any man could be at that age. But with the Lockerbie thing, he adopted a young orphan boy called Michael and trained him in his own image. They act as a team. Creasy can also call on any number of weird and wonderful guys from his past . . . I've met some of them. . . . They saved my life. Believe me, they're the best.'

Gloria was a tough and shrewd old woman who would never buy even an orange without examining it very carefully. 'What has he done since?' she asked.

'I don't know the details,' Grainger answered. 'But some years ago, he and Michael wiped out a white slave ring in Europe. As a result, Creasy ended up with a sort of adopted daughter. She's seventeen now.'

The old woman leaned forward and said, 'How come?'

The Senator shrugged.

'It seems that Creasy and Michael rescued her from the slave ring when she was only thirteen. She had run away from home after being sexually and mentally abused by her stepfather. The white slavers had forced her on to heroin. While Creasy went after them, Michael took her away and helped her go cold turkey. When the whole thing was over, Creasy decided there was no way he could send her back to where she came from. Don't ask me how, but he arranged adoption papers.'

'Does she work with him and Michael?'

'No. At first, she wanted to. She wanted Creasy to train her as he had trained Michael, but a couple of years later, she had a kind of delayed reaction trauma. When she came out of it, she decided she wanted nothing to do with weapons or violence. I went to visit with them last summer, by which time her ambition was to become a doctor. She's very bright and, because of her experiences, much older than her years. I've arranged to get her into college here in Denver, and she'll stay with me during her studies . . . In fact, she's due to arrive next week.'

The old woman was nodding thoughtfully.

Grainger said, 'She'll be company for me, and bring a bit of youthful spirit into this house.'

It was as though Gloria Manners had not heard the words. She was deep in thought. She lifted her head and asked, 'Where does this man Creasy live?'

'He lives on an island in the Mediterranean . . . in a house on a hill.'

'How do you contact him?'

'By phone. If you like, I'll phone him tonight.'

Very slowly, she nodded and said, 'Please do that, Jim.'

CHAPTER 2

Tommy Mo Lau Wong reached forward and delicately picked up a strip of raw beef. He dropped it into the simmering water that formed a moat around the copper stove. Seconds later, his four lieutenants followed suit.

They were sitting in a private room of a small, exclusive restaurant in the Tsimshatsui district of Hong Kong. The restaurant specialised in Mongolian hot-pot, which meant cooking a variety of raw meats in boiling water, eating them, and then drinking the resultant soup.

Tommy Mo had the face of a cherub and the eyes of a great white shark. He always spoke in a sibilant whisper, but his lieutenants always heard him, even from a distance. He started laughing to himself. It began as a quiet chuckle and ended in a spate of coughing. The others waited patiently. He looked up, his shark's eyes glittering with mirth.

'Can you believe that fool, Kwok Ling?' He sneered as he pronounced the name. 'Thought himself the best doctor in Hong Kong or the whole of China. Just because he was trained in Europe and America, he took an arrogance above himself.' He leaned forward, as though imparting a great conspiracy. The others also dutifully leaned forward. 'He sent me papers with a trusted messenger. Scientific medical papers to show that rhino horn contains a cancer-causing agent.' He giggled again and the others giggled with him. 'Imagine,' he said, 'the good doctor explained that any old man purchasing rhino horn in order to revitalise his sex life was condemning himself to die of cancer. He sent this to me, perhaps in the hope that I would stop selling it. That I might feel guilty about a bunch of sex-starved old men dying of cancer ... sex-starved old men who would pay a thousand times more for my powder than they would pay for gold ... The fool sent his message to me ... the head of 14K.'

They all laughed.

CHAPTER 3

Father Manuel Zerafa glanced at the girl at his left. She was in her mid-teens, but already very much a woman. Long straight sun-bleached hair, a golden face with high cheekbones, a straight nose and a wide full mouth. She glanced back at him demurely. Had she winked? Or was he mistaken? No, he was sure she had winked, just in that split second that he had first glanced at her. She had winked at Michael, sitting opposite her. That wink meant she held the ace of trumps and she was signalling such to her partner. The priest looked across the table at Creasy who was his partner.

'She has the ace,' he said.

'Maybe,' Creasy answered thoughtfully. 'But she could be bluffing.' Almost imperceptibly, the big scarred man brushed at the left side of his chest, as if to scare away a fly. The priest picked up the signal. Creasy was telling him that he held the queen of trumps.

They were playing a game of cards unique to the island of Gozo. It was called bixla and was much loved by the fishermen and farmers, who would play it for hours on end in the local bars during winter. The essence was to cheat by secretly signalling your partner what cards you held. With people who had played so many hours together and who watched each other like hawks, these signals became bluffs, double-bluffs and even triple-bluffs. The game was never played for money but with great humour and the slamming down of a card when a particular piece of chicanery had worked well.

The priest looked at Michael, who gazed back innocently. A man in his twenties. Jet-black hair and sharp-featured. Tall and as slim to be almost thin, but with a frame like steel wire.

'Maybe Michael has it,' the priest said to Creasy.

Michael laughed and showed two of his three cards to the priest. One was the jack of spades and the other the four of diamonds. His third card was laid flat on the table as if taunting the priest.

Gruffly, Creasy said, 'It's a sure bet that Juliet has it. Play your king.'

The priest played the king. Juliet dropped a nothing card. Creasy cursed and discarded his queen and Michael stood up and slammed down the ace with a cry of triumph.

The priest pushed back his chair saying, 'Liars! A young pair of liars.' He pointed a stern finger at Michael and said, 'Get a cool bottle of the white wine from the case I gave you for your birthday and bring it out to the patio with two glasses.'

Michael said, 'Father, you gave me twelve bottles for my birthday four months ago. There are four left. Of the eight that have been drunk, you've had at least six.'

'Sounds right to me,' said the priest, and walked out on the patio.

Creasy looked after him through deep-set, heavy-lidded eyes. Eyes without emotion . . . but his ravaged face and body could not easily conceal the scars of anger and revenge. He rose and followed the priest, his menacing six-foot frame seeming to shadow him. He had a curious walk, the outsides of his feet making contact with the ground first.

The old stone farmhouse stood on the highest part of Gozo, looking out over the island and across the sea to the small island of Comino and, beyond that, the large island of Malta. It was a view the priest never tired of. They sat down on canvas chairs beside the swimming-pool.

Father Zerafa chuckled and remarked, 'There is a saying on the island: "Lead your life as you would play bixla, and the fruit will fall into your hands".' He gestured at the beautiful house and the view. 'But I guess the fruit has already fallen into your hands.'

Creasy said, 'Father, I disagree with the saying. To play bixla well, you have to cheat. To lead a good life, you have to be honest. To cheat at cards when it is expected and when there is no wager of any kind is just fine. But from what I've known and seen, if you cheat in life, it's not fruit that falls into your hands but a rock on your head.'

The priest sighed and said, 'You should have been a priest . . . I shall use it for my sermon on Sunday.'

Michael came out carrying a tray with the wine in an ice-bucket and two glasses. He poured the wine ceremoniously and then left them. They drank for a while in silence; two good and old friends who did not require the bond of light conversation.

Finally, the priest remarked, 'These past few weeks I see an edge of boredom in your eyes.'

'You see too much, Father. But it's true, I get restless. But since Juliet's been going off to the clinic and the hospital and learning all that first aid and stuff, there's not been much to do. Next week, she's off to the States and to college. Michael and I are thinking of taking a trip to the Far East, to look up some of my old friends. We might even go into China, now that it's opened up.' He glanced at the priest and said, 'You know that in my life I have travelled so much, but when you travel with young people and show them the world, you see it again through fresh eyes. I guess we're ready to go.'

'When?' the priest asked.

'Oh, in a couple of weeks. We'll stop off in Brussels first and see Blondie and Maxie and a few others, and then head East from there.'

They heard the phone ringing from inside the kitchen and Michael answering it. After a while, Michael came to the kitchen door and called out, 'It's for you, Creasy . . . Jim Grainger from Denver.'

Creasy grunted in surprise and pushed himself on to his feet.

He returned to his chair and the wine ten minutes later, his face thoughtful.

'A change of plan,' he said to the priest. 'We leave tomorrow and we go West not East.' He turned to Juliet, who was standing at the open door and said, 'Michael and I are travelling to Denver with you tomorrow.'

CHAPTER 4

Chinese funerals can be very elaborate affairs. Professional wailing women dressed in white mourning robes; the louder they can wail, the more they are paid. Houses, furniture, cars and money are made out of brightly coloured paper and then burned at the temple, so that they pass on to the other world with the deceased.

Lucy Kwok Ling Fong did none of this. She simply had her father, mother and brother cremated. She put the ashes into a single urn and drove with them to an old building in Causeway Bay, where she paid several thousand dollars to have the urn placed on a shelf, together with thousands of others.

As she left the building, a man approached her, a Caucasian. He had short blond hair, a red, round, perspiring face, and was dressed in a light blue safari suit. He introduced himself as Chief Inspector Colin Chapman. She recognised the name. He was the head of the Anti-Triad Department of the Royal Hong Kong Police Force. He had been away on leave at the time her family had been murdered.

'I wonder if we could have a talk, Miss Kwok?' He had a broad Yorkshire accent, which somehow irritated her.

'I think I've told everything I know to your assistant, Inspector Lau.'

'Yes, you've been very co-operative, but I would appreciate just a few minutes of your time.' He gestured across the road at a tea house. She sighed and glanced at her watch.

'Just a few minutes then,' she said reluctantly.

She ordered jasmine tea and he had a San Miguel beer.

'I must first offer my condolences,' he said. 'It was a terrible tragedy for you.'

She took a sip of tea and looked at him. It was noisy in the tea shop. She glanced around the large room. Chapman was the only foreigner in the room and probably within a square mile. She felt her resentment rising and let it come out.

'I find it very strange, Chief Inspector, that an Englishman should be the head of such a sensitive department. It would be rather like sending a German to Sicily to head the Anti-Mafia department there. Surely, it would be impossible for a foreigner to understand the minds of these people.' She gestured around the room. 'Even of these people here. Oh, I'm sure that you passed your Cantonese language examinations and speak it well enough to impress the bar-girls in Wanchai. How old are you, by the way?'

He appeared to take no offence. She noticed that his eyes were very dark brown.

'I'll be thirty-five next week,' he said, pulling a ball-pen from the breast pocket of his safari jacket. He reached for a napkin and pulled it towards him, and very quickly drew on it with the pen. She watched in puzzlement. He put the ball-pen back in his pocket, turned the napkin and pushed it across the table. She looked down at it. After five seconds, her eyes narrowed in deep concentration. Ten seconds later, she felt her skin prickling. She was looking at six Chinese characters drawn by an expert calligrapher. Her skin had prickled because she could not interpret the characters. Slowly she looked up at him. His brown eyes gazed back.

To read a Chinese newspaper requires the knowledge of approximately seven hundred and fifty characters. A university graduate would be satisfied to know three thousand characters. Lucy Kwok Ling Fong was a graduate of the Hong Kong University and was proud of her knowledge of over four thousand characters. She could not read the six characters in front of her.

'What do they mean?' she asked.

'In which dialect?' he replied in his Yorkshire accent.

She smiled slowly and answered, 'Cantonese.'

In flawless Cantonese he told her: ' "Not every stranger is completely stupid".'

Her smile widened and she asked in the same dialect, 'Is that Confucius?'

He shook his head.

'That's Colin Chapman.' He switched to Shanghainese, which again was flawless. 'Or would you prefer to talk in your mother dialect?'

She lifted her head and laughed, and said in Mandarin, 'Very clever, Chief Inspector, but surely you agree that somebody can be stupid in many languages. After all . . . a parrot is just a parrot.'

For the first time, he smiled. He took a sip of beer and said in English, 'That's very true, Miss Kwok, and I don't blame you for having doubts about a *gweilo*'s capability to understand a Triad's mind, but I've had more than ten years' experience. The subject fascinates me and, without any false modesty, I would rate myself as one of the top three experts in the world.'

'Who are the other two?'

'My assistant Inspector Lau, who interviewed you extensively, and a Professor Cheung Lam To at Taipei University.'

She was looking down again at the napkin. She tapped it with a long red fingernail.

'How many?' she asked quietly.

'About eighty thousand,' he answered. 'But of course, one never stops learning.'

She smiled again and said, 'May I borrow your pen?'

He passed it over. She wrote something along the bottom of the napkin and pushed it across. He looked down and read: 'Dis girl vellee solly. She will talk to you.'

He smiled again and said, 'Perhaps we can do it more privately in my office, this afternoon. I need at least two hours of your time.'

'You have it, Chief Inspector.'

CHAPTER 5

The Doberman greeted him like an old friend, despite the fact that some years earlier Creasy had put her into an undignified sleep with an anaesthetic dart. She wagged her stumpy tail and licked his hand.

Senator Grainger gave a firm handshake to Creasy and to Michael, then he kissed Juliet warmly on both cheeks and said, 'Welcome. I hope you'll be happy here.'

She looked around the opulent hallway of the mansion and then at the plump Mexican maid, waiting to take her suitcase.

'I'm sure I'll be happy,' she said. 'It's very kind of you to take me in.'

Five minutes later, they were seated next to the pool with long cold drinks in their hands. The Senator glanced at his watch.

'Your flight was a bit delayed,' he said, 'and Gloria will be here quite soon, so I'll brief you right away.' He took a sip of his drink, absent-mindedly patted the Doberman, and let his mind go back over the years.

'Gloria Manners came from a poor background. Southern white farmers whose farm was too small and the family too big. She got a job as a waitress in a good restaurant here in Denver. That's where she met Harry, who was a regular there. He came from a good property-owning Colorado family, which objected strongly to him marrying someone as low down the totem pole as Gloria. He went ahead anyway, and his Pa cut him off without a cent. Starting with nothing, Harry went right on to build a huge fortune in real estate and oil rights speculation.'

'Sounds like quite a guy,' Creasy commented.

21

Grainger nodded.

'He was a hell of a guy. We had big battles on some real estate deals. He was tough but he was honest. Anyway, he was killed in a car crash about three years ago. Gloria was crippled in that same accident. She's paralysed from the waist down and spends her life in a wheelchair.'

'What sort of woman is she?' Creasy asked.

The Senator took another sip of his drink and answered, 'I never got on well with her. To be honest, I always thought she was a bit of a bitch who got lucky. Since the loss of her husband and her paralysis, she's got worse. She has a mean streak in her . . . but she loved Harry . . . and he loved her . . . so me and most of our friends put up with her, I guess, originally, for the sake of Harry, and now for his memory.'

'Age?' Creasy asked.

'Early sixties, but looks a lot older.'

'Money?'

The Senator thought for a moment and then answered, 'At least a hundred million dollars. She worked with Harry in his business, and I can tell you that she's shrewd and tough. They only had the one child, Carole, who was a fine young woman. Not at all like her mother, although strangely, they got on very well together. Carole's body was flown back for burial in Denver. I went to the funeral. Gloria's face showed no expression. She just sat there in her wheelchair, as though she was carved from stone, but I guess she was hurting bad inside. She's determined to find the people who killed her daughter.'

Michael joined the conversation. 'Jim, if you dislike this woman, why are you helping her?'

Grainger glanced briefly at him and then looked back at Creasy.

'Two reasons. Firstly, because Harry Manners was a friend of mine and Carole was his daughter as well; secondly, because I happen to be the Senior Senator for Colorado and Gloria is one of my constituents. It's my duty to help her.'

Creasy had the open file in front of him. It was all too brief. He flicked through the few pages while everyone looked on silently, then he said to Grainger, 'I have some strong contacts in Zimbabwe. Even now, all these years after independence, and even though I spent some years fighting the present government as a mercenary.' He studied Grainger and then asked, 'What will the deal be, Jim?'

'I guess, any deal you want,' Grainger answered. 'With her wealth and her desire for justice, she'll do anything to find out who killed her daughter.'

As he finished speaking, they heard the chimes of the doorbell. The Doberman growled softly in her throat. Two minutes later, Gloria Manners was being wheeled across the patio by a middle-aged nurse in a starched white uniform. Creasy noted that Mrs Manners' face was etched with many furrows and lines, distorting what had once been a face of immense beauty. Her grey hair and thin face also depicted her tragedy. Despite the heat of this early summer day, she wore a heavy black crocheted blanket around her now useless legs.

Her eyes settled immediately on Creasy and she studied his face in silence. Creasy gazed back at her, looking directly into her bitter blue eyes. She glanced at Michael and Juliet and finally turned to Grainger and said, 'At least he looks the part.' She lifted her head and said to the nurse. 'Run along, Ruby, and come back in exactly half an hour.'

The nurse turned and went back inside the house.

Grainger leaned forward and asked, 'Would you like a cool drink, Gloria?'

She shook her head impatiently. 'Thank you, no.' She was looking again at Creasy. She said in her Southern drawl. 'I understand you're from Alabama?'

'A long ways back, ma'am.'

'Can you help me?' she asked.

'I can try.'

'What will it cost?'

Grainger sighed and started to say something. Creasy held up his hand.

'I have no idea,' Creasy answered. 'It will cost you about fifty thousand Swiss francs as expenses for myself and Michael to go down to Zimbabwe and look around. If, after a couple of weeks, I think there's no chance, I'll tell you that and we'll go on home.'

She moved her gaze to Grainger.

'A few days ago, I talked to a couple of guys that Harry's brother-in-law sent me. They asked for three hundred thousand dollars as an upfront retainer . . . your guy comes cheap.'

The Senator smiled slightly.

Creasy said, 'Ma'am, I don't take money for nothing.' He

tapped the folder in front of him. 'The Zimbabwe police came up with a dead-end and they had a lot of pressure from the American Ambassador down there. I guess there's only a slim chance of finding anything out.'

'And if you do?' she asked.

'Then I'll start charging. I might have to bring some other guys into it. I might have to pay some folding money to get information.'

Now the Senator interjected. 'I have personal proof of Creasy's honesty, Gloria.'

Creasy was still looking at the woman. He went on, 'If I find out who did it, without doubt, I'll charge you half a million Swiss francs.'

'Still cheap,' she said. 'What if you find out who did it and they have political or other kinds of protection? Understand, Mr Creasy, I want justice.' She spoke the last words quietly but with great intensity.

He leaned forward and also spoke quietly and again tapped the file. 'Ma'am, my intuition is that whoever killed your daughter, did so because she happened to be with that guy Cliff Coppen. I guess he was their target and, for them, her death was incidental.'

'In a way, that makes it worse.'

'I agree. If I find them and they have such protection that they cannot be brought to trial, I'll kill them myself. That will cost you a further million francs.'

There was a silence around the pool and around the garden. For the first time, her ravaged face showed slight animation. She glanced down at the gold watch on her bony wrist, and then said to Grainger, 'Jim, if you're serving lunch, I'd like to stay.'

They had cold meats and salad, together with an ice-cold bottle of Frascati, served to them at the pool by the Mexican maid. Creasy told Mrs Manners that he would need a full personal history of Carole and plenty of photographs. She assured him that he would have everything he needed later that afternoon, and asked when he would leave for Africa.

'Tomorrow,' he answered. 'Via Brussels, where I have to confer with a friend.'

The old woman nodded her head and said, 'The sooner the better. I wish I could go with you.'

For the first time, Juliet joined the conversation. 'Why don't you?'

The woman looked at her and, with her fist, hammered the arm-rest of her wheelchair. 'Isn't that obvious?'

Juliet shook her head.

'No, it's not. You got from your house to this house. From what I know and have seen, you're paralysed only from the waist down.'

'Only!' the woman snapped.

'Sure,' Juliet answered. 'You can use your arms and your brain, and the wheelchair looks like the top of the range model to me. It will work as well in Zimbabwe as it does in Colorado.'

Grainger saw the anger building up in the older woman's eyes and said quietly, 'Juliet, perhaps you don't undestand . . . Maybe you will when you are a little older.' Abruptly he saw the anger growing in the girl's eyes.

'Mr Grainger, I don't have to be one day older to know about suffering. You know my history.'

Total silence, and then Juliet turned to the woman again.

'Mrs Manners, we learned earlier that you have a fortune of over one hundred million dollars. Creasy could have ripped you down for a couple of million at least. You have enough money to take your nurse along and even hire a back-up, and to travel first-class and have your wheelchair shipped along with you. I'm told they have good hotels in Harare.' She paused, and then said quietly, 'I don't know how it feels to rear an only daughter and then have her shot for no apparent reason, but I do know that if it was me and I had a hundred million dollars, I wouldn't just hire a top pair of mercenaries . . . I would want to be close to the scene.'

The old woman was silent.

Juliet glanced at Creasy and caught the look in his eyes and immediately shut her mouth and kept it shut.

'It's not a good idea,' he said, looking at the woman. 'Juliet is forgetting some things. Even flying first-class is going to be inconvenient for you. We go from here to Brussels and spend one or two nights there. From Brussels, we'll probably have to fly to London to connect with a flight to Harare, and that flight will take at least ten hours. After one or two days in Harare, we'll have to go on to Bulawayo and that flight won't offer first-class service. In total, we'll be in the air for about twenty-four hours, plus the usual waiting about in airports. That kind of travelling is very tiring, even for a very fit person. With modern communications, we can stay close in touch with you, right here in Denver.'

Gloria Manners was looking at the table in front of her. She glanced at Creasy and then at Juliet and said, 'I think you're right, young lady.' She turned to look at Creasy and said, 'I understand your argument, and of course there's something else behind it as well . . . You don't savour the prospect of having a bad-tempered old woman tagging along . . . especially one that's paying the bills.'

Creasy shrugged non-committally and said, 'It doesn't matter if you're paying the bills. I never accept interference on a job. It was your personal comfort I was concerned about.'

'Then you don't have to be concerned any more,' she said. 'Juliet was right. You could have shaken me down for a couple of million bucks or more. I'll use that money to charter a private intercontinental-range jet with a full cockpit and cabin crew. I'll take along Ruby, who knows how to look after me. I suggest we meet at the airport at ten o'clock tomorrow morning.'

'You can make all your arrangements, including the jet, by that time?' Creasy asked.

It was Senator Grainger, who supplied the answer. 'Yes, she can . . . money talks in these situations, especially in this country.'

As Ruby wheeled the old woman away, Michael said to Juliet, 'You did us no favours there.'

She was looking at Creasy. She started to mutter an apology, but he held up his hand.

'It's done now. The private jet will save time, and having her along just might have advantages.'

'What advantages?' Michael asked.

'Right now, I can't think of any.' And then shrugged. 'But who knows? Besides, we can't afford to turn this job down. The coffers need replenishing.'

CHAPTER 6

His pleasure was mirrored on his face. She saw it as she crossed the room and shook his outstretched hand. She noticed other men in the bar watching her . . . all the other men in the bar. Colin Chapman pulled a seat back for her and she sat down with a gracious nod of her head at this un-modern courtesy. He sat down opposite her, the pleasure still on his face. A waiter appeared and she ordered a banana daiquiri.

'It is so rare,' he said, 'these days, to see a Chinese woman wearing a cheong-sam . . . which is a great pity, because they are one of the most beautiful costumes in the world.'

Again, she inclined her head and said, 'To tell the truth, Colin, it's the first time I've ever worn one. When I was at school, they were looked on as a bit of a joke, and later on we all wore designer clothes. This morning, when I was packing up my mother's clothes, I found half a dozen which I'm sure she hadn't worn for many years. They fitted me perfectly, which for a cheong-sam is very necessary.'

He was admiring the high mandarin collars and the soft blue silk which flowed over her contours. At the same time, he was thinking that Lucy Kwok was a very practical young lady, perhaps even hard-hearted. After all, her mother had been brutally murdered only two weeks ago, and here she was wearing her clothes.

It was as though she read his thoughts.

'I know it must seem a little strange, but I was close to my mother and she would have approved.' She smiled at him. 'In fact, I wore it because of you, in acknowledgement of your understanding of our Chinese languages and culture. It is also why I invited you to eat at the Dynasty restaurant tonight.'

The policeman looked slightly uncomfortable.

'Of course, I appreciate it. I've heard of the exquisite food, but I could never afford it, not even on a senior policeman's salary.'

Mischievously, she said, 'So now you're worried that you'll be seen there and investigated by the Independent Commission Against Corruption.'

Very seriously, he said, 'Lucy, you must understand that in my particular position I have to be very careful. As soon as I received your invitation this morning, I sent a fax to the head of the ICAC, informing him where I would be dining tonight and why . . . and who'd be paying the bill.'

The surprise showed on her face.

'Are you joking?'

'Definitely not. I even insisted on an acknowledgement of my fax, which came back ten minutes later.'

Her drink arrived and, as soon as the waiter left, he continued, 'Understand that the Triads know me as their enemy. Last year, they managed to obtain my account number at Lloyd's bank in London and paid three million Hong Kong dollars into it, without my knowledge. Fortunately, as soon as I started working in the Anti-Triad section, I took precautions. For the last three years, copies of my bank statements, both in London and here, have been sent automatically to the ICAC.'

'I'm impressed,' she said. 'And the only bribe I will ever offer you is that of friendship. I'm sure the ICAC cannot object to that. Anyway, I don't have a lot of money. It seems that my father spent most of his wealth on his research . . . but tonight I will be extravagant . . . shall we go for dinner?

CHAPTER 7

The first confrontation took place at thirty-five thousand feet, above the middle of the Atlantic Ocean. The private jet was a state-of-the-art Gulfstream IV. Its configuration was a crew-quarters, just behind the cockpit, then a galley and service area and, behind that, a dining area and then a lounge. At the back was a comfortable, en suite state cabin, together with two smaller cabins containing three bunks each.

The two-man cabin-crew had produced a gourmet lunch, and then Michael and Ruby retired to the lounge area and played cards. Creasy and Gloria Manners stayed at the dining-table.

'What's the programme in Brussels?' Gloria asked.

'It's a question of consultation,' Creasy answered. 'I have a friend there, called Maxie MacDonald. Rhodesian born and bred. During the War of Independence there, he fought in an elite unit called the Selous Scouts. They infiltrated what we used to call the Terrorist Organisation and what they used to call the Freedom Fighters. It happens that he operated in the area where your daughter was killed, and knows it intimately. I know how to take care of myself in the African bush, but compared to Maxie, I'm a novice. For a few months, I was attached to the Selous Scouts, but operated mainly on the other side of the country adjoining Mozambique. Maxie and I are good friends. We've worked together over many years. I have good contacts in Zimbabwe, but his are even better. He still has family there. I want to talk to him before we head south. I also want to see a couple of other friends in Brussels and check out the scene. For some reason, Brussels is a kind of information centre for mercenaries. We may need some back-up and we'll certainly need some weapons. I'll arrange all that over the next forty-eight hours.'

Gloria asked, 'What arrangements have you made for me and my nurse?'

'I've booked you a suite in the Amigo Hotel, plus an adjoining room for your nurse. It's more than five star and damned expensive.'

'So you'll meet your friend Maxie at the hotel?'

Creasy shook his head.

'Maxie is retired now. Together with his wife and her young sister, they run a small bistro. Michael and I will have dinner there tonight. I'll brief him on the situation and then listen to his suggestions.'

He could almost feel the hostility coming across the narrow table.

'And what do I do?' Gloria asked. 'Sit in that hotel and twiddle my thumbs?'

'It's operational,' Creasy answered. 'It's a significant part of my preparation. Maxie's knowledge and contacts are important.'

The reaction was immediate. Gloria Manners rose slightly in her wheelchair and said, 'I don't want to be a simple onlooker. I have an alternative suggestion. You invite this Maxie MacDonald and, if necessary, his wife and even her sister, to dinner at my hotel and then I can listen in on what's going on.'

Creasy shook his head.

'I can't do that. Maxie and his family run a business with a local clientele. They just can't close down for a night. Michael and I will go in and have a late supper, when Maxie's got time to talk to me.'

Gloria Manners reached forward and pressed a button on the bulkhead. Ten seconds later, the steward appeared. Gloria Manners looked at Creasy and said, 'I'm going to have a cognac. Do you want something?'

'I'll join you with a cognac.'

They remained silent until the steward brought the drinks, and then Gloria leaned forward and said, 'We had better examine the parameters of this relationship.'

'I guess so.'

'You work for me.'

'So?'

'When someone works for me, they do what I tell 'em.'

Creasy smiled. It was the first time she had seen him smile, but she didn't get the reaction from a normal smile.

He said, 'Mrs Manners, I work for you because I choose to. As a matter of fact, I need the money that you're offering . . . but I don't need it so bad that I have to take bullshit from anybody. We do this my way, or when we land in Brussels we say goodbye and you fly, in your plane, back to Denver and hire a bunch of ex-Green Berets, who would be about as comfortable in the Zimbabwe bush as I would be in a society cocktail party in Hollywood.'

She took a sip of her cognac, watching him all the time over the rim of her glass. She said, 'Jim Grainger told you about me?'

'Told me what?'

'That I'm a difficult bitch.'

'No one needed to tell me that.'

'He never liked me.'

'Why not?'

'Maybe there's a reason. But it's none of your business.'

'It's immaterial,' Creasy answered. 'Whether you're difficult or not only affects me as to this operation. You're paying me a modest sum to find out whether there might be any reason to continue looking for your daughter's killers. If we continue, you have to fall in line. You don't tell me how to handle my contacts and my friends. You don't tell me how to handle the operation. Make your mind up now.'

As they looked at each other across the table, Creasy realised that it was a make or break situation.

The old woman said, 'I didn't come along to stay in a suite in a luxury hotel . . . I need to be part of it.'

'You will be. But on my terms.'

'What are your terms?'

'I'll give you an example. If you want to be in on the conversation with Maxie MacDonald, then I'll arrange a special car to bring you from the hotel to his bistro and you join us for dinner. Of course, you have Ruby with you.'

Another silence, while they eyeballed each other across the table. Then her head dipped in the merest nod of acknowledgement.

She said, 'You booked me into the Amigo Hotel with my nurse. Are you and Michael staying there too?'

Creasy shook his head.

'No. Michael and I are staying in a whorehouse.' He stood up, glanced down at her shocked face and said, 'I'll tell you about it when we get to Brussels.'

He walked down the plane to the lounge area. From behind him, Mrs Manners voice called out imperiously, 'Ruby! I need you.'

The nurse sighed, tossed her cards into the middle of the table and stood up.

Creasy sat down in her chair and watched as Michael stacked the cards.

In a low voice, the young man asked, 'Why do we have to work for a bitch like that? Why do we even have to spend more than thirty seconds in her presence? I don't give a shit who killed her daughter. In fact, if we find out who did it, maybe we'll point them at the old bitch herself.'

Creasy looked at his adopted son and said in a very reasonable voice, 'There are two reasons, Michael. One is that I was asked to do the job by Jim Grainger, and he's been a good friend to both of us. Right now he's looking after your sister in America. The other reason is that, although we're not broke by any means, we need the money. That last operation cost a fortune.'

Michael was shuffling the cards. He looked up and said, 'You once told me that we don't work for anyone we don't like.'

'That's correct.'

'I don't like Gloria Manners.'

Creasy's voice lost its reasonable tone. 'You make judgements after just a few minutes' conversation with somebody?'

Michael was obstinate. 'It doesn't take more than a few seconds to know whether you like somebody or not.'

Creasy leaned forward and his voice now became harsh. 'That makes you stupid, and I don't like to work with people who are stupid. It can be fatal. Personally, I don't like Mrs Manners – but I don't dislike her. I'm reserving my judgement. I advise you to do the same. Otherwise, when we land in Brussels, you can fuck your little girlfriend and then go back to Gozo, while I find someone intelligent to work with me. Believe it when I tell you that there would be many takers. The money is good and the target is a criminal. We stand on moral ground.'

There was a long silence as Michael continued to shuffle the cards, then he said, 'It's just that I hate that bitch . . . Maybe it's my background. Maybe all those years of being told what to do and not having any way out made me hate people like Gloria Manners on sight.'

Creasy said bluntly, 'You had better stop feeling sorry for yourself, and you had better make up your mind before we land in Brussels in a couple of hours. I don't take orders from Mrs Manners and neither do you. But you damn well take orders from me. If you don't like that you can fuck off.' He stood up and began to move further down the aircraft.

Michael's voice stopped him. 'Creasy. Of course I'll follow your orders. Just keep me away from her.'

Creasy turned, looked at him and said, 'Understand something, Michael. If I tell you to kiss her ass every morning you had better do it. Or I'll get Frank Miller or Rene Callard to replace you.'

Another silence, then Michael nodded and said, 'Can we make it her hand instead of her ass?'

'I'll think about it.'

CHAPTER 8

The shark's fin soup was the clear indicator. It is a dish which must be included in every Chinese banquet and its quality is the benchmark for the whole meal. If the shark's fin soup was of the top quality, it meant that the following dishes would be of a similar excellence ... and massively expensive. The very top quality is pure top-grade fin and exorbitant. It is also somewhat slimy and glutinous. Colin Chapman tasted it and looked across the table and bowed his head slightly. Lucy Kwok smiled in acknowledgement and then, while he ate, she talked.

'Since you know so much about the Chinese and our culture, you can understand us better than most *gweilos*. Perhaps you understand that in our nature, when something bad is done to us we desire not so much justice but vengeance. You also know that we are generally very patient people ... but I am not patient. I want vengeance against the people who murdered my family. Not only the ones who physically hanged them, but the ones who ordered it.'

A waiter came close to the table, ready to ladle out another serving of shark's fin soup.

Colin Chapman said to him in Cantonese, 'It was delicious and I could eat it until the sun comes up, but I know there's much more to follow.'

The waiter's eyes widened and he slid a glance at Lucy.

She smiled and said in the same language, 'In a desert, one can find a diamond.' She looked again at Chapman and, as the waiter went away, her face turned serious and she hammered gently on the table with her small fist, to emphasise her words. 'I want vengeance on the man who ordered it.'

Equally emphatically, Chapman answered, 'The one who ordered it was Mo Lau Wong. Of course, you know who he is.'

'Yes, I know who the bastard is. He is head of the 14K. Everyone knows who he is, but it seems the wonderful Hong Kong police force can do nothing about it. I tell you that if this was China, the authorities would have shot him years ago.'

The waiter brought the next dish, which was whole ouma abalone in oyster sauce. After he had served it and left, Chapman said, 'Lucy, you have a false impression of what goes on in China these days. The authorities there arrest and execute low-level drug dealers, pimps and small-time thieves or embezzlers. They don't shoot people like Tommy Mo Lau Wong.'

She was looking at him sceptically.

He shrugged and continued, 'Tommy Mo visits China frequently. He has business interests all over the country, but particularly in Canton and in all the new economic zones. He has a very ornate villa, five miles outside the city on the Pearl River.'

'Do the communist authorities know about this?'

He gave a short, cynical laugh. 'Of course they know. We've given them all the necessary information. They choose to turn a blind eye and to give him protection. They do this for many reasons, not least for the palm money he hands out . . . The new economic order has brought vast corruption to China. It's not like twenty years ago. The other reason they protect him is because of the situation in Hong Kong itself. Should there be difficulties between the Chinese and British governments in the final run-up to the hand over of Hong Kong in 1997, then the Chinese government would use Tommy Mo and his twenty thousand-odd followers in the colony as a threat against the British.' He shrugged again. 'We cannot arrest him here even though we have strong Triad laws, simply because we have no hard evidence.' He laughed again, cynically. 'We cannot even get him on tax evasion charges. Ostensibly, he lives a very simple life in a fifth floor apartment in Happy Valley. He claims a modest income from a small rice distribution company. He is never, ever present at the scene of a crime. But the reality is very different. Apart from the villa in China, there is another one in Sai Kung, in the New Territories. It's owned by a company in Taiwan, which we suspect is a front for the 14K. That villa is a fortress, with a high stone wall all around the gardens and the most sophisticated security system outside of Fort Knox. We suspect that it's where the Triad initiation ceremonies take place. Tommy Mo spends a lot of time there, but still maintains his address at the little shabby apartment in Happy Valley. Of course, he employs the best lawyers and accountants, or at least the Taiwanese front company does. We can't touch him.'

They had finished the ouma abalone. The waiter was not close to the table because when they had sat down, Lucy had told him only to approach when she beckoned. She did so now, and he brought the next dish. It was roast lung kong chicken.

Chapman tasted it and said to her, 'I have truly never eaten such a meal.'

She nodded absently. Her mind was elsewhere. She had hardly touched the delicious food. She looked up at the Englishman again and asked, 'Can you not turn one of his followers, just like the Italian Anti-Mafia police turn some big fish?'

'We've been trying for years. We've offered them new identities in foreign countries as far away as Australia or South America. I can tell you, unofficially, that I have the authority to offer huge sums of money as a reward for information. Lucy, the Triads may seem similar to the Mafia on the surface but, believe me, they are very different and infinitely more dangerous.'

She had ordered a bottle of Le Montrachet. She reached for the bottle and refilled their glasses. The waiter, standing just out of earshot, adopted a pained expression but did not move.

She took a sip of her wine and said, 'Of course, I know about the Triads as every Chinese does, but I bow to your superior knowledge. At that long meeting in your office. I meant to question you then, but you were the one asking all the questions about me and my family. I would be grateful if you would educate me a little now, about the Triads.'

'I'll be pleased to sing for such a supper . . . Let's start at the very beginning.'

He talked uninterrupted for the next half hour, first explaining that the Triads had their origins during the fifth century AD, in what was then called the White Lotus Society, which had very strong Buddhist overtones. But it was more than a thousand years later that the numerous Triad Societies blossomed throughout China. They wanted to throw out the hated Manchu Ch'ing Dynasty and restore the Ming Dynasty. Their aims were both patriotic and laudable and they received grass-roots support. This anti-foreign patriotic posture was retained until 1912, when Dr Sun Yat-sen formed the first Chinese Republic. Up to that time, the vast majority of the population had viewed the Triads with respect and vied to become members. Then the whole thing changed. Once their original purpose had been accomplished, the Triads turned to crime, much like the Mafia in Sicily, but on a vaster scale. Their elaborate initiation ceremonies still retained a quasi-religious atmosphere, and even Taoism crept in. But the ceremonies' only purpose were to terrify initiates into believing that the Society was all-powerful and that any deviations or disclosures would be fatal, both to mind and body. Over the next fifty years, the large Societies fragmented. Some of the fragments withered away, while others flourished. The whole of the colony of Hong Kong split into territories, and the different Triad societies fought for every inch of those territories. They also branched out into South-East Asia, where there was a sizeable Chinese population, and so came to control crime in Singapore, Malaysia, Indonesia and the Philippines. During the last few generations, they also spread their tentacles to Canada, America, Europe and Australia. By 1990, they had become the most powerful global criminal organisation. They have elaborate hand signals and coded speech signals, not just to indicate their membership of a Triad Society, but also their position in the hierarchy. They also entered big business: property, construction and finance. They are known to control several Public Companies. They are adept at bribing public officials, including the police and judiciary. The extent of their hold on their membership is so great that a Society member will willingly accept a suicide mission or kill himself before giving away information. It is estimated that by the mid-twentieth century, one in six of the Hong Kong Chinese population was affiliated to a Triad Society. The Societies have no other purpose except the pursuit of crime and power.

Her face was tinged with anger and sadness.

'So, it seems that the man who ordered the murder of my family is unlikely to be brought to justice.'

He peeled an orange and said, 'If I believed there was no chance at all, then I would resign. I have to keep a belief in the work I do. We have had successes, and if my department were not efficient the Triads would be totally out of control and there would be no law . . . But, Lucy, I have to be honest. The chances of us arresting Tommy Mo for the murder of your family are slight. The chances would be better if we could establish a direct contact between your late father and Tommy Mo himself. I say that because the nature of the murders was a direct warning to others. It's why I've had protection around you twenty-four hours a day, and why I urge you to emigrate to a country which does not have a large Chinese community.' He noted the surprise in her eyes. 'Yes, Lucy, you would not have noticed the protection. My men are skilled and loyal . . . as to the possibility of emigration, I want you to think about it carefully.'

'Never!' she said vehemently. 'It would be running away.'

'You have to understand,' he answered, 'I can only protect you for a limited time because I have limited resources. I would say only for another month. I'm glad you decided to stay on at the house instead of moving to an apartment, because it's difficult to approach that house without being seen.'

She twirled the last of the wine in her glass, looking at it thoughtfully, and said, 'Do you have any idea of the motive? After all, my father was not in business. What would the 14K have against a research doctor?'

'I have no idea, but you must try to think carefully about all the conversations that you had with your father, mother or brother over the past months. There must be a clue somewhere.'

She nodded and said, 'I will do everything I can.' A smile touched her lips. 'It will mean I will have to see quite a lot of you.'

He also smiled slightly.

'I'm afraid so. I regret imposing that burden.'

CHAPTER 9

Ruby wheeled Gloria down the ramp at the side entrance of the Amigo Hotel. A stretch limousine was waiting. It was specially adapted for wheelchairs. The chauffeur lowered the ramp, and two minutes later, Gloria was in the back. She found Creasy sitting in the armchair-like seat next to her. Ruby climbed into the front seat, next to the driver, and they moved off through the busy city.

Creasy turned and gave Gloria a careful appraisal and then nodded in approval. She was dressed in a full-length emerald silk gown with a black shawl draped about her shoulders. She had applied subtle make-up which softened the lines of bitterness on her face. She did not look like the woman of confrontation with whom Creasy had flown across the Atlantic. She soon dispelled the illusion.

'Do you mind telling me why you left a message with Ruby that I should dress up tonight? Who are you to tell me what to wear for a dinner in some cheap bistro?'

Creasy was looking at the bright lights of the city. A light rain had begun to fall.

He turned back to her and said, 'Mrs Manners, I'm not only telling you what to wear but I'm also going to tell you how to behave tonight.'

She snorted in derision. 'I need a hired hand to teach me how to behave?'

'Listen to me, lady! I regret that you lost the husband you loved. I regret that you lost your only child. I regret that you're doomed to live in that wheelchair for the rest of your years. You can view me as a hired hand – which, technically, I am – but, whether you

39

like it or not, as from the moment we lifted off from Denver Airport. I'm running this operation.' She started to say something and he held up a hand. 'Mrs Manners, unless you listen to what I have to say, and unless you do what I ask of you, I going to have this car turned around and take you back to your hotel. And you can kiss your hired hand's ass goodbye.'

They drove in silence for a couple of minutes, and then she said, 'It will be a waste of money.'

'Why?'

'Because I chartered that goddamn Gulfstream jet for another two weeks. Do you know how much those things cost?'

'I can guess.'

'OK. So I listen to what you want me to do, but I make no promises.'

'You make one promise first. You don't interrupt me with a single word until I've finished talking.'

After a pause, she nodded. He turned in his seat to look at her.

'We are not going to have dinner in a cheap bistro. We are going to have dinner at the invitation of two good friends of mine. It happens that they both work in their bistro and so that's where they have to entertain us. It also happens that I need his advice. I need that advice because it could help me find out who killed your daughter. So this dinner is what we call 'operational', and on an operation, everybody involved has to be co-ordinated. That includes you. Now, having talked to you for some hours, I realise you have the impression that you can wave your magic wand and everybody will fall into line and lots of miracles will happen. But sometimes your mega-bucks and your wand won't work. This dinner tonight is one such occasion. Maxie MacDonald doesn't believe in magic wands. If he's going to help us, he has to like you or, at least, respect you. And that goes for his wife Nicole, as well.'

She opened her mouth to speak but saw the look in his eyes and shut it.

He went on, 'There is another aspect. You know that Michael and I are staying at a whorehouse. I told you a little bit about Blondie, the Madame. She's about seventy years old, Italian by birth and not blonde at all. She's been a friend of mine since I was in the Foreign Legion, twenty-five-odd years ago. I won't bore you with the reasons why she's such a close friend, but she is. It so happens that Maxie's wife Nicole used to work for Blondie. I borrowed Nicole to act as a decoy, in Washington back in '89. It was part of the operation I had going there with Jim Grainger. In fact, Jim met her there. Maxie was also on that operation and worked with Nicole. It was a dangerous time and, as happens at such times, Nicole and Maxie fell in love. When they returned to Europe, she quit her job with Blondie and he gave up being a mercenary. They bought the bistro and run it with Nicole's younger sister.' He paused and glanced at his watch and then his voice quickened slightly. 'Now this afternoon, I got a hell of a surprise. Blondie announced that she would come with us to dinner. She hardly leaves the Pappagal and, in my memory, never at night. But she's very fond of Nicole and I guess, in a strange way, she's paying Nicole an honour. Because of that, Blondie has dressed up as though she's going to a very important occasion, even though it's taking place in a modest bistro. That's why I left a message with Ruby asking you to dress up. The point I am making is that tonight you're having dinner with the Madame of a whorehouse. If you offend her, you will offend Nicole, and if you offend Nicole you offend Maxie. Of course, he will still answer my questions and give me advice, but there is something else I want from him.'

She couldn't help herself. The question came out. 'What?'

Again, he held up his hand.

'That will have to wait until later, after I have judged his mood and Nicole's, but Blondie could be a help.'

The limousine turned into a side-street and pulled up in front of a building with a small neon sign, reading 'Maxie's'.

Creasy said, 'So, Mrs Manners, it's important that tonight you control your natural impulse for abrasiveness.' He pointed at the bistro. 'You can't wave your magic wand to get those people to do what I want.'

They stared at each other and then she asked, 'Do you know what time it is?' she asked.

'Yes. Around ten o'clock.'

She nodded.

'I usually take dinner at eight. I'm damned hungry . . . Let's go.'

Inside, the bistro was small and warm. On one side of the room was a long bar. There were only eight tables, covered by blue and white gingham tablecloths. Michael was sitting at a corner table together with an old woman dressed in a long turquoise gown. Her face was heavily made-up and diamonds and gold, glistened on her wrists, fingers and in her ears. Her jet-black hair was carefully coiffeured on top of her head. Her thin lips were bright crimson. There were only six other diners at an advanced stage of their meals. The bartender came round from behind the bar and greeted Creasy in a strange manner. The two men put their left hands behind the other's neck and kissed each other briefly but hard on the cheek, close to their mouths. Then Creasy turned and introduced him to Gloria. She was then introduced to Nicole and her young sister, Lucette. Creasy gestured to Ruby to push the wheelchair across the room. Michael stood up and introduced Gloria to Blondie.

For the next half an hour, Gloria was uncharacteristically subdued. She sat across the table from Blondie, who was obviously in her element, half-*grande dame* and half-coquette. Lucette served the food, and it wasn't long before Gloria could see that there was something between her and Michael. Every time she leaned across the table to place a plate or retrieve something, her arm managed to touch his.

At first, the conversation was mostly between Blondie and Maxie, as they discussed old friends and acquaintances. Ruby sat on Gloria's right and didn't utter a word, but she hardly took her eyes from Blondie's face.

Suddenly, Blondie was talking to Gloria in her heavily-accented English. 'Creasy told me about your daughter. I'm very sorry. I also lost a daughter once. Of course, the pain never goes away, but I can tell you that the passing of time makes the pain easier to bear.'

'How old was your daughter?' Gloria asked.

'She died the day after her sixth birthday.'

'Any other children?'

'No. I can't understand why, but after that I did not want any more . . . and the times were not good. It was just after the war and those days in Italy were hard days . . . have you always been rich, Mrs Manners?'

Creasy was watching Gloria. He saw her shake her head as she said, 'No. I know what it's like to be poor.'

Creasy saw the faintest smile cross her lips.

She said, 'To quote Eartha Kitt: "I've been rich, and I've been poor . . . and being rich is better".'

Blondie gave a deep chuckle. The other customers had left and now Maxie and Nicole joined them at the table, while Lucette cleared away the plates. Then the young girl brought espressos and a bottle of cognac and abruptly the mood changed.

'So what do we have?' Maxie asked Creasy.

'We have a murder. As you know, it was Gloria's only daughter and only child. It happened by the Zambezi . . . in an area near to the Cheti. You know it well.'

'I know it very well. That was my area of operation for more than half a year in nineteen seventy-eight.'

Creasy turned to Gloria and explained. 'As I told you on the plane, Maxie was more or less a founder member of the Selous Scouts. I was attached to them for a while in 'seventy-seven, but I operated on the other side of the country, near the Mozambique border. I need to tell you a bit more about the Selous Scouts. They were a very elite unit of the Rhodesian Army and named after the famous nineteenth-century explorer, tracker and hunter. The idea was to turn captured terrorists, or what are now known as freedom fighters, who were infiltrating across the Zambezi from Zambia on the North-West border and across from Mozambique in the East and then send them out in the bush with some of our own troops, who were pretending to be terrorists, using Chinese or captured weapons. Obviously, there were only a few white Selous Scouts.' He smiled across the table at Maxie and went on, 'But if you drink in bars from Harare to Cape Town, enough whites will tell you that they were Selous Scouts to tilt the whole of Africa. In fact, there were never more than a hundred whites in the unit. They also raided terrorist headquarters and training camps in Zambia and Mozambique with great success. They were probably the best trackers in the world, and could live off the land with only their bare hands for any length of time. The point is, Mrs Manners, that with the end of the war and the coming of independence, the Selous Scouts just sort of drifted away into oblivion. No photographs were taken of the black members, unless their faces were covered. All records were destroyed. Many of those black members are now in positions of authority in that country, while others went back to their villages. With independence, the new black government carried through, after some years, a remarkable policy of conciliation between the forces who fought for independence and the forces who fought against it. They created a cohesive single army, some of whose members were Selous Scouts.' He turned back to Maxie and said, 'The police made exhaustive enquiries, particularly as they were highly pressured by the American government, a major aid donor to the country. Mrs Manner's daughter, Carole, had been spending a few days at camp with a white South African friend. He was an eminent zoologist and was doing research work in the Zambezi Valley on the after-effects on wildlife after the creation of Lake Kariba. He was thirty-five years old and well versed in bush lore. So much so, that he liked to be on his own without African helpers and, as a matter of principle, never carried a gun.'

Maxie muttered something under his breath.

Immediately, Gloria asked, 'What did you say, Mr MacDonald?'

He shifted his eyes from Creasy to her. 'It was just a curse, Mrs Manners. I know the type. In a way, it's kind of a macho syndrome, to go out in the bush and commune with nature. That's fine, if you do it totally on your own and accept the risks . . . but you don't do it with a companion, especially not with a city girl . . . and especially not in an area like that, where elephant and rhino poachers roam around with high-powered assault rifles.'

Gloria was nodding, but she said, 'I cannot blame the man entirely. His name was Cliff Coppen and while he spent a few weeks in Bulawayo, Carole fell very much in love with him. She wrote me a letter, saying that she wanted to go on a field trip with him, but that he had refused because of possible danger. In that letter, she also told me that she knew where his camp was going to be, and that she was going to travel to Victoria Falls, hire a Landrover and driver, and have him take her to that camp . . . You have to understand, Mr MacDonald, that my daughter was a headstrong and determined woman . . . and a very beautiful one. I don't think that an idealistic zoologist would have been much of a match for her.'

Maxie smiled slightly.

'She was your daughter, so I get the picture.'

He looked again at Creasy and asked a one-word question. 'Poachers?'

'Possible but very doubtful. There are few rhinos left in that area. The Zimbabwe police report also shows that an anti-poaching patrol had passed by only forty-eight hours earlier. They had seen and spoken to Cliff Coppen and Carole. There were no tracks anywhere around the camp. The motive was not robbery because nothing was taken. The bodies were not discovered until three days later, by which time there had been heavy rainfall.'

The two men began to speak in a sort of jargon.

'Bullets?'

'7.62 millimetres.'

'How many?'

'Three, same rifle. Two in the man. Stomach and upper spine. The bullet that killed Carole was a heart shot.'

'A loner?'

'Looks that way.'

'Close target?'

'Penetration gives an estimate of four to six hundred metres.'

'A pro?'

'Looks like it.'

Creasy sighed and looked at Gloria. She was sipping her brandy, looking down at the table. Creasy switched his gaze back to Maxie and said, 'Coppen was clutching a long stick. The end was blackened. They were shot by an open wood fire. My guess is that Coppen was on his haunches prodding at it, with Carole standing beside him – I've seen a position drawing. The gunman shot her first because she was standing and could move faster. The fact that it was a heart shot shows that he knows his business. He would have shot Coppen as he rose. With that movement, Coppen took the first bullet in his stomach. He was spun around and knocked flat because the second bullet was angled towards the neck.'

'He didn't waste bullets,' Maxie said. 'No tracks at all?'

'Everything washed out.'

'Casings?'

'None.'

'A pro.'

'Yes, a pro.'

The two men fell silent into thought. Nicole was looking at Gloria, who was still holding her glass near her lips and taking frequent sips.

Blondie broke the silence. She said to Gloria, 'It is a fact that

45

Creasy is probably the most effective soldier roaming around this globe, and I well know that Michael has been trained by him in his image. I also know that Creasy came here, not just to see me, but to dig into the mind of Maxie. You are leaving for Zimbabwe early tomorrow morning. I think, in the back of his head, Creasy would be happy if Maxie goes with you too, because Maxie was a Rhodesian. He will not ask him because, when Maxie married Nicole, he promised to give up that work. But three years ago, Nicole pushed him out to destroy some very evil people. That is how Juliet came to be Creasy's daughter.' Blondie was looked directly at Nicole. She went on, 'I know my Nicole. She loves her man and is confident in his love for her. But she is wise enough not to hold him back from something he wishes to do ... and something he feels he should do.'

Immediately, Nicole answered, 'We have a part-time bartender who can become full-time anytime. Maxie still has distant cousins in Zimbabwe and many friends. Some of them come here to see him, but others cannot afford to leave Zimbabwe. Maxie should see them. If he wants to go, I raise no objections.' She smiled. 'In fact, for the past few weeks, he's been restless. Maybe some time in the bush will do him good.'

Gloria turned to look at Creasy.

'Do you need him?'

Maxie himself answered the question. 'He doesn't "need" anyone. He won't admit it, but he knows the bush, as a whole, as well as I do. On the other hand, he does not know that area of it as I do. Creasy has friends in Zimbabwe, but since I was born and grew up there, I have more friends ... and more contacts. And I also have cousins there. Creasy would never admit to needing me but, as Blondie said, in the back of his mind he's sitting across the table in my bistro because he wants me out there in the bush. He wants me because he knows that if we find a clue as to who killed your daughter, it's more likely that we'll find that clue somewhere in the bush, near the Zambezi.'

Again, Gloria glanced at Creasy. He simply nodded.

The Gulfstream IV lifted off from Brussels airport at nine o'clock the next morning.

CHAPTER 10

Lucy found the file after four days.

During those four days, she realised the extent of her father's life-work, the esteem in which he was held by others in the field, and the vast number of overseas contacts. He was not only a graduate of Guy's Hospital in London, but also had a Master's degree from John Hopkins University in America. His speciality, however, was in Chinese medicine and its relationship and possible influence, both past and future, on modern Western medicine. The walls of his library were filled from floor to ceiling with ancient books and the walls of his laboratory were lined with bottles and flasks containing the plants, herbs and liquids and animal parts and organs which were all part of Chinese medicine. The files of correspondence with other experts from both the West and the Eastern world were voluminous. Every evening, Colin Chapman would arrive at the house, have a quick dinner with her, and then help. Because of his vast knowledge of written Chinese, he concentrated on the correspondence between her father and the professors and doctors on mainland China, while she went through the English language correspondence.

On the first evening, she had looked up at him across the large refectory table. He wore thick horn-rimmed spectacles which, she thought, suited him.

She had remarked, 'This is a wild situation. Here I am, Chinese, reading the English stuff and there you are, a *gweilo*, reading the Chinese.'

He said seriously, 'Lucy, your father was a very learned man, much more learned than I had known. Did he ever actually practise medicine?'

'No. Only in an emergency. Soon after he left John Hopkins, his father died and left him a substantial sum of money. His first love had always been pure research and so he never really had to make a living as a doctor. He returned to Hong Kong, bought this house and set up his laboratory and library and study. He made many important discoveries and, as you know, wrote several books. He was a happy man in all his work and in all his life. Lately, he had become fascinated with the advent of genetic engineering, because he was able to show that many traditional Chinese medicines thousands of years old have a scientific basis.' She gestured at an old desk in the corner, on which sat a word processor. 'He was half way through a book on the subject when he was murdered. It's my job now to make sure that all his papers and research go to the right people, so that it can be continued.'

Chapman went back to studying his file. She pulled another box file in front of her. Her father's handwritten words were on the front. There were just two of them: 'Rhino Horn'. Underneath were the Chinese characters. It was a thick file and, after she had leafed through it for half an hour, she suddenly lifted her head and said, 'Colin, I think I have something.'

Half an hour later, Colin said, 'That must be the connection.' He was sitting beside her. He leaned back in his chair and spoke out loud, but as though talking to himself. 'For centuries, it has been firmly believed by the Chinese that the horn of the rhino is a potent aphrodisiac. The powder made from that horn has always been tremendously expensive as wealthy old Chinese men try to satisfy their young concubines. But now, with the rhino almost facing extinction through poaching, that powder has become the most precious substance on earth. Rhino horn is also used by Yemenis for ornamental dagger handles, but the most valuable market is here in Hong Kong and in Taiwan. That market is controlled by one Triad . . . the 14K.'

Colin had extracted one letter from the file. It was in English and dated one month earlier. He read it out loud: ' "My dear Cliff, I have some truly astonishing news, and since you were such a vital part of my project, I hasten to write. It was four months ago when you were able to obtain for me the fifty grams of black rhino horn. I had put aside most of my other projects while I worked on it. My experiments came to fruition at about two o'clock this morning, when I discovered that, far from being an aphrodisiac, the substance actually diminishes male potency and contains a carcinogenic-causing agent called Hetromygloten. The thing is, I cannot understand why it contains such an agent. Then it occurred to me that perhaps it came into the fibrous hair of the horn through certain grasses or plants that are part of the black rhino's diet. Naturally, I have no knowledge of that diet, but I'm sure you do. Of course, it might also be in minerals contained in the water that they consume or in the soil of their habitat.

' "I'm sure that my findings have deep implications. As I write this, I have beside me your letter of the 26th, where you state that the fight against the poachers is being lost and that even the programme to dart the black rhinos and then de-horn them is proving futile, since poachers still kill them because it saves tracking a useless animal. If, however, my countrymen can be convinced that by imbibing even a small particle of black rhino horn their sexual potency will be markedly reduced – and that they also risk cancer – then the market for it will cease immediately. For this campaign, we will need substantial funds, but I'm sure that this will be forthcoming from worldwide conservation organisations and perhaps certain interested governments. However, the next step must be that I do more work on the subject and then publish an academic article in *Nature*. That article can then be quoted in newspapers and magazines as part of the educational campaign.

' "As you well know, such things take time. It could be six months or even a year. I know from your letter that the black rhino does not have much time and so I have a ploy which might end the trading almost immediately. I phoned an old British acquaintance of mine who had recently retired from the Hong Kong police force, and asked him which Triad gang would have control of that particular trade. He immediately made enquiries with the Anti-Triad Branch, who told him that, without doubt, the 14K is the largest, most dangerous and has world-wide connections. It is headed by a man called Tommy Mo Lau Wong.

' "I intend to communicate with this Tommy Mo and inform him of my findings and warn him that, unless the business ceases forthwith, a large advertising campaign will shortly appear with my findings. Like any astute Chinese business man, Tommy Mo will realise that any rhino horn powder he is holding, or has in the pipeline, will become worthless. He will immediately sell all his stocks and not take any more. Obviously, if this works, the expensive advertising campaign will not be needed and the money can be used elsewhere. I will let you know the result, if any. Again, my thanks for your considerable help. With warmest wishes, Kwok Ling Fong." '

Chapman turned to look at Lucy and said, 'I'm afraid that, like most academics and scientists, your father was somewhat naive about the real world out there.'

She nodded. 'I'm afraid he was . . . He must have made contact with Tommy Mo, who had him murdered and then tried to burn the evidence.' She shook her head and said, 'To think that my whole family was murdered just because of some animal horn.'

'Not just that,' Chapman answered. 'Although rhino horn powder has a huge value per gram, there is very little of it around. The turnover in that business would have been relatively small-beer compared to the 14K's total turnover . . . You must understand the Triad mind. Your father threatened Tommy Mo. That itself was reason enough to have him killed, together with your mother and brother. Tommy Mo would have made it known among the 14K why he had your father killed . . . It is their way.' He turned back to the letter and read out the name of the addressee. ' "Cliff Coppen, c/o The Ministry of Natural Resources and Tourism, Harare, Zimbabwe".' He then said thoughtfully, 'There is no reply in the file . . . which is strange because, with such news, you would have thought there would have been.'

'What now?'

The Englishman looked at his watch.

'It will not be hard to find out who the recently retired policeman was. If he did phone anybody in my department, the call should have been logged.' He tapped the file. 'At the date of your father's letter to Coppen, I was out of the colony.' Again, he glanced at his watch. 'Zimbabwe must be six or seven hours behind us. I'll have my office phone their Ministry of Natural Resources and Tourism and find out where this Cliff Coppen is at the moment, and try to get a contact fax or phone number. I'm very interested as to why there was no reply to your father's letter . . . unless, of course, Coppen called him on the phone.'

'But how can this man Coppen help?'

'I don't know yet, but we follow up every lead.'

He reached for the phone, dialled the number and issued a series of instructions. When he hung up, he said, 'They'll phone me back shortly . . . What will you do with this house? Sell it? It must be worth a fortune.'

Her short laugh held no mirth. 'It will be sold, but it's been mortgaged and re-mortgaged. Unlike his father, my father had no head for money . . . He didn't gamble or play the stock market or anything, but by the time he had given me and my brother expensive educations, and with all the money he spent on his work and the laboratory, there won't be much left, if anything.'

'What will you do?'

'I have three months' paid leave. When the house is sold I'll probably move into an apartment with another air hostess.' She saw the concern on his face and said, 'You know the Triad mind, Colin, but you don't yet know my mind. I'm not going to be chased out of town by any bastard Triad. Not Tommy Mo or anybody else.'

For the next five minutes, he tried to convince her of the dangers of staying in Hong Kong. He was still trying to convince her when the phone rang. She answered it, listened and then passed it over to Chapman.

He listened for several minutes, occasionally asking a one-word question, then he hung up, turned to her and said, 'Assuming that a letter from here to Zimbabwe takes about a week, then at about the same time as Cliff Coppen got your father's letter, he was shot dead, together with an American girlfriend on the banks of the Zambezi River. The Zimbabwe police are faxing me a full report.'

'Coppen's death could be a coincidence . . . after all, Africa can be a dangerous place.'

The Englishman shrugged.

'So can New York, Rio or a little village in the country. When it comes to the Triads, I don't believe in coincidences.'

CHAPTER 11

The Gulfstream IV was equipped with a satellite telephone. Maxie MacDonald used it first. As they flew across the Alps, he spoke to his cousin, seventy miles outside Bulawayo, Zimbabwe's second city. He spoke in a language which Gloria did not understand.

She looked at Creasy across the table and asked, 'What is it?'

'Ndebele.' Creasy answered. 'It's the language of the Matabele, which is the main tribe of that part of the country.'

'Do you understand it?'

'A little. Maxie and his cousin speak it perfectly.'

'Why aren't they speaking in English? Is it some secret you're keeping from me?'

Creasy kept the irritation out of his eyes.

'We're keeping nothing from you, Mrs Manners, not at the beginning of this trip or now. It's just that we don't know how secure this satellite link-up is. Maxie is talking about weapons. We don't want anybody eavesdropping.'

'What weapons?'

'Well, obviously, Maxie and I are not going into the bush looking for murderers with our bare hands. We need rifles and hand-guns. The plan is that we will leave Michael in Harare for a few days, to nose around. He's good at that and no one knows him there. You have to understand that, although it's a big country, the cities and towns have a village mentality, especially among the white community. After leaving Michael in Harare, we'll fly to Bulawayo and spend one day there, and then fly on to Victoria Falls, which is the nearest town to the operational area. There are some good hotels there. That will be your base while Maxie and I go into the bush.'

'What will you be looking for, exactly?'

'Nothing, exactly. All tracks of the killer or killers have been lost.'

'So what's the point of going into the bush? Are you just going to be playing at boy scouts?'

Again, Creasy kept the irritation out of his eyes.

He said, 'Mrs Manners, so far, apart from the hiring of this jet, this operation is costing you relatively little. If Maxie and I don't stumble across something in the bush – and if Michael draws a blank in Harare – then we'll go home.'

There must have been an edge of sarcasm in his voice because she immediately bristled.

'Is that what you want?' she snapped.

He shook his head.

'Let me explain further, Mrs Manners. Usually, I'm very choosy about who I work for. In fact, given the choice, I wouldn't be working at all. I ended my career with a nice nest-egg, but events over the past two years have whittled that down. I'm not poor, by any means, but I like to have a good reserve. So I'd be very happy to find something in the bush that relates to your daughter's murder, and then go on to collect the big payment. So will Maxie and Michael.'

'What you're saying is that if you still had this nest-egg, you wouldn't have taken on this job?'

'I'll tell you the truth, Mrs Manners, I don't know. Jim Grainger's a friend of mine.'

Maxie had finished his telephone conversation. Creasy turned to him and asked, 'So?'

'Ian has all the weapons we need and they're fully licensed, but there's one small problem. He can only lend them to us with written police permission. By law, they have to be in his possession. Obviously, he can't afford to break the law.'

'I anticipated that problem,' Creasy said. He glanced at his watch. 'Quite soon, Jim Grainger will be waking up in Denver. I'll phone him and ask him to use his influence through the State Department to ask the American Ambassador to apply a little pressure on the Zimbabwe authorities again.'

'OK,' Maxie answered. 'But now there's something else. Ian confirms that the Commander John Ndlovu is the one and the same ZAPU officer we fought against back in the seventies. He also says that he's well-respected, both by blacks and whites and, as far as is known, he's not corrupt.'

'What's all this about?' Gloria asked.

Creasy explained. 'ZAPU was one of the two guerilla armies fighting for independence against the Rhodesian forces. Ndlovu was a good commander, operating mainly in the eastern Highlands. I almost managed to catch him a couple of times, but he was clever. He will know all about me and Maxie.'

'That's not good news,' Gloria commented.

'It's not necessarily bad news. There's been a major reconciliation in Zimbabwe between the different forces.'

'So, you think he'll co-operate?'

Creasy looked at Maxie for the answer.

Maxie said, 'Well, if he's getting pressure from his Minister, he'll probably co-operate, although with some reluctance. After all, no policeman anywhere likes to come up with a dead-end in a case, and then have a rich woman arrive with a bunch of mercenaries to open the whole thing up. Especially when he gets pressure to issue those mercenaries with temporary permits for half a dozen guns. However, there is a plus. My cousin knows Ndlovu personally and gets on with him OK, and since they're his guns, it might make it more acceptable for Ndlovu . . . We just have to wait and find out.'

Further back in the plane, Michael was playing gin rummy with Ruby the nurse, and losing. She was a woman in her mid-forties, with a severe face but pleasant eyes.

'You have a tough job,' Michael commented.

'You mean Mrs Manners?'

'Yes. She can't be the easiest of patients.'

'I've had worse,' Ruby said, with a slight smile. 'But not many.'

'How long have you worked for her?'

'I was about number six. The others all quit within days or weeks. I guess by that point, she realised she'd have to soften up a bit or she'd never get anyone to stay.'

'You mean she's softer than she was?'

Again the nurse smiled. 'Marginally, but enough to be bearable. Besides, the pay and conditions are very good. There's another factor. I have an only daughter . . . Her father ran off years ago. She's in college now, and we're very close. I know how much bitterness I would feel if she was murdered in a far-off country, like Carole Manners was.' She laid down a full gin and said, 'You're not concentrating, Michael.'

It was true. He ruefully counted his cards and made a note on the scoresheet.

She said, 'Anyway, I'm enjoying this trip. It breaks up the routine and I've never been to Africa before.'

'Neither have I,' Michael said. 'I'm looking forward to it.'

Further up the plane, Creasy finished his brief telephone conversation with Jim Grainger and then said to Gloria, 'He'll get back to us either before we land in Harare or at the hotel tonight.'

She had been listening to Creasy's side of the conversation.

'What did he ask, which made you reply, "No, she's fine."?'

Creasy glanced at Maxie and then said to her, 'He asked me whether you were being a damned nuisance, but then he would, wouldn't he?'

Slowly, she nodded. 'Yes, I guess he would.'

CHAPTER 12

The other customers did not exactly bow or scrape when Tommy Mo walked into the restaurant, but they did fall silent and watch as he walked with his entourage between the tables to the private back room. He was known in Hong Kong as 'Wu Yeh Tao Sha', which translates as 'the knife that never sleeps'. Since he owned the restaurant, the food and service was outstanding. The manager, chef and waiters were all members of the 14K and Tommy Mo could talk freely.

His number one lieutenant was a short bald Shanghainese in his mid-sixties, who had the nickname 'Shen Suan Tzu', which translates as 'the fragrant brain.' At meals, he always sat on Tommy Mo's left side. As the first course was served, he informed his boss that the police and other security services had gone on to red alert at 6.15 p.m., fifteen minutes after he personally had phoned through to police headquarters, using a recognised code, informing them of an impending terrorist attack within the next twelve hours, either at the airport or the sea terminal. Through their informers within the police, they knew that security was now concentrated on those two areas. The security guards from around the house of Lucy Kwok Ling Fong had been observed leaving at 7.30 p.m., but their departure had coincided with the arrival of Chief Inspector Colin Chapman.

Tommy Mo's face hardened at the mention of the name and he muttered curses in his native Chui Chow dialect. Fragrant Brain went on to explain that the attack on the house was planned for midnight but, obviously, if Colin Chapman stayed late they would have to delay it. Then Fragrant Brain got a major surprise.

Tommy Mo shook his head and said, 'Let fate decide.' He

referred to Colin Chapman by his derogatory nickname 'Yin Mao' which translates as 'one pubic hair'. 'Maybe it is time that he stopped bothering us.'

The astonishment showed briefly on Fragrant Brain's face.

'There will be an uproar,' he said. 'The *gweilo* government gets very upset when even a Chinese policeman is killed, but when a *gweilo* policeman is killed they go crazy.'

'Let fate decide,' Tommy Mo repeated. 'Back in the old days, we just used to bribe the Anti-Triad Police, who co-operated well. If a crime was committed which did not involve us, then we used to help the police catch the criminals. Then the idiots brought in the Independent Commission Against Corruption under that crazy Irishman and they threw all their best policemen in jail. That was all right because then they had to promote and bring in inexperienced idiots. But now we are facing people who understand us and how we think, and the most dangerous is Yin Mao. He speaks our languages better than we do. I could hardly believe it when I heard the bastard speaking Chui Chow. I never knew a *gweilo* like that one. He is dangerous, and I have weighed up the advantages and disadvantages of killing him. They are balanced, and so I will let fate decide. If he remains at that house after midnight, then he will die with the woman.'

CHAPTER 13

'Have you alerted Hong Kong?'
       'Of course I have, damn it!'
Rolph Becker shouted down the phone, the anguish showing on his face. He stood on the patio facing the dark lake, lit by the merest sliver of a moon, a cordless phone to his ear. It was close to midnight. Half an hour earlier, Rolph Becker had arrived home from his weekly visit to Bulawayo. He had immediately phoned a partner in Harare and informed him of the news that, far from the Coppen/Manners murder being all but forgotten, the woman's mother had arrived from the States by private jet, together with three hard mercenaries, one of whom was Maxie MacDonald, an ex-Selous Scout who knew the area like the back of his hand and spoke Ndebele like a native. He had discovered this while having lunch at the Bulawayo Club. Nothing happened in that city without it being gossiped about.

On hearing the news, his partner had simply said, 'If they go in the bush they'll find nothing . . . Selous Scout or not.' It was then that he asked whether or not Rolf Becker had been in touch with Hong Kong. A question that incurred Becker's wrath.

'There were two mistakes made.' Rolph Becker said bitterly. 'The first in Hong Kong, when that idiot Tommy Mo didn't realise that the bloody house of that Chinese professor had a sprinkler system, which we know saved a lot of his documents. The other mistake was made here. We should never have allowed that woman to be shot. If only Coppen had died, nobody would have minded much, especially since he was an orphan. But when a woman gets shot, it's different . . . Even more so, when that woman has a multi-millionairess for a mother.'

'So what's our strategy?' the partner asked.

Becker's voice went quiet and cold. 'Our strategy is to have Maxie MacDonald and his friends watched closely. And if they go into the bush, your job is to make sure that they don't come out alive. Meanwhile, I've strongly suggested to Tommy Mo that he takes care of Professor Kwok's daughter, and this time to make sure that the Professor's study is completely incinerated, which should have happened in the first place.' He was gazing out across the black lake, and his voice took on a hard edge. 'I've decided that we have to try to hit Gloria Manners. She holds the purse-strings, and once she's out of the way the others will go home . . . Yes, I know it's dangerous, but we can't stop now. I've lived here all my working life. I've watched this lake grow and I grew with it . . . I came from being a poor white in South Africa, looked down on by everyone, to being somebody . . . a man people look up to . . . No one's going to take that away from me. No one's going to put me in prison. No matter who has to die.'

CHAPTER 14

Lucy was in the garden, sitting on a canvas chair reading, when he arrived. He parked his black Volvo by the gate and climbed out. Colin Chapman was definitely not a handsome man, she decided, but he carried himself with assurance . . . with a slightly cheeky air.

She watched as he moved across the road to another car, leaned down and spoke to the driver, who then sounded his horn twice. A minute later, two men materialised from the sides of the garden wall and climbed into the car. As he walked to the gate, the car drove away. It, or one like it, had been parked there every day and night since the death of her family.

She stood up, and he kissed her lightly on the cheek and explained, 'We had what we call a red alert, both at the airport and the sea passenger terminal. This afternoon we had a strong tip-off of a terrorist attack and so we've had to pull in all our security people. That included my people who were protecting you.'

As they walked into the house, she said, 'Well, it's no problem. I'm sure I'm not a target.'

'I'm sure you're at risk,' he answered. 'I cannot put my people back up here until tomorrow morning, which means I have to stay the night.' They were now in the lounge. He turned and smiled at her. 'That might sound like the greatest line a man ever made but, Lucy, I assure you that the red alert is genuine and that the threat to your life is real in my mind.'

With a half-smile, she said, 'Colin, I have two questions. First, if I was a seventy-year-old lady, would you also be offering to stay the night? And second, if this house is attacked by Triad hitmen tonight, would you be able to protect me?'

He said, 'If you had been a lady of seventy, I would have insisted that at least two of my men remained on watch, even if it meant a clash with the Commissioner. But I must be honest. I find you attractive and also enjoy your mind and your company. So, since you had invited me for dinner anyway, I thought I could sleep on your settee until my men come back in the morning.'

She reached up and kissed his cheek and said, 'After dinner, will you write me poems in Chinese?'

He nodded solemnly.

'If that's what you'd like . . . As to your second question: of course I'm not Rambo, but I have been well-trained.' He reached under his jacket and pulled out a large pistol. 'I know how to use it.'

'Have you ever killed anybody?'

'No, but if anyone breaks into this house tonight, I will kill them.'

'I will sleep easy then,' she said. 'Is there any news on the case?'

'There is . . . I had a long fax from the Police Commander in Zimbabwe who is handling the Coppen/Manners case. Very informative and interesting. I'll tell you about it over dinner.'

She surprised him by cooking a traditional English dish of roast lamb. She knew how to do it because one of her early boyfriends had been a chef at a smart English-style restaurant in a hotel in Causeway Bay. She had shown interest and he had taught her several traditional dishes.

Colin Chapman was massively impressed, especially because she had not overcooked the meat and she had made the perfect mint sauce. She explained that she had cooked it for him because, although she knew he liked a wide variety of Chinese food, she also knew he sometimes had to eat too much of it. Her father had enjoyed good wine and she took a bottle of Château Margaux from the storeroom. They drank it both before and during the meal, and it went so quickly that she fetched another bottle, and by the end of the meal she was feeling light-headed.

As she brought in the coffee, he pulled out the fax from Zimbabwe. It ran to several pages. He said, 'This is from Commander John Ndlovu, Head of the Matabeleland CID. He headed the investigation. He is clearly intelligent and articulate. He mentions that he was under great pressure from the US Government through his Ministry. Obviously, the mother of the murdered girl pulled powerful strings. Ndlovu reached a dead-end. No motive, no tracks, no weapon . . . nothing.'

'But you think the motive could be connected with the death of my family? Have you replied to his fax?'

Chapman shook his head and then smiled at her.

'This afternoon, I took a decision. Tomorrow, after the red alert is over, I'm going to pull in Tommy Mo for questioning. It's never happened to him before and it was a decision I took only after consulting the Commissioner . . . it's time Tommy Mo came under the hammer.'

'Will it serve any purpose?'

'It will hurt his dignity . . . he will lose face. We will arrest him at his usual restaurant, which we are sure he secretly owns. It will be full of people. I will personally frogmarch him out.'

'To what purpose?'

He took a sip of coffee and said, 'I'll have to let him go after a night in the cells, but it will unbalance him, and when criminals are unbalanced they sometimes do stupid things.'

'So it's just a faint hope?'

'Faint, yes . . . but still a hope.'

'And if he does nothing stupid . . . what then?'

He sighed, gave her a speculative look, lowered his voice to a serious tone and said, 'You must go to Zimbabwe. I would like to go myself, but it's impossible.' He tapped the pages in front of him. 'What's happening down there is interesting. Gloria Manners, the dead girl's mother, has arrived by chartered jet, together with a man simply called Creasy, his son Michael, who is apparently adopted. They are both mercenaries. There was also a man called Maxie MacDonald, whom Ndlovu informs me is an ex-Selous Scout, which was an elite Rhodesian unit in the War for Independence.' He tapped the papers again. 'According to Ndlovu, Creasy and MacDonld are going into the bush in the area of the murders.'

'Will they find anything?'

His answer was measured. 'I wouldn't have thought so, but then, at the end of his fax, John Ndlovu mentioned that he made an enquiry to Interpol, both about Creasy and Maxie . . . not that they are criminals, but since the mercenary activity in Africa in the sixties and seventies, all intelligence information on mercenaries has been filed and collated by Interpol. Obviously, they charge a fee for their information and the fee has a scale of three, ranging from very brief details to their complete file.' He read from the fax: ' "Chief Inspector Chapman, my budget is such that I could only afford to obtain brief details on the subject Creasy, which I enclose. Since your budget must be greater than mine, perhaps you might wish to extract the full dossier from Interpol on both men. If so, I would be grateful for a faxed copy. I will keep you informed of any developments here and will be grateful for the same from your end. Signed, John Ndlovu (Commander CID)" '

Colin looked up and said, 'So I sent a fax to Interpol for full dossiers on both men. You may or may not know it, but Interpol is not a police force as such. It is simply an office with some bright men and women and sophisticated computers. They correlate information from just about every police force in the world and, in some cases, such as this one, from intelligence organisations. The information on these two men came back within an hour.' He passed her over a sheaf of faxed papers. 'I think you should look at them.'

She read the pages, and when she looked up he saw the glint of excitment in her eyes. She said, 'So, Creasy is the lead man. MacDonald works for him. A few years ago Creasy wiped out an entire Mafia family down the length of Italy.' She pulled the last page in front of her and read out the words. 'The subject is not in the mould of the normal mercenary profile. Although he works for money, he is extremely discriminating about whom he works for. There is no knowledge of him ever having been involved in criminal activity or acts of terrorism or atrocity. From tragedies in his personal life, he appears to have developed a particular abhorrence for organised crime.'

As she spoke the last words, Colin smiled, and then said, 'Yes, Lucy, you could definitely describe Triads as organised crime. But from what you tell me, you don't have the money to hire such a man and the team he would certainly need.'

'It's true,' she said sadly. 'But if Creasy finds something out in Zimbabwe, it's possible there may be a connection which you could use here.'

'Yes. It's why I think you should go – and soon. I'll phone John Ndlovu and ask him to give you his co-operation.'

She gave him a hard look.

Are you suggesting that I go to Zimbabwe just to get me out of danger here in Hong Kong?'

'Of course I want you out of danger here, but I have to admit that I'll miss your company. The simple fact is, Lucy, I'm convinced that the two cases are linked, and if this man Creasy discovers something in Zimbabwe, we might get something on Tommy Mo. The Commissioner would never let me send one of my officers out there on pure speculation, but I think you should go and make contact with the man and with Mrs Manners.'

She looked at him across the table and said, 'So, you'll miss my company?'

He nodded firmly.

'Understand something. I've spent years studying Chinese culture and languages and, of course, I'm surrounded by Chinese police officers, and count several as good friends. But I've never had much to do with Chinese women. I'm not one to go to the bars in Wanchai or Kowloon. Yet, these last few days, I feel that in a small way, I've managed to cross the culture gap.'

She nodded in agreement.

'I feel the same, but we Chinese stick to our own. Being a modern Chinese girl in Hong Kong is not always simple. Within my race there is still a great deal of prejudice towards *gweilos*. Many still refer to you people as *Sun Ging Fang Gweilos* – barbarian foreign devils. Even among the educated. A woman in my position is forced to make a choice early on. If she goes out with a *gweilo*, then she is sort of contaminated in the eyes of Chinese men. The first man I ever went out with was an Englishman and although I took that decision. I have always felt somehow uncomfortable.' She smiled. 'But not with you, Colin. The other night in the restaurant, when you spoke to the waiter in the Fukien dialect, I was very proud to see the respect in his eyes. So somehow, for me, you have crossed that racial divide. I also enjoy your company. I know that I put on a strong face, and some people I know are amazed that I show no emotion about what has happened to me. They cannot understand how I continue to stay in this house where my family were murdered. They don't understand that I cannot bear to leave it, because I feel their spirits are still here and will remain here until I go far away. But inside of me there is terrible emotion. I loved my family, and I feel as though part of my heart has been cut away. Your concern and your friendship have been more important to me than I can put into words.'

It moved on from there. They went into the lounge and Chapman phoned the office to check on the status of the red alert, which, he was informed, was still in effect. The cruise liner QE2, on her round the world trip, was due to berth at the sea terminal in the early hours of the morning, and Intelligence had suggested that it might be the target of a terrorist attack.

They sat on the settee together and watched CNN news. After that catalogue of worldwide disasters, she put on some classical music, which she knew he liked. As Chopin's Nocturnes drew to a close, she found her head resting on Colin's shoulder and her mind both emotional and – for the first time in a long time – very relaxed.

His arms slid around her shoulders. She lifted her face and they kissed. Her first thoughts were that, although he could read and write eighty thousand Chinese characters, he was not exactly an expert in kissing. But somehow his clumsiness was endearing. After a minute, she pulled away and, for something to say, remarked on how nice he smelled. He immdiately looked embarrassed.

'It's aftershave lotion,' he said. 'I don't usually wear it.'

'It's nice. What is it?'

'Versus by Gianni Versace.'

'Hmm, that's expensive . . . a present from a girlfriend?'

He looked discomfited and shook his head. 'No . . . well . . . actually, I haven't had a girlfriend for a long time.'

She put her hand on his cheek and smiled.

'Did you buy it yourself?'

'Yes.'

'When?'

'Well . . . this afternoon.'

She laughed. Not at him but with him. 'Did you plan all this?'

'Well, no . . . Let's say it just happened. I put on Versace and you put on Chopin's Nocturness, which always make me romantic.'

They moved to the bedroom. He admired the bed and she explained that it had been passed down through her family for several generations. It was a massive four-poster opium bed, ornately carved out of mahogany and ebony. She told him it was so heavy that when they had moved it into the house, twenty years ago, it had to be dismantled and then reassembled inside the bedroom.

As they undressed each other he asked, 'And do we get to smoke opium in it?'

'Certainly not. First of all, I would never offer opium to a Chief Inspector of Police and, secondly, opium diminishes the sex drive.'

She led the lovemaking. He ran his eyes and his hands over her slim body in silent wonderment, and then stroked the thin band of silky black hair between her thighs. Gently she pulled his head down to guide his lips to kiss her there. His body was impatient. He was breathing quickly. She slid under him and guided him into her and within minutes he was gasping with pent-up relief.

She was not disappointed. Her instincts told her that it must have been weeks or months since he had last made love. But he was intensely embarrassed. She used the necessary words to comfort and reassure him, and then she slipped out of the bed, went into the bathroom and ran the hot tap over a small towel and took it back and gently wiped his genitals.

They lay side by side in silence and just before she fell asleep, he murmured, 'En goi ne' . . . 'I love you' in Cantonese.

She gave him a feathery kiss but did not answer.

She woke up three hours later, and lay with her head on his chest, and looked across at the bedside table, where he had left his shoulder-holster and gun. It seemed incongruous. She could not imagine him firing a gun. She could not imagine him as her lover, but she had no regrets about being in bed with him and lying in his arms. She felt not love, but a warm glow. She would leave in the morning for Zimbabwe. Maybe she would not come back. Maybe destiny would find a new life for her. She smiled at herself, thinking of destiny. She and Colin had discussed it a few times. He was very interested and knowledgeable about the myriad super-stitions and beliefs in Chinese society, ancient and modern. He could understand how it might dominate the lives of poor people, but not modern, highly educated Chinese. She explained that, no matter how Western-orientated a Chinese might be, he always kept his ancient superstitions. Her father was a Western-educated scientist, but when he had built this house, he employed a Fung Shui expert together with the architect, and the two men had

66

worked together so that the spirits, inside and outside the house, would be calm.

Colin laughed and shook his head in surprise and asked, 'Do you also believe in such things?'

'Oh, yes. Very much. I believe the spirits affect the destiny of all of us.'

It was ten minutes later when the window shattered . . . ten minutes after midnight. The light was still on and her eyes still open. She saw the oblong black object arcing across the room and, although she had never seen one before, she recognised it as a grenade. It hit the far wall, bounced off the white Tientsin carpet and rolled under the bed.

She felt Colin's body jerk beside her, and then the massive bed lifted and tilted with the explosion. She lay stunned on the carpet, but within seconds he was on his feet, grabbing at the gun and pulling her down behind the bed which had lost one leg. Two more grenades followed. The first one shattered into shrapnel. She felt a sharp pain in her arm and heard a grunt from him. The second grenade exploded into white flame and for several seconds she was blinded. She heard several explosions in other parts of the house and then voices shouting in Cantonese.

Chapman was at the broken window, standing naked, the gun raised and firing rapidly. The door burst open and Chapman ducked and turned. There was a black-clad Chinese at the door, holding a machine-pistol. The phosphorous grenade had dimmed but it still gave a faint glow. The Chinese man's eyes were darting around the room, looking for targets.

A second figure appeared, also clad in black and also holding a machine-pistol. Next to her, Chapman fired and one of the men spun away. The other pulled back into the corridor. Then in a blurred sequence, she saw Colin hurl his now empty weapon at the door. She felt his arms around her and heard his voice screaming, 'Run!' And then he had lifted her off her feet and flung her through the window that was no longer there.

As she rolled over the grass lawn, she heard the staccato sound of firing from inside the bedroom. To her left, another black-clad Chinese was lying moaning, his hands clutching his belly. She started back towards the window and then she saw Colin's face there, twisted in agony.

'Run!' he hissed, and then his head lifted as more bullets slammed into his back. His naked torso slumped over the window-sill among the broken glass, and she saw the blood all over his back. She heard more shouting from inside the house and from the other side of the garden, and instinct made her run. Instinct made her stop by the pool and told her that she could not run fast enough. She was beside the small stone structure that housed the filtration plant. She pulled open the old wooden door, crawled in beside the round orange filter and the pump, and pulled the door closed. The shouting went on for another two minutes, then she heard more explosions from inside the house. She twisted and looked through the crack in the door. All she could see was flames. She could only hear the crackle of those flames and the roar as cars revved up outside the gates. Then she heard the scream of spinning tyres

Two minutes later, above the roar of the flames, she heard the howling of sirens. She pushed open the door and fell out beside the pool. She lay there, naked, feeling the slight wound in her shoulder, feeling hatred consuming her mind and her guts.

CHAPTER 15

The Ambassador arrived at the Meikles Hotel half an hour after they had checked in. He was tall, grey-haired and courteous. Gloria received him in the lounge of her suite. Creasy, Maxie and Michael arrived a few minutes later. Creasy immediately noted the change in Gloria's attitude. She was being pleasant.

After a waiter had served coffee and departed, the Ambassador glanced at Creasy and said, 'Of course, I know what you are and who you are. So do the Zimbabwe police. In fact, Commander John Ndlovu tells me that some years ago you and he chased each other around the mountains in Mozambique.'

'That's correct,' Creasy answered.

The Ambassador said 'Well, now he's a very good policeman. And, from what I hear, not corrupt.' He turned back to Gloria. 'Mrs Manners, I assure you he carried out a thorough investigation. I don't think he can be blamed for not coming up with the suspects.'

'Will he co-operate with us?' Creasy asked.

'Yes, although with some reluctance. Under such circumstances, in a murder investigation, no policeman likes a bunch of outsiders interfering.'

'What about the firearms permits?' Maxie asked.

The Ambassador's smile was a little grim.

'That too,' he said. 'But it took a lot of persuasion.' He glanced again at Creasy. 'Are you still an American citizen, Mr Creasy?'

'No. Like many Foreign Legionaries, I took out French citizenship after my first five-year stint.'

'I'm pleased to hear that. As American Ambassador here, I'd prefer not to have armed American mercenaries roaming the

69

country, even if they do have police permission. What about your son?'

'I have a Maltese passport,' Michael answered.

Maxie chipped in. 'And I exchanged my Rhodesian passport for a British one after Independence.'

The Ambassador was looking positively pleased. He turned again to Gloria. 'Mrs Manners, I would have liked to invite you to the residency for dinner, but I understand that you're only staying for one night. And, unfortunately, tonight I have to attend an official function. What are your plans from tomorrow?'

Creasy answered the question. 'Tomorrow, Mrs Manners, myself and Mr MacDonald, fly to Bulawayo. We stay only briefly to take delivery of the weapons and then fly on to Victoria Falls, where Mrs Manners and her nurse will stay at the Azambezi Lodge Hotel. Mr MacDonald and I will go into the bush and take a look around the murder site.'

'And your son?'

Again, Michael answered for himself. 'I'll be staying on in Harare for a few days. I've been very busy lately. I could use a little time off, especially the evenings.'

The Ambassador nodded thoughtfully and said, 'There's a surprisingly wide and varied nightlife in Harare, but I suggest you stay away from the clubs in the townships. They can be a bit dangerous. There's so much unemployment in the country, the crime rate in the cities is soaring.'

'Thank you,' Michael said. 'I'll keep that in mind.'

The Ambassador stood up, saying, 'But phone me at the Embassy, if you need anything.' He turned to look down at Gloria. 'Mrs Manners, that also applies, of course, to you. If you run into any problems or need any assistance, don't hesitate to phone me. I know the reason for your visit here is not a happy one, but I hope you'll be able to relax a little at Victoria Falls. The Azambezi Lodge is a wonderful hotel and very peaceful.' He looked at his watch. 'Commander John Ndlovu will be here in a few minutes, so I'll leave you to it.' He reached down and shook her hand.

She gave him a rare smile. He did not shake the hands of the three men, but gave them all an appraising stare and then said, 'Good luck, gentlemen.'

As the door closed behind him, Gloria looked at Creasy and,

with an edge of triumph in her voice, said, 'So you see, Creasy, I do have a magic wand. He was extremely courteous and helpful.'

Creasy grunted to himself and then said, 'He was courteous and helpful because he's a Foreign Service Career Officer and not a Presidential Appointee. Jim Grainger is a very powerful Senator who sits on the House Foreign Service Committee. The Ambassador had a phone-call from the Senator, which is why he's being so sweet. Anyway, the result was satisfactory. Without those weapons permits, we would have had to carry our guns illegally and that could have caused problems.'

Before she could say anything, a soft tap came on the door. Creasy stood up, walked over and opened it.

John Ndlovu was a tall thick-set ebony African. He was dressed in an extremely smart suit, with a white shirt and some kind of regimental tie. His black shoes had a mirror-like polish. The two men looked at each other for a long time and then Creasy said, 'Of course, I've seen your photograph and would recognise your face anywhere.'

The African nodded.

'And once I had you in the sights of my rifle,' he said. 'It was a very long shot, and I decided to get closer. It was a mistake. You got away and, later that night, killed four of my men.'

'It was a war.'

The African held out his hand, saying, 'Yes, it was a war. It's good that we can meet now and have a drink, instead of shooting at each other.'

Creasy took the proffered hand and shook it warmly. Then he ushered the policeman into the room and introduced him to Gloria and the others. After shaking hands, John Ndlovu looked at Maxie MacDonald and said, 'Another name out of the past. Have you been back to this country since Independence?'

'No. I decided to stay away for a while and let things cool down.'

The African gave him a half-smile. 'It was a wise decision at the time, for a Selous Scout . . . but there is no acrimony now.'

Creasy had moved to the drinks cabinet in the corner of the room.

'What can I get you?' he asked.

The policeman accepted a scotch and water and then told Gloria of his regret that his force had not been able to track down

71

her daughter's killers. He assured her that they had made extraordinary efforts and would continue to do so. Such a murder case had become rare in Zimbabwe in recent years. There was no obvious motive. Unfortunately, the rain had washed away all signs of tracks. In spite of that, he had borrowed four expert trackers from the anti-poaching department. After a week, he had had to return them, but by that time, it was clear that there was nothing to find. He could think of no political motive and there had been no robbery. He expressed his regret again and his condolences.

'I understand the situation,' Gloria said. 'I've read your report and I've no doubt that you've made every effort. But you'll understand a mother's feelings. I hope you don't mind that I've brought these men down here?'

He shrugged.

'I've been asked by my Minister to give you and them, my co-operation. Of course, I would have objected if you had brought in a bunch of ordinary mercenaries. Some of them are nothing more than thugs, but Creasy and Maxie MacDonald are not exactly ordinary. I know from experience that they're both experts at tracking in the bush and living off the land. If there's any chance of finding something out there, which my men may have missed, then they are the men for the job. Naturally I've studied Maxie MacDonald's file these past days. He speaks fluent Ndebele and some of the tribal languages of the area. That's an advantage.' He turned to Creasy. 'When will you go into the bush?'

'How do you know we are going into the bush?'

The policeman smiled. He said, 'You didn't come here to go fishing on the lake.' He gestured at Michael. 'Does this young man know anything about the African bush?'

'It's his first time in Africa,' Creasy answered. 'He'll be staying in Harare for a few days to unwind a bit. He'll join up at the Falls with us later.'

The policeman reached into the top pocket of his jacket, pulled out a card and handed it to Michael, saying, 'If you run into any trouble, phone me.'

Michael thanked him and tucked the card away. Then, from the inside of his jacket pocket, John Ndlovu pulled out a sheaf of papers and gave it to Creasy. 'Those are the temporary firearms permits. I'd be grateful if you didn't carry those weapons in view when you're in an urban area. The permits are good for thirty days. After that, I have permission to extend them, depending on the circumstances.'

Creasy handed the papers to Maxie, who flicked through them and then nodded. Creasy said to the African, 'Thirty days should be more than enough. Either we will have come across something, or we'll be out of the country.'

'I assumed so,' the policeman said. His voice took on an edge of authority. 'I expect you to keep in touch with me and inform me of any developments, and to keep in mind, at all times, that you're on my territory. Those weapons are only to be used in self-defence. Just remember that if you make progress, there'll be no summary justice.'

'I understand,' Creasy answered. 'We're just going looking – nothing else.'

Abruptly, Commander John Ndlovu turned to Maxie MacDonald and began speaking to him rapidly in a language the others could not understand. Creasy recognised it as Ndebele. Maxie began to nod slowly, never taking his eyes off the African's face. Finally, the African produced yet another piece of paper and passed it to Maxie. Maxie studied it carefully and then nodded again, folded the paper and tucked it into his back pocket.

The policeman turned to Gloria and reverted to English. 'Mrs Manners, I sincerely hope that your men will succeed where we have, so far, failed.' He reached down and shook her hand, and then shook hands with the others. At the door, he turned and said to her, 'If I can be of any help at all, don't hesitate to contact me.' He gave her a wry smile. 'Or, of course, contact your Ambassador. That man seems to be able to get things done around here.'

As soon as the door had closed behind him, Gloria looked at Maxie and said impatiently 'What were you talking about in that language?'

Maxie looked at Creasy and said, 'We were talking about two things. Ndlovu suggested that when we go into the bush, we take some sovereigns or gold krugerrands with us. Especially the latter. The police are not allowed to offer rewards to informers, but we have no constraints. It's a very poor area of the country. Ndlovu also pointed out that it's illegal to import gold into the country without a licence, and he doesn't want to know anything about it.'

Gloria said, 'So how the hell do we bring in sovereigns or krugerrands?'

Creasy and Maxie glanced at each other and then Creasy tapped his metal-studded belt and said, 'People like us never travel without a few gold coins. The metal studs disguise them from the airport scanners. We have enough to bribe a couple of villages up there.'

Gloria said, 'And the other thing you discussed?'

Maxie hesitated and then pulled out the piece of paper and handed it to Creasy. Creasy unfolded it, read the official words and smiled slightly.

'Well?' Gloria snapped.

Creasy looked at Maxie and then said to her, 'It seems that sometimes there is summary justice in Zimbabwe. This is addressed to Maxie. Being an ex-Selous Scout, he was an ex-member of the Rhodesian Armed Forces. After the war, those armed forces were merged with the guerilla forces. Technically, Maxie never resigned, nor was discharged. He just disappeared over the border. This piece of paper, signed by the Minister of Wildlife and Tourism, is both an order and a permit. If, in the bush, we come across any rhino or elephant poachers, Maxie is to shoot them on sight. If he comes over any tracks which indicate that poachers have been in the area within the past forty-eight hours, he is to follow those tracks for a minimum of seventy-two hours or until such time that the spoor indicates the poachers have crossed back into Zambia.'

'What the hell's going on?' Gloria asked. 'I mean, who's paying you guys?'

Creasy passed the paper back to Maxie and said to her, 'It's very unlikely that we'll come across any poachers in the area – it's mostly been poached out. And anyway, solving this murder takes priority over everything else.'

Maxie nodded.

'That's true,' he said. 'But if we do come across any of those bastards, it will be my pleasure to shoot them.'

CHAPTER 16

The funeral is tomorrow.'
   'What time?'
'Four o'clock, in the afternoon.'
'I'll be there.'
Inspector Lau sighed. He looked down at Lucy Kwok in the hospital bed and said, 'Miss Kwok, I just spoke to your doctor. He wants you to stay here for at least another three or four days. The wound is not serious, but you lost a lot of blood and there is the shock factor.'
She shook her head.
'Forget about the shock factor. I'm becoming immune to shocks. As for the blood, they gave me a massive transfusion as soon as I got here and another one this morning. I'm going to be at Colin's funeral.'
Inspector Lau saw the determination in the woman's eyes and nodded.
'I'd be grateful,' Lucy said. 'If you could send a police car to pick me up, at three o'clock.'
'I'll pick you up myself, and bring you back here after the funeral.'
She shook her head.
'After the funeral, I'll be going to the airport.'
'Where are you going?'
'To Zimbabwe. There's a flight to London and I'll connect from there to Harare.'
'You should rest a few more days, but I think your decision to leave Hong Kong is a wise one.'
At once, he saw the anger in her eyes and heard it in her voice.

'I'm not running away from Tommy Mo and 14K. I agreed with Colin that I would go to Zimbabwe and try to find the link between the murders there and those of my family. Colin was sure there's a link and it may lead to Tommy Mo. Has there been any other word from the Zimbabwe Police?'

'Yes. There was a fax this morning. Mrs Manners arrived by private jet yesterday with the three mercenaries. Commander John Ndlovu has promised to keep me informed.'

She gestured at the phone beside the bed. 'I'll make my flight arrangements this afternoon and then phone you. I'd be grateful if you'd fax Ndlovu and give him my arrival time.'

'I'll do that. Shall I ask him to book you a hotel?'

'No, the airline will do that. Being a stewardess, I get huge discounts.'

The Inspector walked across the room and looked out of the window. They were in the Matilda Hospital, high on the Peak. He was looking down at the high-rises of Victoria and beyond them, Kowloon. The faint hum and buzz of one of the busiest cities in the world drifted up. He turned to her and said, 'Colin was my friend. He never said very much, but I understood him. I think, during the time that you worked with him on your father's files, he became very fond of you.'

Lucy Kwok was silent for a while, then she said, 'He told me on that last night that he was in love with me. It must have been true. He threw me out of that window. He could have followed and tried to escape. He had already fired all the bullets in his gun . . . but he stayed there and died.'

Inspector Lau walked back to the bed and looked down at her again and said, 'Were you in love with him?'

Slowly, she shook her head.

'No. But I was coming to like him very much. Maybe love would have followed. Who can say? That's destiny. Maybe *gweilos* fall in love more quickly that we do.'

Inspector Lau walked slowly towards the door. Then he turned and said to her, 'Colin Chapman looked like a *gweilo*, but he was not a *gweilo*. His heart and his mind and his soul came from the middle kingdom. All I want now is the heart and the mind and the soul of Tommy Mo. Either locked up in a prison cell . . . or dead.'

From across the room, she asked, 'Would you kill him yourself?'

76

'No. I'm a policeman. But sometimes I wish I was not . . . I'll pick you up at three o'clock tomorrow, then I'll take you to the airport.'

CHAPTER 17

It was only a one hour flight to Bulawayo. The Gulfstream touched down just after 9 a.m. It taxied behind the Land-rover with the flashing light to an area away from the main terminal. The police car was waiting and another civilian Land-rover. The steward lowered the steps and within minutes two men had climbed aboard, both white. One was in the uniform of an Inspector of Police and the other was clad in the typical clothes of a white farmer: khaki shorts, khaki shirt and rough suede ankle boots. The farmer carried a large canvas bag.

Maxie knew them both. The farmer was his cousin. The weapons were in the bag. Although he had not seen his cousin for more than fourteen years, they greeted each other casually, as if it had only been yesterday. It was the way of Rhodesians. The Inspector was in his early fifties. He shook Maxie's hand warmly and Maxie said, 'This is a surprise.'

The Inspector said, 'I guess it must be. I decided to stay on for a year after Independence. At first, things were rough but I stuck out a second year and then things improved, so I'm still here.'

Maxie grinned. 'Christ! They even made you Inspector.' He turned to Creasy and said, 'This is Robin Gilbert. We were at school together.' He then introduced the Inspector to Gloria, who had spent the short journey reading the local newspaper.

The policeman said, 'I understand you're going straight on to Vic Falls, so let's get this business over with.'

The farmer lifted the canvas bag on to the saloon table and unzipped it. Creasy took out the sheaf of papers that Ndlovu had given him in Harare, and passed them to Robin Gilbert. It took ten minutes for Gilbert to check the weapons against the licences. He then countersigned the licences and handed them back to Creasy, saying, 'Mr Creasy, whenever you or Maxie or Michael Creasy are carrying one of these guns, always have the relevant licence on your person.'

'Understood.'

Gloria was looking at the assortment of rifles and pistols. She said, 'God Almighty! There's only three of you. This is enough for a small army.'

Creasy explained. 'They serve different purposes for different occasions. We're not going to carry them all around at the same time.' He pointed. 'That's a high-velocity rifle for long-range. Next to it is a lightweight .22 with silencer. Those other two rifles are AK47s for close work. The pistols are Colt 1911s and very effective.' He picked up one of the AK47s and one of the pistols and put them back into the canvas bag, together with two of the licences, and said to the farmer, 'Please be sure they get to Michael in Harare before nightfall.'

The farmer nodded.

'I'll be there by late afternoon.' He had a small battered satchel over one shoulder. He lifted it off and tossed it to Maxie and said, 'Biltong. Made from young kudu.'

Maxie's eyes literally sparkled with pleasure as he unstrapped the satchel and lifted out what looked like two kilos of dark leather.

'What the hell is that?' Gloria asked.

Creasy explained. 'It's dried and salted meat. What we call "jerky" in America. Over there, we make it mostly with beef, but here they use game. You might say it's an acquired taste, but a man could live in the bush for many days on that much biltong and nothing else except water.'

The farmer picked up the canvas bag, made his farewells and left. The policeman gestured to Creasy, who followed him down the aircraft. Once out of earshot, he said, 'I understand you're going straight from here to Vic Falls.'

'That's correct.'

'I'm going up there today myself, to do a couple of weeks' duty in the area.'

'Was that a sudden decision by Ndlovu?'

'I guess so. I got the orders last night.'

'He's sending you up there to keep an eye on us?'

Gilbert shook his head. 'I think not. It would be a waste of time, my trying to keep an eye on you two in the bush . . . You'd lose me in about sixty seconds . . . No. Ndlovu knows that I was friendly with Maxie. It makes sense to have someone like me close to the area. Maxie's more likely to confide in me than in some black policeman he doesn't know.'

'Sounds likely,' Creasy said. 'So, you'll base yourself at Vic Falls?'

'Not exactly. I'll move back and forth, between Vic Falls and Binga. I'll be in radio contact with the stations at both places. If you come across anything, just get in touch.'

'Will do.'

Gilbert hesitated and then said, 'Do you think I could hitch a ride on this thing? It would save me a boring four hour drive.'

Creasy smiled wryly. 'I'll ask Mrs Manners. But she's a bit of an old bitch, and not in a very good mood this morning.'

Creasy walked back up to the saloon, followed by Gilbert. Gloria was being served a cup of coffee by the steward. She was still reading the newspaper.

Creasy said, 'Mrs Manners, Inspector Gilbert is also traveling to Vic Falls today. His first job is to check your security at the Azambezi Lodge. If we take him with us, it will save him a four hour journey by car.'

Gloria looked up and stared at the policeman for several seconds, and then said, 'Sure. Why not?' She turned to the steward. 'Give the man a cup of coffee.'

Creasy moved further forward towards the cockpit, saying, 'I'll tell the pilot to get going.'

Again, the policeman followed him, and at the cockpit door he tapped Creasy on the shoulder. Creasy turned.

'How did you know?' Gilbert asked.

'Know what?'

'That at the top of my list of orders from Commander Ndlovu is to arrange total security for Mrs Manners?'

'It wasn't hard to work out. The last thing Ndlovu needs is for another American to get shot in his country.' He pointed back down the aircraft. 'Especially one like that.' He turned back to the cockpit door, opened it and said, 'Let's get this mother off the ground.'

The row erupted about fifteen minutes later, as they flew over Matabeleland. Creasy and Robin Gilbert were sitting to the rear of the aircraft. Creasy was picking the policeman's brains about the local conditions and the policeman was briefing him on the situation regarding local politics and economics and the poaching problem. Maxie was up front in the saloon, drinking coffee with Gloria and Ruby. Gloria had tried a piece of biltong and didn't like it. She had finished reading the newspaper and was obviously bored. She showed no interest in the scenery unfolding below.

'When are you and Creasy going into the bush?' she asked Maxie.

'At dawn tomorrow.'

'When will you reach the site?'

'It depends.'

'On what?'

'On how fast we move.'

'Goddamn it! You don't know how fast you're going to move?'

'No. It could take two days or three days.'

'Why?'

Maxie sighed and tried to explain. 'We'll be looking for spoor . . . tracks. A lot depends on the condition of the ground. How dry it is, which way the wind was blowing and is blowing.'

She leaned forward and said tightly, 'Don't bullshit me! I've read all the police reports. They had trackers in that area for days and they found nothing.'

'Mrs Manners, we're not looking for tracks that will be weeks old. We're looking for recent tracks.'

'Why?'

'Because other people may have been in the area when your daughter was killed and they may have gone back into that area.'

Gloria leaned even further forward, and in her tight voice said, 'You'd better understand something. I don't want you chasing after some goddamn poachers and wasting my money. You work for me, not for the Zimbabwe Wildlife Department!'

She was suddenly looking at a pair of very cold eyes. The voice was equally cold, but Creasy heard it from the back of the plane. He stood up and starting walking to the saloon.

Maxie said, 'Wind in your neck, lady. I am not working for you. I came down here on expenses only. You paid my hotel bills and you paid my food. But if you have your accountant examine the bills, you'll find out that you never paid for any of my drinks at the hotels. I'll tell you why. Many years ago, I spent a couple of years as a hunter, working for a safari company. We had many American clients, most of whom were spoilt over-rich idiots. When the professional hunters used to meet up with each other back in Bulawayo and ask how each other's trips went, we used a very cryptic phrase. We either said, "I was drinking their whisky" or "I was drinking my own whisky." It meant that the clients were either friendly and co-operative or they were unfriendly morons. And let me tell you lady, so far on this trip, I've been drinking my own whisky. I don't pretend to like you, although I'm sorry about your problems. Now understand one last thing: if I come across the fresh spoor of rhino poachers, I'm going after them. That's how it is, and if you don't like it, I'll get off this plane at Vic Falls and head home.'

The woman sat rigid, and then looked up to see Creasy standing above them. She said, 'Did you hear what this bastard said to me?'

Creasy nodded.

'Yes, He took the words right out of my mouth.' Ruby was looking on in fascination. Creasy continued, 'Maxie is right. We don't work for you. That was the deal we made in Denver. We came down here to have a look. If we find something that makes it worthwhile continuing, then you start paying. I hope we do find something, because it would give me pleasure to start spending some of your money. We'll know one way or another within four or five days. Until that time, I suggest you keep control of yourself, otherwise, even if we do find something, we're likely to piss off and drink our own whisky.'

CHAPTER 18

In spite of the air-conditioning, the sweat poured off Michael's face. The dance-floor was packed and gyrating to the rhythm of the eight-piece African band. The sound system was antique, as were the instruments, but the music was straight from the soul of Africa and nothing like the sounds of those Zimbabwe bands that had been 'discovered'' and then sanitised in European recording studios. The girl in front of him was called Shavi and was Indian; part of the community that had remained in the country after Independence. She was small and slight, with huge luminous eyes and a curved red mouth which was constantly breaking into a smile.

There were few white faces on the dance-floor or at the long white bar which only served beer and soft drinks. The club was located in a township ten kilometres from the city centre and was wonderfully unsophisticated. He had met Shavi in the disco at the Sheraton and quickly warmed to her maverick nature. Over a drink, she had explained that the substantial Indian community, which had first been brought to Rhodesia by the British as skilled labourers on the railways, had over the years become a sort of middle-class, mainly involved in retailing and property. Her family owned a large garment store. They would not be pleased that she was consorting even with a European, and they would be horrified if they thought she went out with an African. She was the new generation. She had been born in the country and it was as much hers as anyone else's and she would go out with who the hell she liked . . . even a Maltese. Michael had looked around the sophisticated disco and remarked that it would not have been out of place in any big European city. She had immediately suggested a change of venue and after a taxi ride and a fifty cent entrance fee, they had walked into Mushambira Club in the suburb of Highlands and its pounding music.

He was surprised that the almost entirely black clientele were so well-dressed, the men in suits and ties and the women in brightly-coloured well-made dresses. Shavi explained that after the first flush of being able to go into the sophisticated white clubs in Harare, a lot of even wealthy blacks prefer the raw music and atmosphere of places like the Mushambira Club Bagamba. They felt more relaxed among their own, and the few liberal-type whites who went there were simply tolerated.

'And you?' Michael had asked.

She had laughed and answered, 'I'm unique. Perhaps the only Indian woman who's ever walked through these doors. I speak perfect Shona and have no prejudices and they feel that. I've also been here with an African boyfriend who I met at university. He's now on a scholarship in London.'

'Did you love him?'

'Oh, yes. But London is far away and I'm only nineteen with much to do.'

They danced almost non-stop for about an hour, to the Blacks Unlimited band, until finally Michael took her by the hand and said, 'The bar and a cold beer beckons . . . And I'd like to meet a few of the locals.'

Like all the others, they drank the beer straight from the bottle. There was a giant of a man behind the bar with a permanent wide smile and sweat pouring down his face. Shavi introduced him as the bar-owner. He looked Michael up and down and then asked her something in Shona.

She shook her head and answered, 'No, Maltese.'

The black face looked puzzled and she spoke to him again in Shona, obviously telling him of the place she herself had only learned about a few hours earlier. He nodded and held out a huge hand to give Michael a surprisingly light handshake in the African manner.

He said in English, 'By your looks, I thought you might be Greek. And I hate those bastards. They'd steal your wallet as fast as your woman. I never had a Maltese in here before. You're welcome. Especially when you come with the beautiful Shavi. She decorates my place.'

With his left hand he pulled out two bottles of Lion beer from the cooler, grabbed one of the many openers on the bar and flipped off the tops. He banged the bottles down in front of them and said, 'On me', and then moved down the long bar to serve other customers.

Michael turned to look at Shavi. Even at the bar, her body still moved slightly to the music, and he felt himself doing the same. Back at the Sheraton she had asked him what he was doing in the country. He had told her that he was taking six months off before going to university in America and that he had decided to have a look around Africa and see the sights. She had looked a bit thoughtful at that, but said nothing.

Now she swayed closer to him, looked up and asked, 'Why did you lie to me?'

'Me?'

She looked around.

'Do you see anybody else I'm talking to?'

'Why should I lie to you, and what would be the lie?'

Her mouth was still smiling but her eyes held a challenge in them.

'This is a big country,' she said. 'But in a way, Harare is like one large village. We all know what's happening here. Your name is not John Grech. It's Michael Creasy. You are staying in a suite at Meikles Hotel and you are a mercenary.'

He kept a poker face and remained silent. There was no more challenge in her eyes, just humour.

'Back at that disco,' she said, 'I was with a group of friends when you asked me to dance. One of them is a ground hostess at the airport and saw you get off a fancy private jet with two other men, and a woman in a wheelchair.'

'And you know who they were?'

'Oh, yes. All of Harare knows that she is the mother of the American woman who was murdered a few weeks ago. The man with the scars and the grey hair is your father. Apparently, he is a famous mercenary. The other man is well-known in this country. He was a Rhodesian and a Selous Scout. In fact, his father used to buy his clothes from my father's shop. You are here to find the murderers. So I'm a little surprised that you are in this club, dancing with an Indian girl.'

He took a swig from the bottle, looked down into her dark eyes and asked, 'OK. Your friend at the airport, I understand. But how do you know about my father and why we are here?'

'I told you, this city is a village. Maybe you noticed the very well-dressed young African who was in my group at the disco. He works for the CIO – the Central Intelligence Office. They keep tabs on every foreigner entering the country. He told me that the crippled woman is richer than God, and that she hired the best mercenaries in the world to hunt down her daughter's killer.'

Michael said, 'Well, if your well-dressed African friend is some kind of intelligence agent, he shouldn't be shooting off his mouth in some disco to young women. Especially since the government here is giving us full co-operation.'

'That's true. But then, you see, he was trying to impress me.'

'Why?'

'Because he's in love with me.'

Michael laughed. 'Is everyone in this village in love with you?'

Solemnly, she answered, 'Of course. Don't you think I'm beautiful and charming?'

'Oh, yes. And also inquisitive. Are you an informer for the CIO?'

'No, but you can be sure there are several here and the CIO will know your movements all the time you are in Harare. We are not a police state, but most young countries and their politicians are paranoid about security.'

'I guess you're right,' he said. 'But there's nothing sinister about what we're doing. The police have tried hard on this case but haven't come up with any answers. It's natural that a very rich woman would spend some of her fortune to try and find out who killed her only daughter.'

'Yes. But you didn't answer my question. If she's paying you what must be a lot of money, what are you doing chasing innocent Indian girls in discos and nightclubs?'

Michael spoke in a bantering tone but his mind was ice-cold. 'Can't you guess?'

'Oh, yes. But I'll only tell you when I have a fresh cold beer in my hand.'

It was hot in the club and Michael was still sweating, but the girl's face and dark olive body were completely dry. She wore a white cotton and chiffon blouse with no bra, and emerald silk trousers flowed around her legs. She had straight jet-black hair which reached down to her small rounded bottom. She tilted her head back and drained half the bottle of beer and then put her head to one side as she looked up at him.

'Your father knows Africa. He brought the Selous Scout MacDonald with him because he's the best. Because he's reputed to be the best. You are young, but you have never been to Africa before . . . so I guess your father told you to stay in Harare and find out about the local gossip and, if necessary, seduce innocent young girls to do so.'

Michael said, 'Well, the only information I've learned so far is that so-called innocent young girls know exactly what I'm doing here.'

She laughed. But then her face went serious and she leaned closer. 'You must be careful. Maybe that American woman and the man with her were killed for some political or financial reason. Having you and your father and the Scout MacDonald sniffing around could make them nervous and that could be dangerous. Life is not valued here as much as where you come from. You could be struck by lightning.'

'Lightning!'

'Yes. Didn't you know?'

'Know what?'

'It's in *The Guinness Book of Records* – more people are killed by lightning, per capita, in Zimbabwe than in any other country in the world. I think it was more than five hundred last year.'

'Are you serious?'

'Of course, it's mostly in the tribal lands where they live in mud and wood huts and don't know about lightning conductors.'

He smiled but her face remained serious.

'I like you,' she said. 'You're handsome and intelligent and you dance well. I don't want to see you struck by lightning.'

'Shavi, you can be sure that I know all about lightning conductors. Now, come on, introduce me to some of your African friends.'

She turned and looked down the bar and suddenly he heard her curse, even above the music. She was looking at a group of three men about twenty metres away. They were in their late twenties and dressed in green suede jackets and white open-necked shirts and smart jeans. They all wore polished brown shoes. Her gaze moved to the dance-floor and she spotted someone else and cursed again. She turned back to the bar.

'What is it?' Michael asked.

She sighed. 'It's a friend of mine. He's being stupid.' She gestured at the dance-floor. 'He's out there dancing with a girl, the beautiful one in the long white dress. He should never have brought her here . . . but as well as being stupid, he's arrogant. He brought her to the wrong territory.'

'Why?'

With her chin, she pointed at the group of three men. 'One of those used to be her boyfriend. He's obsessed with her. About two weeks ago, my friend out there took her away from him. She's beautiful but she's a bitch. She must have persuaded my friend to bring her to this club, knowing that it would enrage the other guy. This is his territory. He deals on the black market with his friends and sometimes in drugs. The clothes they wear are a sort of trademark. They are more or less a gang and very tough.'

Michael studied the three men and then looked across the dance floor. The girl in the long white dress was indeed beautiful, almost as tall as himself, with a neck like a gazelle. Her tight hair was threaded with tiny multi-coloured beads that glistened in the light. She danced like a dream. Her face and arms were the colour of ebony. Every once in a while, she threw a slanted glance at the group of three men at the bar. Her partner was also tall and very slim and dressed in a ruffled white shirt, open almost to the waist, dark blue trousers and white leather shoes. He was also black but paler than her. He had a gold chain around his neck and a gold wristwatch.

Michael turned back to Shavi and asked, 'Is your friend also in the black market?'

'No, my friend is at college. He has a rich father . . . but his father can't help him tonight.'

Michael glanced around the huge barn-like room with its raised stage at the far end. There were at least four hundred people dancing or drinking or rapping in the corners. He asked, 'Your friend has no support here at all?'

'None. He's not even a Shona . . . He's a Manica from Mutare down at the Mozambique border. No one here will interfere. They sure won't help a stranger against their own.'

Michaeal gestured at the huge man behind the bar. 'What about him?'

She shook her head again.

'He won't have any trouble in here – but it's when my friend leaves the place. They'll follow him out.'

'What will they do?'

She looked down grimly at the bar and said, 'They won't kill him, but they'll come close. In such matters, where a woman is concerned, they'll cut his face and kick his balls in.'

'Will they be armed?'

'No. Not even with knives. They'll take bottles out and smash them in the car-park and use them on him. What happens outside is no one's business in here.'

Michael looked at her and saw the concern and even fear in her eyes. He had attempted to use her and, in a way, he had succeeded. He had learned through her that anyone of importance or interest that he talked to would know what he was doing. He also knew that this girl had a magic about her which could probably unlock doors and men's voices. He asked her, 'Is this friend important to you?'

'Yes. It's a long story, but he once helped me when I was very young, and in helping me caused himself such trouble. He was never my lover and never will be, but he's a good friend. I want to leave now and get to a phone and try to get some help for him.'

'Is that easy?'

'No. His friends will not want to come to this territory . . . But I have to try.'

Michael took his decision. He asked, 'Do you want me to help your friend?' She looked at him without comprehension. He repeated the question. 'Do you want me to help your friend?'

'But how? And why?'

He was looking at the three men in their suede jackets. His gaze then swept around the room at all the other black faces. He asked, 'I'm a white man. If I get involved against those three, are the rest of this lot going to lynch me?'

She shook her head.

'No. Even though it's their territory, that gang is not popular. The others will not be offended if a stranger went against them. Even a white one.'

Michael turned again to look at the dance-floor. Shavi was standing close to him. He could feel the warmth of her arm against his. He asked, 'If you go on to that dance-floor and talk to your friend, will he do what you tell him?'

89

She was looking at her friend and the girl in the white dress who was swinging her tightly-clad bottom in the direction of her ex-boyfriend, and obviously revelling in the situation.

'He will do exactly what I tell him,' Shavi answered. 'I can see even from here that he's frightened and wishing to God that he never let her bring him here.'

Michael glanced at the three men again. 'I told that taxi driver to wait for us at the corner. Do you think he's still there?'

'Definitely. You gave him ten dollars – he would wait there for a week. But what can you do? You may be tough, but so are they, and I think that my friend is not tough. He would not be much help.'

She saw Michael smile slightly.

He said, 'The last thing I want is his help. You will make him understand that.'

'Are you armed?'

He could feel the shape of the Colt 1911 pistol nestling in its chamois shoulder-holster under his armpit. He said, 'No, I'm not armed.' He leaned closer to her ear and gave her his instructions. When he had finished she looked up at him.

'I should be terrified for you, but for a reason I cannot understand, I'm not . . . I feel a little frightened of you.'

'Go and do it,' Michael said.

As Shavi moved from his side, he turned back to the bar and beckoned to the owner. The huge man moved forward and took Michael's outstretched hand. Michael said, 'I've enjoyed your club and the music and the good cold beer. If you ever come to my island, you ask for me and I'll be your host.'

The man's face split into a huge grin. He said, 'I'll do that. But don't expect me next week.'

Michael released the hand and turned back to look at the three men. They were watching the dance-floor. They all held dark-brown bottles of beer. Michael noted that two of them held the bottles in their right hands, while the other one, the girl's ex-boyfriend, used his left hand. He turned his head to look at the dance-floor. Shavi was gripping her friend by the shoulders and talking urgently into his ear. He was nodding and looking frightened. He glanced at Michael and then at the ex-boyfriend. The ebony girl in the white dress was standing with her arms crossed, looking very irritated.

90

Michael felt under his wide leather belt and found the flap and eased out three gold krugerrands. From the corner of his eye, he saw Shavi heading for the door with her friend close behind. The girl in the white dress was shouting at him above the music. He did not look back.

The ex-boyfriend and his two partners were moving. As they came past Michael, he moved with them. They seemed not to notice him. The door was narrow and led on to a dusty yard with a few wrecks of cars scattered around. Michael reached the door just in front of the ex-boyfriend. He saw Shavi about twenty metres away, pulling at her friend's arm, trying to drag him away. Her friend was looking back at the door. Michael cursed under his breath and then turned, opening his left hand. The three gold krugerrands glinted on his palm. Loudly, he said, 'I'm a tourist! I know it's illegal, but I want to change these. Are you interested?'

The ex-boyfriend was trying to brush past him, the beer bottle in his left hand. His two partners were pushing from behind. He was looking at Shavi and his enemy, but for a fraction of a second – he glanced down and saw the glint of gold. He turned and shouted, 'Wait! I'll be back.'

It was almost the last thing he said. Michael pivoted and his fist slammed into the man's solar plexus. It had nothing to do with any form of martial arts. It was pure street-fighting, at which Michael excelled. The air in the black man's lungs whooshed out as he doubled over, sending his face into Michael's slamming left knee. He rebounded backwards into one of his partners. The other man was trying to react, smashing his bottle against a door-post and turning, but Michael took one fast stride and kicked him in the testicles with his right foot. He screamed and dropped the bottle, grasping for his groin. Michael hit him with a short, vicious uppercut and pushed his body away. The second partner was struggling to get up from beneath the ex-boyfriend. Michael kicked him in the head and he rolled away, moaning. They lay in a triangle in the dust. It had taken about five seconds.

Shavi and her friend were standing like statues. Michael tossed the three gold coins into the centre of the triangle, and walked briskly towards them, saying, 'Let's find another club.'

CHAPTER 19

Creasy was squatting on his haunches on the bank of the Sebungwe River, his rifle held loosely but ready. Maxie was wading across the river. The water was up to his chest, and he held two rifles high above his head. Creasy's gaze was intent as he scanned the river and opposite bank for signs of crocodile. It was the third day. They had crossed the Gwaai and Mlibizi Rivers, and this was the last river they would cross before trekking to the murder site on the lake. They had passed through a land which Creasy had found strangely satisfying. During his time as a mercenary in the Rhodesian War of Independence, he had served mainly on the Mozambique border in the Eastern highlands, and the topography there could well have been Northern European, with mountains, pine forests, trout streams and very little game. But during the last three days, he had been walking through the real Africa. The terrain was undulating, with high outcrops of basalt rock. The dry Kalahari soil supported mopani woodlands between grasslands and jessie bush. The river valleys were studded with evergreens, particularly the Zimbabwe ebony and baobab trees.

The area was Maxie MacDonald's backyard and because of his impressive knowledge and the studied casualness which masked total awareness, Creasy had done something out of character. As they had climbed out of the Land-rover and watched it drive away, three days earlier, he had tapped Maxie lightly on the shoulder and said, 'You've done jobs for me off and on over the last fifteen years. I've always been the boss. But while we're in this part of the African bush, you're the boss and you give the orders.'

Maxie grinned with pleasure and said, 'OK. You don't have to call me sir, unless we meet up with anybody in a sort of social activity.'

As he turned away, Creasy kicked him in the backside, and then they went into the bush.

Although they were not expecting to find anything until they were in the region of the murder, Maxie's eyes rarely left the ground in front of him, while Creasy took a broader view. They had decided to take three rifles: a high-velocity 300.06, an AK47 assault rifle, in case they ran into a bunch of poachers, and a very lightweight, single-shot .22 with a silencer to shoot small game, in the event that their trapping was unsuccessful.

They had not had to use the .22. On the first two evenings, Maxie had laid traps on game-tracks near the rivers. The traps were simple but effective. A branch was pulled down and stressed with thin twine against a catapult-shaped branch, pushed hard into the ground with a toggle behind it. A thin twig rested on one side of the toggle and the twine was fashioned into a noose with a slip-knot and placed over and around the trip twig. As soon as anything touched that twig, the toggle was released, the branch whipped back and the noose was tightened. On the first evening, they caught a bush-buck, on the second evening, a small duiker. Apart from their rifles, their only other implements were hasp-knives and many metres of thin strong twine wrapped around their waists. The meat was tough and rangy and would have tasted better after having been hung for a few days, but still, as they ate the charred meat with their hands, they felt that they had never dined better in their lives.

Game was plentiful. Impala, zebra and giraffe, an occasional buffalo, which they left at a wary distance, and the beautiful kudus with their spiraling horns and regal expressions. They skirted a breeding herd of elephants, and on the previous afternoon had briefly tracked a rhino, which was rare because they had been mostly poached out in that area. They had spotted it after an hour and Creasy felt a strange anger as he watched the beast and listened to Maxie's words.

'It has been dehorned by the game department, in an attempt to save it from the poachers who come across from Zambia.' Maxie had sighed. 'But it doesn't help. The poachers kill them anyway.'

'Why?' Creasy had asked. 'If they have no value.'

Again, Maxie sighed, more in anger than in sorrow.

93

'There are two reasons. First, so they don't waste time in the future, tracking that particular animal – sometimes tracking takes several days. Second, and more disgusting, their bosses pay them the same money for killing a dehorned rhino as for one with horns.'

'But why?'

'It's incredible but simple. Just five years ago, there were more than two thousand black rhinos in Zimbabwe. Today there are only about three hundred and fifty, of which half are on private land and well-protected. The people who pay these poachers have big stocks of rhino horn and they sell very little of it, to keep the price astronomically high. It's their intention to make wild black Rhinos completely extinct. The day that happens, the value of their stock will shoot through the roof. In the Far East, ten grams of rhino horn would become more valuable than a pure white nine-carat diamond. It's estimated that those bastards have stocks of up to five tons. We're talking tens of millions of dollars . . . it's pure filthy economics.'

Creasy had looked at the once-beautiful but now unbalanced creature and his anger had mounted.

'How much do the poachers get for a horn?' he asked.

'On average, about five hundred dollars . . . That's a year's normal wages in Zambia, but the risk is high. The game department wardens have a licence to kill, and they do it often. Trouble is, there aren't enough of them and they only have a single helicopter for the whole damn country.'

They turned away from the animal and Creasy said, 'Well, if we come across any of the bastards, we'll shoot to kill. You have the licence.'

'It's unlikely,' Maxie said sadly. 'They operate further to the west. That rhino will have great difficult finding a mate in this area, and so his line will die out anyway.'

Creasy thought about that and then muttered, 'Well, we can live in hope.'

Maxie had reached the opposite bank and reslung the .22 over his left shoulder. Without looking back, he moved cautiously through jessie bushes, holding the AK47 at the ready. Creasy knew that he would do a circuit to make sure that his landing area was not threatened, either by man or animal.

It was fifteen minutes before Maxie reappeared on the bank. His eyes swept the river for any sign of crocodile and then he beckoned and Creasy waded across.

They picked up the tracks about fifteen kilometres from the murder site. Maxie squatted and studied the dry soil for several minutes, while Creasy sat and watched. Then Maxie moved in widening circles, until he stopped and crouched again and then beckoned to Creasy. He pointed to the signs: the flattened grass, the broken twigs and the scuffed dirt.

'This was their camp last night,' Maxie said. 'Two of them. Afs.'

'You're sure they're Afs?'

'Definitely. They're wearing sandals made from cut-up car tyres.' He pointed to an imprint on the ground. 'Whites would be wearing Fellies or bush boots like us. They're not Wildlife Rangers and they don't have much money, otherwise they'd have decent boots or shoes.'

'Rhino poachers?'

'I doubt it. Those guys usually wear army boots, either from Zambia or Zimbabwe. These two are probably local poachers after meat and skins. They'd be using the same sort of traps as we have during the last few days.' He gestured to his right. 'There's a Batongka village about twenty k's over there. The tracks show that they came from that direction. They'll be heading for the lake and, from the spoor, I guess they'll end up a few k's north of the murder site.'

'You're the temporary boss,' Creasy said. 'What do we do?'

Maxie straightened and looked at his watch. He turned away to his left, in the direction of the lake, and then thought out loud. 'If they're from that village back up the river, they probably poach this area on a regular basis, and be sure they know it like the backs of their hands. They might have seen something about the time of the murders. Now that kind of poaching gives them only a subsistence living. If they did see something or cross some tracks before that big rain, then their information could be useful. If they're Batongka, then they're traditionally tight-lipped, but for a little gold they might loosen up.'

'Let's talk to them,' Creasy said. 'Can you track them?'

Maxie nodded.

'They're being careful but I can track them. You remember the technique?'

'Sure,' Creasy said, and looked at his watch. 'We have five hours to sundown. Let's get going.'

Maxie walked over to a mopani tree and ripped off a branch about one metre long. With his knife, he stripped off the twigs and leaves and then moved forward. Creasy waited until he was about fifty metres ahead and then followed, watching him closely. It was classic two-man tracking. Maxie followed the spoor closely in front of him and, with his stick, pointed out the signs of the spoor for Creasy to see. A bent clump of grass, showing the direction, an imprint on the soil or a dislodged twig. If Maxie lost the spoor, Creasy would stand beside the last sign, while Maxie would circle around to find the spoor again. Within the next two hours it happened twice on outcrops of basalt rock, and Maxie had to circle at a distance of several hundred metres before he picked up the spoor again on softer ground. Creasy was a well-trained and experienced tracker himself, but on these occasions, he marvelled at Maxie's skill.

After three hours, Maxie stopped, crouched down and closely examined the soil. He picked up some earth on his finger and smelt it and let it dribble from his finger. Then he beckoned Creasy forward.

'They stopped here and took a piss,' he said. 'Not more than an hour ago. We do the same.'

'Why?' Creasy asked impatiently.

Maxie explained. 'Because ten minutes ago we scared a white-crown plover from its perch, and that bird makes a lot of noise. Five minutes before that, we disturbed those baboons and that coughing bark of theirs can be heard over a long distance. About ten minutes before that, a Greater honey-guide bird tried to attract us to a bees' nest . . . and that bird's call is also clear over long distances. If those two boys up front are very experienced, they'll relate the noises to our movements. So we stop for half an hour to ease their minds.'

Creasy grinned down at him. 'You're not just a pretty face, Maxie.'

Maxie stood up and grinned back. He said, 'I spent about three years during the war in this bush. If I just had a pretty face, you wouldn't be looking at it now. You'd have to dig six feet down to look at a pretty skull.'

Creasy pointed at the darker areas of earth, where the men had urinated. 'Do you think those men are armed?'

Maxie had unzipped his trousers and was taking a pee.

'I can't be sure,' he said. 'If they are, and they're caught by the game rangers, they'd get an extra five years in jail.'

'Do you speak their language?'

Maxie nodded.

'Not brilliantly, but enough to get by. But they probably speak Ndebele as well. Most of the smaller tribes in this area do.'

They caught up with them an hour before sunset. Maxie had paused again for half an hour on two occasions when they had disturbed the birds. Creasy had felt no impatience, just admiration for his friend's caution and uncanny skills, as he had pointed out with his stick the almost invisible marks of the spoor.

They were only two kilometres from the edge of the lake when they held a brief, whispered conference.

'They won't go to the edge of the lake itself,' Maxie said. 'By now they would have made camp about a kilometre from here, and they would be setting out their traps on the game trails. They'll work individually, each setting up about four traps each. They'll go back to those traps just before dark, and then bring whatever they've caught back to the camp. That camp will be in a hollow or dip, so that when they light their fire, it will be undetectable from a distance. We move in just before nightfall. I go first, just wearing my shorts and unarmed. You cover me with the 300.06. I'll approach from an angle, so you'll have an open field of fire.'

Two hours later, Creasy was chewing on the scorched haunch of an impala, and listening as Maxie spoke in a strange language to the two Africans sitting across the fire.

They had lain in an outcrop of rocks as the sun went down, watching as the two Batongka tribesmen returned to their camp. One carried an impala doe over his shoulder, and the other, two small duikers under his arms. The one with the impala carried a rifle in his left hand. They had watched as the animals were expertly skinned and the skins hung up to dry over the branches of a nearby tree. The rifle had been leant against the trunk of that tree.

The Africans had just begun to light their fire, when Maxie passed the two rifles to Creasy, took off his shirt and walked in a semicircle towards the fire, his arms held away from his body. They spotted him when a hyena scuttled away from a clump of bushes. Immediately, one of them ran to the tree and the rifle.

Creasy lined him up in the sights of the 300.06; but it had not been necessary to fire. Maxie called out in Batongka. He lifted his arms horizontally to the ground. The African with the rifle held it with the barrel pointing to the ground, and Maxie walked forward, talking confidently and reassuringly.

They turned out to be two brothers. As soon as Maxie assured them that he would not report them to the authorities, they welcomed him and Creasy to their camp, and from their ex-army rucksacks pulled out a goatskin gourd containing a local brew made from fermented bananas. By the time it had been passed round the campfire a few times, the mood was mellow.

Maxie talked and translated each sentence for Creasy's benefit.

'We are here because of the murders of the two white people near here, a few weeks ago.'

The elder brother, who was old enough to have greying hair, nodded solemnly. 'It was a bad thing, and also for us. There were police and trackers all over the area and we could not go hunting for at least two weeks.'

'Do you make a living from your hunting?' Maxie asked.

The grey-haired African shook his head.

'Not what you'd call a living. We sell the meat for very little, and once a month a man comes from Bulawayo and takes the skins. We get fifty cents for a good impala skin and we know he sells it for three dollars back in Bulawayo.'

'Why don't they sell them themselves in Bulawayo?' Creasy asked.

'Because the bus trip to Bulawayo could cost them a couple of dollars plus two wasted days. Even if they could find a dealer there,' Maxie told Creasy. He turned back to the older man and asked, 'Do you know anything about who might have shot those two people?'

Twin shields came down over the older man's eyes as he shook his head. He glanced nervously at his brother.

'We know nothing. The police came to our village and questioned everybody.'

'We are not the police,' Maxie replied. 'And whatever we learn, we will not tell them about it.'

The African shook his head.

'We know nothing. We were not in the area at that time. The police had their own trackers and they could find nothing because there had been a big rain in the morning, and by then the killer would have gone.'

As Maxie translated that sentence, somethinc clicked in Creasy's head. He reached out and tapped Maxie's wrist and asked, 'Are you sure he said killer and not killers?'

'I'm sure.'

Creasy looked at the fire, deep in thought, and then said, 'From your experience, how often would these two men be poaching in the bush?'

Maxie immediately got his drift and answered, 'Very frequently and only in this specific area, because there would be several poachers in the village and all of them would have their own patch. I know that from my days in the Selous.'

Creasy was nodding thoughtfully.

'And being poachers, albeit small-time, they would be on the look-out for any human tracks, in case game rangers might be in the area.'

'They would,' Maxie agreed.

Creasy reached down and felt for the slit at the back of his belt, eased out the gold krugerrand and tossed it across the fire between the two brothers.

They glanced down as it lay, glittering in the firelight. Five years' work. Slowly their gaze lifted to look at Maxie, who said, 'That's to pay for our meal and the drink.'

They looked at each other again, then it was the younger brother who spoke, 'Who sent you here?'

'The mother of the murdered girl,' Maxie answered. 'She owns a million cows.' He pointed with his chin at the gold coin. 'And maybe a million of those. She wants vengeance on the man who killed her daughter.'

For a long time, the only sounds were the crackling of the fire, the laugh of a distant hyena and Creasy, munching on his impala haunch as though he didn't have a care in the world. Then, very slowly, the older brother reached down and picked up the gold coin and tucked it into the pocket of his frayed khaki shorts. He glanced again at his brother who gave him an almost imperceptible nod.

He said to Maxie, 'There is a man who hunts here. He has done so for many years. He hunts for the leopard and for cheetah. He does it for his pleasure, not for money. We know his tracks well . . . he smokes cigarettes which cost much money.'

'He is an African?' Maxie asked.

'He is not black,' came the answer. Then he gestured to his left, down the lake. 'He comes and goes from that direction.'

Maxie translated that for Creasy and said, 'He must come from Binga and, for sure, he's a white man. This man knows more than he's saying. They are very cautious people. If that man has been hunting leopard and cheetah for many years here, they will have seen him. Only white men smoke expensive cigarettes.'

'Press him,' Creasy said.

Maxie turned again to the older brother. 'Have you seen this man?' he asked.

'Look beyond Binga,' the African said. 'But not much beyond. Just about five k's.'

Maxie translated that and then added, 'There are very few white people living in Binga on a permanent basis. Some missionaries, American Peace Corps workers and doctors at the regional hospital. Five k's beyond Binga there are some holiday cottages owned by wealthy whites out at Bulawayo. There are two or three other white families who farm crocodiles and have Kapenta fishing licences . . . We'll find our man there.'

'How long to get there?' Creasy asked.

'It's a two-day trek.'

The younger brother had passed the gourd back to Creasy. He took a swig and decided that it was definitely an acquired taste. He passed the gourd on to Maxie, saying, 'So we leave at first light.'

CHAPTER 20

'My name is N'Kuku Lovu . . . but you can call me Monday.' Michael could not keep the surprise from his face and the grey-haired African laughed and explained. 'Under the white man's rule, every black child born in Rhodesia had to have a pronounceable English Christian name to go on to the birth certificate together with a tribal name. I was born in the remote province of Binga, sixty years ago, and the clerk who registered my birth did not have much imagination. Since I was born on a Monday, I was called Monday.'

Michael smiled and remarked, 'It's as good a name as any . . . and not one to forget.'

They were sitting in an elegant office on the fifteenth floor of a modern building in central Harare. Michael was dressed in shorts and a short-sleeved shirt and flip-flops, and was slightly cold within the air conditioning. His host wore a perfectly cut grey, pin-striped suit with a blue shirt and a cream tie.

The African leaned back in his chair and gazed out of the floor-to-ceiling window across the skyline of Harare. Then slowly his eyes moved back to Michael and he said, 'I asked you to come here to receive my thanks for saving my wayward son from at least a terrible beating and maybe even death. In many ways he is a pride to his father, but he has a weakness for women. Perhaps he will have learned something from what happened last night.'

'Perhaps,' Michael agreed. 'It was about three years ago that I found myself in a similar situation or worse . . . it was also because of a teasing woman. It sure as hell taught me a lesson. But, Monday, the person you should really thank is Shavi.'

'I have already done so.'

A silence developed. The African was in deep thought. When Michael had entered the office, two minutes earlier, the African had pressed a button on his intercom and instructed his secretary that he was not to be interrupted until further notice. Since he was obviously a busy man, Michael assumed that, having received his thanks, he should leave. But, as he started to rise, the African held up a hand.

'I should have invited you to my home so that my wife could have also thanked you, but I thought it not a good idea that you should come to my home.' He gestured at the office around him and went on, 'I must tell you also that this is not my own office. That is in the penthouse ... I own this building ... I have borrowed this office from a friend for this meeting.'

Michael had settled himself back into his chair. The African smiled and pointed to a cabinet in the corner. 'But I know that is a well-stocked bar. What can I get you?'

It was late afternoon. Michael thought for a moment and said, 'A gin and tonic would go down well.'

The African glanced at his watch, smiled and said, 'I will join you with that, but if you ever meet my wife, be sure not to mention that I've been drinking before sundown.'

As Michael took the first sip of his drink, the African looked at him across the rim of his own glass and stated, 'They are planning to kill you.'

Michael lowered his glass and asked quietly, 'Because of last night?'

The African shook his head.

'Oh, no, those from last night are small people with small minds and you frightened them very much. The people who want to kill you are big people with wide minds and much power.'

'Who are they?'

Again, the African's brooding eyes were looking out over the skyline. Michael waited patiently until the African had made his decision. Monday N'Kuku started to talk about his business. He had grown up in the Zambezi Valley and had been educated at a mission school. Both the school and his village had to be relocated when the mighty Kariba dam had been built and Lake Kariba formed. As a boy, he had managed to get a job on a white farm. It paid only subsistence wages and the farmer had been brutal, and so Monday N'Kuku had formed an early hatred for white people.

That hatred had lasted five years until the white farmer had sold out to another white farmer when the troubles had started. His new boss had been a totally different human being. He had shown kindness to his black workers and they had responded and the farm had prospered. Every white farm had a small village that housed its workforce. The new boss had spent some of his profits in improving that village, by installing running water and electricity. He had arranged for his workers to be medically examined once a month. The boss's wife had started a kindergarten, with lessons for the young children at the farm village. She quickly discovered that Monday N'Kuku had a basic education and so, at the age of twenty, he had been brought in from the fields to run that kindergarten. His new boss and his wife encouraged other white farmers in the area to send the black children of their workers to attend what soon became a small school. Monday N'Kuku was sent to Bulawayo to study to become a real teacher. Four years later, he had returned to the school. But he had only stayed two years. The boss's wife had recognised his intelligence and one evening had simply told him to go to Bulawayo to see a man called John Elliot, who owned a factory making and selling fencing materials. John Elliot had given him a job as a very junior clerk. During the next twenty years, Monday N'Kuku had worked hard and risen to be sales manager of the entire company. He had also obtained a wife and three children and a small house in an African township. Michael listened patiently as the African described the troubles that came with Ian Smith's declaration of Independence from Britain and the war that followed. The owner of the factory decided to sell up and move to South Africa. Monday N'Kuku did not like the new owners. He had saved some money and so he resigned, moved to Harare, which was then called Salisbury and opened his own small business, selling machinery to farmers, both black and white. The business had prospered and as the war for black liberation intensified, Monday N'Kuku had the wisdom to start donating money to the eventual victors. He was well rewarded and, five years after black rule, he was one of the wealthiest black businessmen in the country, with very powerful connections both inside and outside the government.

He finished his story by saying, 'It has been the rule all my life always to pay my debts. It has been a good rule and I will continue to follow it. So now I have to repay my debt to you, but in doing so I cannot compromise others. Of course, like everybody else, I know what you are doing here and your father and his Selous Scout friend, MacDonald, and the American lady paymaster, Mrs Manners. I know the whole story because we are a village and I am in the centre of the village.' He smiled. 'We sit in air-conditioned luxury in a Westernised world, but the old tribal drums still beat. You are a white man . . . you cannot hear them. But the drums tell me that very soon some people will try to kill you and your whole party.'

'Who are those people?' Michael asked.

Again, a silent survey of the skyline of Harare, and then the grey-haired African said, 'We have criminals in Harare. Very many. Some small and some big. Among the big ones are a gang who carry out assassinations for money.' He smiled again slightly. 'I suppose you could call them mercenaries. Most of them came out of the war to find no place in our new society. They are led by a man I know well. Ostensibly, he is a businessman, but that is just a cover. He has political protection from certain quarters but, of course, so do I. Early this morning, his gang was hired to murder Mrs Gloria Manners, yourself and your father and MacDonald.' He smiled again. 'It will be difficult in the extreme to find your father and the Selous Scout, because they have gone into the bush, and even though they are white men, they are both men who know the bush. After last night, I also realise that you would not be an easy target . . . but Mrs Manners in her wheelchair at the Azambezi Hotel will be very exposed . . . I know that two members of that gang took the lunchtime flight to Bulawayo. From there it's a four hour drive to Victoria Falls. You can be sure that they will make their move on Mrs Manners sometimes tonight.' He paused and watched Michael's face and could almost see his brain working. Then he continued, 'The beating drums also tell me that Commander John Ndlovu is co-operating with Mrs Manners and her people, due to pressure from the American government. He is an honest and efficient policeman.' He pointed at the phone on the desk. 'That phone is secure. I suggest you phone John Ndlovu immediately and have him put tight security on Mrs Manners.'

Michael looked at the phone and then shook his head. He asked, 'Who hired this gang of assassins and why?'

Monday N'Kuku leaned forward and said very quietly, 'A man from Binga, from where I came from. A white man called Rolph Becker. His father came from South Africa many years ago, and settled and eventually died in the Zambezi Valley. His father was my first boss, who used to beat me as a fourteen-year-old, to give him pleasure. I hated his father and I hate Rolph Becker and I hate Becker's son, Karl, who thinks he is a bush man and who yesterday morning left the family home at Binga and went into the bush.' He pointed again at the phone. 'Now call Commander John Ndlovu.'

'Why did Becker hire this gang of assassins?'

The African shrugged.

'There is no proof to show that Becker arranged the killing of Mrs Manners's daughter and her boyfriend Coppen. But since he has now hired people to kill you all, you might say the circumstantial evidence points to him being behind those first murders. Now, phone John Ndlovu.'

Again, Michael shook his head. He said, 'If I phone John Ndlovu, he'll want to know how I got that information. He will certainly want to talk to me and could detain me at a time when I need to move quickly.'

'That's true,' Monday conceded. 'So what are you going to do?'

'I'm going to ask a favour of you,' Michael answered. 'I want you to arrange for John Ndlovu to receive an anonymous telephone tip-off from somebody speaking Shona. Then, for sure, he'll arrange tight security on Mrs Manners.'

The African thought for a moment and then said, 'That's no problem. You're right. The Azambezi Lodge will be swarming with policemen. I'm sure Ndlovu has already arranged security, but after that phone-call it will be doubled or tripled. But what about you?'

Michael was thinking. He was trying to think as Creasy would think. He went through the options. He could simply fly to Vic Falls and wait for Creasy and Maxie to come out of the bush. He could, of course, go and see John Ndlovu and tell him what he had learned without divulging his source, and then Ndlovu would definitely bring the Beckers in for questioning, but there would be no proof. He went through the facts of the situation and what he knew. Within the hour, Gloria Manners would be totally protected. Yesterday, Karl Becker had gone into the bush, presumably looking for Creasy and Maxie. He looked up at the African and asked, 'What can you tell me about this man Karl Becker?'

Monday thought about it for a moment and then answered, 'He comes from a long line of evil men. As I said before, I have been involved with that famly and it was not pleasant. But Karl Becker is the most evil of them all. He enjoys hurting people . . . and, above all, killing them. Age or sex matters not. Better still, if they are black.'

'How good is he in the bush?'

'Very good indeed, for a white man.'

'As good as Maxie MacDonald?'

The African smiled.

'Becker is a good amateur, but MacDonald was a Selous Scout and therefore is a total professional. Do you play football, Michael?'

Michael nodded.

'Yes. I used to play frequently and I still do occasionally.'

Monday spread his hands and said, 'I used to, as well, and I still follow the game worldwide on TV. The comparison between Karl Becker and Maxie MacDonald in the bush is that of a good club player to Pele on the football pitch.'

Michael went back into thought and Monday waited patiently. Michael had to assume that Maxie and Creasy would capture Karl Becker. They would question him severely. Creasy's decision would not be to take him straight to the police but to take him to his father, and also question the father. Creasy never liked involving the police. Michael suddenly felt young. He just wished he could communicate with Creasy – but on this occasion he had to make his own decision. Another minute passed. Then he made his choice. He would get to Binga, locate himself close to the Becker household and be ready, in case Creasy and Maxie needed back-up. He looked at his watch and said, 'Monday, I would be grateful if you could arrange to get me into Binga unseen, by dawn tomorrow.'

'That presents no difficulties. I have business there. In an hour, one of my trucks will leave Harare with a trusted driver and with you hidden in the back. It's a twelve hour journey. He will drop you off within a mile of Becker's house before dawn. Meanwhile I'll have someone tip-off Commander Ndlovu that Mrs Manners is in great danger.'

Michael stood up and held out his hand and the African rose to shake it.

'Thank you, Monday. 'As you say, you are a man who pays your debts.'

CHAPTER 21

The stewardess served the duck *à l'orange* and refilled the champagne glass. Lucy Kwok gave her a conspiratorial smile of thanks.

Wherever airline personnel travel in the world, they get massive discounts on their own airline and others. It is a kind of mile-high mafia. Lucy had flown Cathay Pacific to London, spent a free night at an airport hotel with the cabin crew and then got a stand-by flight on British Airways to Harare. When she boarded the plane, the senior stewardess had recognised her from a holiday she had enjoyed in Hong Kong two years earlier.

She had whispered in Lucy's ear, 'Just wait by the staircase. I'll get the others settled and then have a word with the captain.'

Fifteen minutes later, Lucy was ushered into the luxurious cocoon of first class, and was given her first glass of champagne only seconds after settling into her comfortable armchair.

There were only three other first-class passengers. A black politician and his wife, and a middle-aged white businessman who had tried to chat her up soon after take-off. She gave him the standard brush-off, explaining that her husband was waiting for her at the airport.

The ten hours had passed quickly and comfortably, and with the good food and champagne, she should have been relaxed. But as the plane swept down from the dark African skies and landed at Harare Airport, Lucy's mind was in turmoil.

She had travelled widely in her work and on her subsidised holidays, but this was her first visit to Africa. There was a tension in her. She was not sure if she would ever return to Hong Kong. With the death of her family and then Colin Chapman's death and the destruction of her family home, she felt that her links with the place were falling away. She mourned for her family with a constant inner pain and mourned Colin Chapman with a sense of guilt. She kept telling herself that the guilt was illogical, but there was no denying that he had died protecting her.

The first-class passengers went through immigration and customs first and the wealthy white businessman looked somewhat surprised as he followed her out into the arrivals hall and saw her being greeted by a tall well-dressed African.

Commander John Ndlovu shook Lucy Kwok's hand and took her overnight bag, and nodded to the porter carrying her other luggage to follow them. Five minutes later, they were driving into the city, side by side in the back of an unmarked police car.

'It's more modern than I had expected,' she remarked, looking at the first high-rise buildings.

'Well, it's not Hong Kong,' the African answered, 'but perhaps it's the most modern city in Africa north of Johannesburg.' He suggested that after she had settled into her room at the Meikles Hotel, they meet for a drink in the bar.

Half an hour later, in the newly-opened Explorer Bar of the hotel, she sipped a highball and listened while John Ndlovu brought her up to date. It only took a few minutes for her to learn that Gloria Manners was staying in a hotel at Victoria Falls, that Creasy and Maxie MacDonald had disappeared into the bush for several days, and that Michael, who was supposed to spend a few days in Harare, had checked out that very morning and simply vanished.

'What do you suggest I do?' she asked the policeman.

He shrugged.

'I'm afraid there's nothing you can do, Miss Kwok, except wait. I expect that Creasy and MacDonald will stay in the bush no longer than a week. If they haven't come across anything by then, they'll come out and everyone will go home. I suggest that you wait at Victoria Falls with Mrs Manners. It's much more pleasant than Harare and she'll be the first to know if anything happens. After all, she's funding everything.'

Lucy thought for a moment and then said, 'What sort of woman is she?'

The African made a gesture with his hands.

'She's in her sixties and obviously very wealthy. She spends her life in a wheelchair. She lost both her husband and her only child, so her immense wealth means nothing. I'd say she's a bitter lonely woman.'

'Sounds like good company,' Lucy said ruefully.

The African took a last sip of his drink and said, 'Well you could spend time looking at the Mosi-Oa-Tunya.'

'What's that?'

'Victoria Falls. The locals call it "the smoke that thunders".'

'I'm not here on a tourist trip,' Lucy said.

'I understand that. But there's nothing you can do for the next few days except wait. That's what Mrs Manners is doing . . . and that's what I'm doing.'

'Well, I can't get to Victoria Falls until tomorrow. I checked in London and all the flights from Harare are booked.'

He beckoned to the red-jacketed bartender and said, 'Joseph, please give me the phone.'

The bartender lifted the phone on to the bar. Ndlovu dialled a number and then spoke a few short words in Shona. Without waiting for an answer, he cradled the phone and said, 'You are booked on the 8.00 a.m. flight in the morning to Vic Falls . . . Perhaps a tourist will have to wait another day before getting wet from the smoke that thunders.'

'I'm very grateful to you, Commander.'

He glanced at his watch and then reached into his top pocket and gave her a card. 'I have to leave now, Miss Kwok. Call me if you need anything.' She took the card and thanked him and he asked, 'Are you going to bed now?'

She shook her head. 'I've got massive jet-lag from flying East to West and then South. I'll have a couple more drinks here.'

He nodded solemnly and looked around the crowded room. It was filled with well-dressed men, both black and white, and only a few couples. Again, he beckoned the bartender, a huge East African.

He turned back to Lucy and said, 'Meet Joseph Tembo. He's been head bartender here for many years. He will keep an eye on you while you are here.'

'Is that necessary?'

The African nodded.

'A single woman in Harare would not usually drink in a bar on her own unless she is a little loose. Consequently, some of the men here might bother you. Joseph will not let them bother you, unless you wish it. Tembo is Swahili for "elephant" and he can sure charge at someone, if they annoy you.'

'What did you tell him?'

'I told him to tell them that you were my sister.'

She lifted her head and, for the first time in a long time, laughed. 'I doubt they will believe him.'

'Perhaps not . . . but they will get the message.'

CHAPTER 22

Gloria Manners felt trapped and irritated. It was early evening and, with the help of Ruby, she had prepared herself to go down into the beautiful gardens by the River Zambezi to watch the famed sunset. Later they would have dinner *al fresco*. But five minutes earlier there had been an urgent knock on the door. It was Inspector Robin Gilbert. He explained that he had just received a tip-off from Commander Ndlovu that some criminals had left Harare to make an attack on her person. She was therefore to stay in her room together with Ruby and take their meals there until the criminals had been tracked down. Meanwhile, he had received reinforcements. Many of them were already on the grounds of the hotel. They were all in plain clothes or disguised as waiters or porters. The two men who would bring their meals would be his men.

He had left without giving Mrs Manners a chance to argue. She remained in a bad mood throughout the meal, and until she finally fell asleep after drinking one scotch too many.

She came sharply awake just after midnight.

She turned and saw Ruby sitting up in the twin bed. They could hear gunfire just outside the building and much shouting. Abruptly, the window smashed and Mrs Manners pulled herself under the covers and shouted to Ruby to do the same as glass littered their beds and the floor.

The firing stopped as suddenly as it had started. Then they heard footsteps running down the corridor outside. Gloria was filled with fear until she heard the voice of Inspector Gilbert shouting out to them to stay still and that everything was all right. Seconds later he was in the room.

'I managed to get one shot off,' he said. 'And of course it had to come through your window. Is anybody hurt?'

'No,' Gloria said. 'What about the man who did it?'

'They're both dead, Mrs Manners. Please don't move. There's glass everywhere. I'll have some maids here in a couple of minutes to clean the place up and move you to another suite. You can spend the rest of the night in peace.'

'Peace!' she said. 'I doubt I'll ever find peace in this country.'

CHAPTER 23

They moved fast about a kilometre in from the lake itself. They would not be stopping to trap that night. They simply chewed on strips of biltong. Maxie's plan was to skirt behind the village of Binga and come in at right-angles to the ridge where the small white community lived. The country was very sparse and dry and they sweated under the rising sun. They walked side by side, but there was very little conversation. They trudged on with an air of impatience.

It was late afternoon when Maxie reached out a hand to stop Creasy.

'Someone's tracking us,' he said.

Creasy wiped the sweat from his face with the back of his hand and grinned.

I was waiting for you to tell me,' he said. 'I picked it up ten minutes ago.'

Maxie grinned back.

'You're a smartass, Creasy. I picked it up an hour ago, and deliberately took us close to that bunch of baboons to give them a fright. They got another fright, fifteen minutes later and I heard their chattering. Then, whoever was behind us disturbed some crowned plovers and ten minutes ago, they disturbed the very noisy honey-guide – that's what you heard.'

'Why didn't you tell me?'

'I wanted to be sure. I needed to establish a pattern from the disturbances behind us and the timing of them. There's no doubt now that whoever's tracking us is keeping about a k behind. He's probably waiting for us to camp and then he'll close in.'

'Do you think it's those two Batongkas from last night? Maybe they're looking for more krugerrands.'

'I doubt it. First, they know I'm an ex-Selous and I tracked them, even though they took great care. They know what I'm capable of. They also know where we're going, which is why I've taken this route. You may have noticed that we kept to high ground, to avoid the chances of being ambushed from the front. If they were tracking us, they would not have been so clumsy. My guess is, that by now, they're back in their village, getting drunk out of their minds.'

They were walking again. Maxie said, 'Don't look back. Whoever is behind us is over-confident.'

'Let's do a buffalo circle on him,' Creasy said.

Maxie shook his head.

'Creasy, you're brilliant in most terrains and especially in urban situations. There's no one better than you in the desert.' He smiled to take away any offence. 'But this is my territory and here, I'm ever so slightly better than you.'

Creasy grunted in half-agreement. 'Maybe. But you're sure as hell enjoying that fact. So let's do a buffalo circle.'

Again Maxie shook his head.

'A wounded buffalo circles back on its tracker and waits in thick bush, just a few metres from its own track, and then charges the tracker. The problem is, we don't have any thick bush in this vicinity. We just have those mopani trees and sparse shrub.'

They walked in silence for a while, and then Creasy said, 'There's a low hill a couple of k's in front of us. So when we pass out of his sight, I'll just pop off to the left and wait for him.'

'Do you want to kill him or catch him?' Maxie asked.

'Catch him, of course.'

'Then you don't just drop off to the left. We have to assume that, even though he's arrogant, he's a good tracker. On this loose soil, he'll be tracking at least fifty metres ahead. He will see the tracks diverge and then he'll back off fast.'

'So what do we do, smartass?'

Maxie turned and grinned at him. After three days in the bush, they both looked and smelled like tramps. Maxie was enjoying his rare moment of superior knowledge.

'We do sticks and boots,' he said.

'I've heard about it but never been involved in that situation. Explain in detail.'

'Well, we've got to make him think that he's tracking the same two men and not just one.' He gestured ahead. 'When we pass out of sight, around that low hill, we stop and have time to pull a couple of small branches from a tree. We tie one end of the branches to your boots. You wrap your feet in your shorts and your shirt and you tiptoe your way to the left, for at least half a k and then circle round behind our tracks and slot in behind him or them. Beyond that small hill, there's a series of three more, so I'll be out of sight. I'll make camp beyond the third hill. All the way, I'll be carrying those sticks with your boots on the end and I'll plant your bootprints next to mine. You need to be close up behind him, or them, by the time they get near to my camp, which will be about four k's from here.' He glanced to his right at the evening sun. 'I'll time my arrival for dusk and set up a rough dummy by the fire to impersonate you. They won't move in before dark, by which time you'll be right behind them. Now, keep looking behind you, once in a while, like you normally do as the backmarker. When we get round the edge of that low hill, do exactly as I tell you.' He turned and grinned at Creasy again, who grunted something inaudible.

Twenty minutes later, Creasy carefully followed the instructions. They had walked alongside a mopani tree.

'Stand still and don't move,' Maxie said. He reached up and pulled himself into the tree and climbed through it and around it. From the back, he stripped down two branches. He climbed back and handed them down to Creasy, and very carefully lowered himself so that his own feet descended exactly on to the last two bootprints he had made. Then he issued instructions.

'Carefully take off your shirt and your shorts, but each time you lift a leg, make sure you put your boots back on to exactly the same spot. Lay the shirt and the shorts on your left, side by side, then step out of your boots, leaving them exactly where they are and put one foot on your shirt and one on your shorts. Do not lower your rifle to the ground.'

Creasy handed him back the branches and looked down at his boots. They were Fellies, much beloved by white Zimbabweans, made of suede and laced up to the ankle. He took off his green cotton shirt, placed it beside him, and then stepped out of his green shorts and placed them next to the shirt. He was naked except for dark blue briefs.

'Very tasteful,' Maxie commented. He received another grunt and then Creasy was unlacing his boots. He stepped carefully out of them and on to his shorts and shirt, then watched as Maxie went to work. He had chosen two branches with a cluster of smaller branches at the ends. He picked up one boot and forced it over the small branches and then took twine from several loops around his waist and tied the boot firmly into place without running any of the twine under the sole. He repeated the process with the other boot, and then placed both boots exactly on the spot where Creasy had stepped out of them. He said, 'For the past few minutes I've watched your spoor and I know exactly the length of your stride. You tend to walk on the sides of your feet, like a cowboy. I'll duplicate your spoor. I know only one man who could ever have noticed the difference between the spoor that I'll make and the genuine article.'

'Maybe he's the one behind us,' Creasy said.

Maxie shook his head.

'Definitely not. He was a tracker for ZAPU. I killed him eighteen years ago. About twenty k's from here.' He tapped his left side. 'He left me with a little trademark. That scar under my ribs.'

'OK. I'll see you in about an hour. Get going.'

He watched for a couple of minutes as Maxie moved across the ground, reaching out with his hands far to his left and planting Creasy's boots in an exact rhythm. Creasy bent down, wrapped his shirt and shorts round his feet and fastened them with twine. Then, as though walking on cut glass, he moved away to his left.

Karl Becker tracked with assurance and pleasure. He loved his work, but he infinitely preferred tracking humans to animals. The end result gave more satisfaction.

It had not been difficult. He had spotted them early in the morning, moving in the direction of Binga. The Envoy L4A1 rifle was slung from his right shoulder. He padded along confidently. He did not track the twin spoors from behind, but criss-crossed them in a zig-zag manoeuvre which took him four to five hundred metres away from the spoors on either side. It was a tiring and time-consuming way to track, but it diminished the possibility of an ambush. He knew what he was up against and it sent a sudden thrill through his body. He was tracking a Selous Scout and a man who he knew was a legend among mercenaries. He felt no fear. He was on his own territory. His rifle was on his back and his instincts were honed. He knew that he had not been spotted. He could have tried two long-shots, but they had moved through open country on the high ground and his approach would have been difficult. Now dusk was coming and soon they would have to camp in a more bushy terrain. He would have cover enough to get within one or two hundred metres. He would shoot the Selous Scout first and he would shoot him twice, to be sure. He felt more confident about having to track down the mercenary.

Maxie stopped and looked around and then picked his spot. His arms were tired from the constant rhythm of planting Creasy's spoor. He tossed the sticks and boots aside and worked quickly. He gathered bushes and, using the twine looped around his waist, tied them into the shape of a torso and a head of a size resembling Creasy. Then he built a fire and placed the dummy torso on the far side from their tracks. The fire blazed and Maxie crouched on his haunches beside the dummy, laid his rifle beside him, pulled a strip of biltong from his pouch and started to chew on it.

Twenty minutes later, Karl Becker carefully circled the edge of the low hill and spotted the fire about a kilometre away. It was almost dark, and he chuckled inwardly as he took in the scene. There was a clump of bushes about a hundred metres between him and the fire. It made a perfect hide. He would wait for full darkness and then move in and make the kill. He looked again at the fire and at the two shadowy shapes sitting beyond it. He chuckled again. 'Sitting ducks,' he thought to himself, and moved away to his right, to come in exactly opposite the fire.

Twenty minutes later, Maxie heard the fluttering wings of a bird, slightly in front and to his left. He knew that somebody was out there. The bird would have been roosting for the night and would not have flown unless disturbed. Of course, it could have been a hyena or a wild dog, but every instinct told him that it was a human hunter. He felt no concern. If Creasy had been in any way disabled during the past hour, he would have fired a shot to alert Maxie. The hunter out there was being hunted.

Karl Becker reached a clump of bushes and gently eased his way through them. He had a good view of the fire and the two shadowy figures beyond it. He knew that the mercenary was bigger than the Selous Scout. The larger figure on the left had to be the mercenary. He eased his backside on to the soil and raised the rifle to his favourite position with his elbows resting on his knees. He decided that his targets were not such good bushmen as he had been told. They should have been sitting on opposite sides of the fire, watching each other's back. He laid his cheek against the stock of the rifle and took aim.

A casual but hard voice behind him said, 'Dr Livingstone, I presume.'

CHAPTER 24

Creasy threw him on to the fire. He screamed and twisted, and managed to roll away as a small burning branch slipped down his mottled green and brown shirt. He could not reach it because his thumbs had been tied behind his back and his ankles. He screamed again, rolling over and over, and eventually dislodged the burning twig. He lay gasping and whimpering, his face against the dirt.

Creasy sat alone, chewing on a piece of biltong. Five minutes earlier, Maxie had melted into the dark bush to make sure that their would-be assassin had no back-up out there. He would be gone at least half an hour.

Creasy took a careful gulp of water from his jerrycan, looked at the bound man and said, 'When I ask you a question in future, I'm only going to do it once. If I don't get an answer within ten seconds, I'll toss you back on that fire. And if it's not the right answer, you go back on anyway. Now, what's your name?'

Ten silent seconds passed and then Creasy began to rise.

'Karl Becker!' came the strangled reply.

'Why were you trying to kill us?'

Painfully Becker twisted over. His short hair was singed and his eyebrows and his left cheek black. He looked up at Creasy, drawing in short, shallow breaths. 'I thought you were rhino poachers,' he said. 'There's open licence on them.'

Creasy sighed, stood up, walked two paces, picked him up by his shirt-front and the crotch of his shorts and threw him back on the fire.

Maxie emerged into the firelight half an hour later. Creasy was hunched up, chewing on biltong. The other man was propped up against the thin trunk of mopani tree, five metres away. His chin was on his chest and he was sobbing. Creasy waved a piece of biltong at the sobbing man.

'Karl Becker,' he said. 'Does the name ring a bell?'

Maxie squatted down, pulled his water bottle from his satchel, took several gulps and said, 'There's a man called Rolph Becker who has a crocodile farm at Binga, not far from home. I believe he has a son.'

'That's him,' Creasy said. He pointed at the rifle propped up against another mopani tree. 'That's an old sniper rifle. An Enfield. It even has the original sight and it's 7.62 calibre. This prick used it to murder Carole Manners and Cliff Coppen.'

'He confessed?'

'Sure. After a little heat.'

'Why did he do it?'

Creasy sighed and said in a cold voice, 'Because his daddy Rolph Becker told him to.'

'Why?'

Again Creasy sighed. 'He says he doesn't know. And I believe him. He likes killing people but he doesn't like the heat.'

Maxie nodded thoughtfully.

'So, I guess we go and talk to Daddy.'

'We do. How long?'

Maxie glanced at his watch.

'If we move now, we'll fetch Binga before dawn.'

Creasy pushed himself to his feet and tossed the remains of his biltong into the fire. 'Let's go.'

CHAPTER 25

Michael pulled himself up off the floor of the passenger cab of the eight-ton Leyland truck and settled himself back into the passenger seat.

They had just passed through the small village of Binga, which sat on the south-east shore of Lake Kariba. Being five o'clock in the morning, the streets had been empty, but still Michael had ducked out of sight as a precaution.

He glanced at the driver's wizened black face. He was so small that he had to sit on two large cushions to see over the wheel, but Michael had been impressed with his skill. They had driven for eleven hours, only stopping to urinate and refill the tank from jerrycans in the back. They carried a cargo of heavy fishing nets for the Kapenta contractors, together with boxes of canned meat for a Save The Children orphanage further down the road.

'About another three k's, *baas*,' the driver said. 'You'll see the lights on a ridge on the left.'

'Lights?' Michael asked. 'At this time of night?'

'Oh, yes. That Becker has security lights on all the time. I've passed this road many times, usually at night. The big lights are always on. Maybe it's since the war. This place was very dangerous. They used to come over the lake at night from Zambia. Becker was one of the few white men who stayed in this area during the bad times.'

'Was he attacked?' Michael asked.

'Yes, *baas*, I think three times, but Becker had about fifteen Matabele. Very well armed with machine-guns and hand-grenades and everything. Very tough men. They fought off the freedom fighters, each time and killed men.'

'What happened to them after the war?'

'Well, there was no vengeance for the freedom fighters, because Comrade President Mugabe gave the orders for no vengeance after the war. But they did kill a lot of Matabele who did not accept the election result and went into the bush. But that's finished now.'

'What's your tribe?'

'I'm Shona, *baas*. From the north. The Matabele are tough, but we Shona are smart so we run the country.'

Michael digested that while slipping a Dexedrine tablet into his mouth. He washed it down with a small sip from his water-bottle, then he asked, 'What happened to Becker's Matabele?'

'They still work for him,' the African answered. 'But now they look after his crocodile farm and they look for eggs along the rivers and the banks.'

'Dangerous work.'

The little driver nodded. 'But they are dangerous people, *baas*. He glanced behind him at the shelf of the cab. Michael's small black rucksack lay beside the AK47 assault rifle and a Colt 1911. The driver turned his gaze back to the road. 'I heard the story of you back in Harare, *baas*. I think you're brave for one so young. I'd be careful what you're doing with those people. That Becker is not a good man and his son is worse. He treats his Matabele good but the other workers he treats bad.'

'I'll be careful. Do you think all the Matabele will be there?'

The driver shook his head. 'No. It's the time of year to collect the eggs. Maybe half of them will be camping by the rivers and lake.'

'Close by?'

'No, *baas*. Far away. Maybe ten cigarettes' drive.' He turned his head and grinned. The little man was a chain-smoker, so it was fortunate that thanks to Zimbabwe's huge tobacco production, cigarettes were very cheap. During the long night's journey, whenever Michael had asked how long it would be until they reached the next town or village, the driver had always answered, 'Three or five or eight cigarettes', equating the distance with the number that he smoked before he arrived there. He had invariably been right and it had kept Michael amused through the night. He calculated that ten cigarettes would come to at least eighty kilometres, maybe even a hundred. So half of

Becker's little army would not get back if any action started in the next few hours.

'Do those Matabele still have those weapons?' he asked.

'Officially, no. The machine-guns and grenades were confiscated after Independence for sure.'

'How can you be sure?'

'Because I collected them. My boss had the contract to pick up all the weapons from this area.' He shook his head at the memory. 'I was very frightened, jumping around on this rough road with a lorryload of guns, grenades, ammunitions and mines in the back of the trunk. But Mr N'Kuku Lovu gave me a big bonus.'

With slight relief in his voice, Michael said, 'So those Matabele are not armed now.'

'For sure they're armed. They will have hidden some of the weapons.'

'Like what?'

'Pistols and maybe some AK47s. Also they'll have some licensed rifles because it's dangerous work, collecting crocodile eggs. But they will not have machine-guns or grenades.' He pointed ahead and to his left. 'There, you see the lights, *baas*. We will pass about one k from the house –' He held up a smoking cigarette – 'when I finish this one.'

Michael was wearing black jeans, black boots, a black, long-sleeved shirt and a black knitted skull-cap. He reached behind him, pulled down a heavy flak jacket and struggled into it. From his shirt pocket, he pulled out two ten-dollar notes and put them on the seat between himself and the driver. Then he got a surprise. The driver glanced down at them, took one hand off the wheel, picked them up and dropped them into Michael's lap.

'Not needed, *baas*. Not for this job. My *baas* gave me a good bonus for this trip.'

Michael picked up the notes and stuffed them back into his shirt pocket.

The driver's cigarette had burned down almost to his fingers. Michael looked up to his left. The bright lights were approaching. He reached behind him for the pistol, tucked it into the shoulder-holster and snapped down the restraining strap. He shifted forward on the seat and slung the AK47 behind him with the strap across his chest. Four spare magazines went into a pouch, hanging from the left side of his belt.

'How far is the African compound from the house?' he asked.

The driver pointed. 'There are two compounds. One for the Matabele and one for the others. You can see the lights of both of them. The Matabele are the nearest. That's about half a k from the house. The compound of the other Africans is about one k away. If trouble starts, the other Africans will not get involved. They will stay in their huts with their heads down, holding on to their wives and children . . . they don't get paid enough to worry about Becker's white skin.' He changed down a gear, touched the brake lightly and mashed his cigarette into the overfilled ashtray. 'We're coming to the place now, *baas*. There's big trees and bushes on the left coming up. I go very slow. Good luck, *baas*.'

Michael slapped him on the shoulder. The truck slowed to a walking pace and he opened the door and jumped down. Seconds later, he was in amongst the trees as the truck accelerated away.

CHAPTER 26

Karl Becker was not a happy man. His two captors had no perception of generosity when it came to dealing with someone who had tried to murder them. He had hobbled throughout the night with his thumbs tied behind his back and his ankles attached by a twenty-inch piece of twine. He had stumbled and fallen several times. They had held a water-bottle to his lips twice during the long march and only very briefly.

For the first two hours, he had been building up a hatred, but then his mind turned to how it was possible that he had been trapped. He considered himself the best tracker in the country, black or white, but the two men strolling along behind him had picked him up like netting a butterfly. How could he not have seen the difference in the tracks when the ex-Selous Scout had started the stick walking? How did he miss the spoor of the man called Creasy when he had moved off the track and around behind him?

Slowly the realisation crept into Karl Becker's head that the two silent figures behind him were lethal. He recalled how the man Creasy had totally immobilised him by tying his thumbs behind his back with a single piece of twine, and then asked his first question, and how he himself had shown his arrogance by spitting in the man's face and seconds later he had been sitting over the fire. He had never heard such a cold voice, not even in his father when he was angry. It had come at him as though sliding over ice cubes. After four hours he had begun to fear for his life. He knew that if he and his father ended up in court, his father's powerful friends would be able to pull big strings to get them, if not a suspended sentence, at least a small stretch in jail. But as he stumbled along, he realised the two men behind him would not accept that.

They were approaching the house at right-angles to the lake. It was about three kilometres away. The Matabele compound would be on their left. Karl Becker made a decision. When they were within a kilometre of the compound, he would scream out a warning.

He had no chance. After half a kilometre the cold voice of Creasy told him to stop. A moment later, he felt hard hands gripping his shoulders, then his head was pulled back by his hair and a piece of cloth was forced into his mouth and tied tight behind his neck. The voice of the Selous Scout was whispering in his ear.

'We don't want any singsongs out here. If you try anything at all, you get a bullet in the back of the head.'

The voice carried total conviction. Karl Becker felt a push and stumbled forward towards the house. He had no thoughts of trying to warn anybody. Now it was up to his father.

They stopped about a kilometre from the house. Karl sank to his knees in exhaustion and then rolled over on to his side. The house was very visible under the security floodlights. He listened as the two men discussed their strategy.

'Maybe we work our way around,' Creasy said, 'and cut off the electricity.'

Maxie disagreed. 'He's a rich man. No doubt he's got an emergency generator. There are plenty of power cuts in this area. That generator might automatically kick in. If not, somebody will come from the compound to start it up.'

They squatted in silence for a couple of minutes, and then Creasy prodded Karl with his rifle and said, 'Well. This is the only child. I guess we just walk up to the front door with the gun at the back of his head and ring the doorbell.'

Another silence and then Maxie answered, 'I don't see why not. Let's rig it up.'

Roughly he pulled Karl to his feet. Then he unwrapped a length of twine from around his waist and threaded one end through the trigger guard of his rifle. The other end went round Karl's neck. When the two ends were tied together, the muzzle of the rifle was held firmly at the back of Karl's cranium.

'Don't jerk around,' Maxie told him, 'or your brains get dislodged . . . if you've got any.'

They moved forward again, crossing the scrub very slowly.

Michael picked them up as they entered the outer parabola of light. He immediately recognised Creasy's shape and then Maxie's. He took in the whole tableau and realised what was happening. His first instincts were to move down and join them, but as he rose to his feet he remembered his training: always watch and wait. If you're in the background, always stay in the background until you know what is going on.

Michael flicked off the safety of the AK47 and squatted back on to his haunches. He watched as the trio moved around to the front of the house under the bright lights.

In the large master bedroom of the house, Rolph Becker woke to the high-pitched buzz of the alarm set into the headrest of the bed. The transition from deep sleep to total awareness took less than five seconds. He flicked off the alarm, slid out of bed and padded to the curtained windows. Of course, it could be just a hyena or some other curious animal tht had tripped the infra-red alarms surrounding the house, but as he parted the curtain half an inch, he saw his son, fifty metres away, with the rifle at the back of his head and the two men behind him. He paused only for a silent curse and then moved fast.

Four times in rapid succession he pressed a button by the bedroom door. It connected to a buzzer in the Matabele compound and the four loud buzzes would indicate a total emergency. Then he was through the bedroom door and pulling down a rifle from the rack in the hall. He was dressed only in a brightly-coloured sarong. He leaned against the wall of the hall and waited. He had bought the chimes for the doorbell in Johannesburg four years ago. It had amused him and his visiting friends. Ten seconds later, when the bell was pushed outside, he listened to the opening bars of Beethoven's First Piano Concerto.

He glanced at the sweep second hand on his Rolex and waited a full ninety seconds. It would be reasonable to expect a man to need a minute to be woken at five in the morning and get ready to receive visitors. It would also give his Matabele time to arm themselves and be on their way.

As he took his eyes from the luminous dial of the watch and started to move to the door, Beethoven sounded again, and in his tense mind, Becker thought that the chimes held a note of impatience. Holding the rifle with its barrel pointing towards the ceiling, he unchained the door and opened it. His son was standing five metres in front of him, a look of sheer terror on his face and his voice was gabbling.

'Pa, do nothing stupid . . . This thing is tied round my neck.'

Becker spoke harshly to his son. 'Karl. Keep your mouth shut. Just stand still.'

One of the men was standing behind and slightly to the left of his son, and holding the rifle casually in his right hand, his forefinger on the trigger. Becker knew that he was the ex-Selous, Maxie MacDonald. The other man was standing three metres away from his son on the right. He had one rifle in his right hand, with the barrel resting over his shoulder. He held another rifle in his left hand, pointing at the ground. Becker recognised that rifle as being his son's and he realised that the man holding it must be the mercenary Creasy.

The mercenary spoke. 'If you move the barrel of that rifle even an inch, my friend will pull the trigger of his rifle. And you will be childless.'

'Please, Pa! They mean it.'

'Shut up, Karl!' his father shouted at him. He did not move the rifle. He looked at Creasy and asked, 'What the hell is going on?'

'Your son tracked us through the bush and tried to kill us. Just like he killed Carole Manners and Cliff Coppen.'

Becker's eyes flickered to his son and then back to the mercenary. He said, 'That's nothing but shit! Karl had nothing to do with that. And if he tried to kill you in the bush, he would have succeeded.'

Creasy smiled at him through his grimy growing beard, and slowly lifted the rifle in his left hand. Becker noticed that he was holding it by a strip of fabric.

'This is your son's rifle,' Creasy said. 'He tells me you gave it to him as a young boy. There's no doubt that police forensics will match the murder bullets to this rifle. Your son tells me that he acted under your instructions. So I came to have a chat.'

'My son would never say that,' Becker said. But then he was looking at his son and he saw the scorch marks on the side of his head and the burn marks on his shirt and shorts. His voice turned to a snarl. 'You tortured my boy?'

'I warmed him over a fire,' Creasy answered. 'He was lucky. I usually don't waste time talking when I catch someone trying to kill me or a good friend of mine. They usually get dead very quickly. Now, let's go inside and have that chat, and then we can phone the police.'

Becker's gaze flickered around the darkness beyond the semi-circle of light. He could see nothing and so he played for time.

'Sure, we'll call the police, but if you don't untie my son immediately, you'll be charged with kidnapping, torture and attempted murder. You'll spend the rest of your lives rotting in a very uncomfortable prison.'

Creasy smiled again.

'I doubt it, Becker. Your son gets released when the police arrive and not before.'

Finally, Becker caught a glimpse of movement behind him in the darkness and another to the right. His Matabele had arrived and were taking up position.

From his vantage point, Michael had also watched their arrival. The six men were outlined against the light. Three of them carried what looked like AK47 rifles. The other three held hand-guns. Silently, he edged closer along the ridge.

It was Becker's turn to smile. Creasy heard a sound behind him, twisted his head and saw the six dim black shapes at the fringes of the light.

'There won't be any police here tonight,' Becker told him. 'The odds have changed. You walked through an infra-red alarm.'

'It makes no difference,' Creasy answered. 'Your one and only son is a milli-second away from death. Even if one of your men shoots me or my friend, we will have time to pull the trigger.'

Becker understood the situation very well, but he was still playing for time. He had counted six of his men in the semicircle. He knew that with every passing second, his situation would be improving.

'So let's talk,' Becker said to Creasy. 'You are a mercenary. We'll make a deal. You go back and tell the Manners woman that you reached a dead-end. She pays you and goes home and I pay you also. How about a hundred thousand of your dollars, in cash or in gold?'

Maxie joined the conversation. He said, 'Your research is defective, Becker. We never work for two masters.'

'I know all about scum like you,' Becker answered. 'You'll do anything for money.'

Michael had moved to within a hundred yards of the semicircle of Matabele. He could just hear the conversation. Suddenly, from the periphery of his vision, he saw another dark figure moving in from his left. He would have been invisible to Creasy or Maxie, from inside the halo of light. He saw the figure stop, crouch and then saw the rifle raise.

Michael took an instant decision. He screamed out, 'Creasy! Down!' And then his AK47 was spitting flame at the crouched sniper.

Like all fire-fights, it seemed to go on forever, but in reality it only lasted a few seconds. As Creasy dropped to the floor, Maxie fired his rifle and then the loop of twine pulled back the already dead Karl Becker. Maxie gripped him around the chest, disengaging his rifle and using the twitching body as a shield.

Rolph Becker managed to get off one shot which grazed Creasy's left buttock, and Creasy pumped three quick shots into Rolph Becker, slamming him back into the hall. Creasy rolled rapidly away to his right, twisted and then started firing again.

Maxie was squatting behind Karl Becker's body, firing his rifle with one hand. He grunted as a bullet passed through Becker's body and lodged itself in his right thigh. From the darkness beyond, Creasy heard the deadly fire of Michael's AK47, watched the bodies spinning in front of him and heard the screams.

There came a watchful silence and then Creasy's voice.

'Maxie?'

Maxie's voice cracked back. 'I got a number two or three in the leg.'

Creasy's voice called out into the darkness, 'Michael?'

Michael's voice came back. 'I'm hit.'

Creasy was still lying in the dust with his rifle aiming at one of the Matabele, who was lying on his back, clutching his shoulder and moaning loudly.

'Don't move, Michael,' Creasy called, and turned his head to look at Maxie.

'Are you mobile?'

'Yes.'

'Recce the house.'

Maxie dropped the body of Karl Becker in the dust and moved to the doorway. Creasy followed.

Rolph Becker was lying on his back with his hand clutching his stomach, his face a picture of agony. Creasy kicked the rifle further out of his reach and looked closely at the wound. His three bullets had stitched a line across Becker's naked body. Only Becker's spread fingers were holding in his guts. He would be dead within minutes.

He looked up into Creasy's eyes and said, 'Get me to the hospital, quick. It's only six kilometres away at Binga. Quick!'

Creasy shook his head. 'I'll get you to hospital when you've answered a couple of questions.'

Maxie was moving quickly from room to room, kicking open doors with his rifle ready. The bullet in his thigh was no hindrance. He could feel the outline of it under his skin. Karl Becker had been a good cushion. He found nobody in the house, but in the master bedroom he found a huge wall-safe with a combination lock. He moved back to the hall and saw Creasy bending over Rolph Becker.

'The house is clear,' Maxie said. 'But I've found a big safe with a combination lock.'

Creasy looked down at Becker's twisted face. 'The combination,' he said. 'Then you get to the hospital.'

Becker almost screamed out a series of numbers. Maxie turned and ran back down the hall. In the bedroom, he dialled in the numbers, and pulled down the large handle. The heavy door swung open, revealing rows of files, bundles of money and two pistols. He ran back to the hall. The flesh wound was beginning to send pain through his body.

'It was correct,' he said. 'The safe is open.'

Creasy straightened up, looking down at Rolph Becker.

'Are you going to send him to hospital?' Maxie asked.

Creasy shook his head.

'It would be a waste of petrol.'

Becker's voice came out in a long sigh. He shuddered over on to his side as his hands came away from his belly. His guts oozed out on to the maroon tiles, then he died.

'He confessed,' Creasy said. 'I guess the files in that safe will confirm it. Now, quick, phone the police while I check out Michael.'

Creasy ran up the small slope and through the bushes. Suddenly he could hear Michael groaning, then he saw him lying, sprawled on his stomach. He knelt beside him and asked. 'Where, Michael?'

Michael's voice was clear and firm. 'I took one in the shoulder and it spun me round, then I got one in the back . . . low down.'

'Do you feel pain?'

'I feel nothing.'

'Don't move.'

Carefully Creasy pulled up the blood-soaked shirt. There was just enough light to see the wound in the lower spine. A stream of silent curses went through Creasy's brain, but he said calmly, 'Don't move, Michael. Stay completely still. We'll get you out of here very soon.'

Michael lay with his cheek against the soil. He said, 'I can't move, Creasy.'

CHAPTER 27

Gloria Manners sat in her wheelchair in the garden of the Azambezi Lodge. The great Zambezi River flowed past not more than twenty metres away and to her right, she could hear the thunder as it plunged over the Falls. She sat alone. After lunch, she had given Ruby an hour off to go and see the Falls.

There were birds in the trees above and small vervet monkeys played on the lawn. She had expected to hate this country, especially after the events of last night, and at first she had. But during the day that hatred had faded away. Maybe it was the serenity of the hotel. It was a two-storey structure shaped in a curve, the pool and gardens in front and the wide river beyond. The entire structure was covered in dark thatch. When they had checked in, the African manager had explained proudly that it was the largest thatched building in the world.

Her thoughts turned to the two men in the bush. She expected them to return in a few days and announce that they had found nothing. She had mentally prepared herself for that. At least she would have the solace of knowing she had done everything possible. She thought about Creasy and how, in some ways, he reminded her of her husband. He was certainly one of the few men who had ever faced her down. She would leave Zimbabwe, knowing that she had hired the very best, and if Creasy failed, then there was nothing more she could do. She would simply live out her boring, chair-bound life in Denver. Perhaps it would not be for much longer. She felt no disquiet about that. Suddenly she heard a voice behind her.

'Mrs Manners?'

She saw the young Oriental woman and felt irritation at having her thoughts interrupted. She snapped. 'Yes! I doubt there is another old woman in this hotel in a wheelchair.'

The young woman hesitated for a second and then walked round in front of her and said, 'I'm sorry to disturb you, but I've come a very long way to talk to you. My name is Lucy Kwok.'

'Talk about what?'

'About the murder of your daughter and Cliff Coppen. And the almost simultaneous murder of my father, mother and brother in Hong Kong.'

After a pause Gloria said, 'You've come from Hong Kong to talk to me?'

'Yes. I think the murders are connected. So do the Hong Kong Police. I know that you're here, trying to find the killers.'

The old woman gestured and said, 'Pull up a chair, Miss Kwok.'

They talked for twenty minutes, by which time Gloria had recounted the events since her arrival in Zimbabwe and Lucy had explained why there was a connection between the murders in Hong Kong and the ones by Lake Kariba.

Gloria turned her head to gesture for a waiter, but instead saw Inspector Robin Gilbert walking across the lawn towards them. He pulled up a chair and sat down. Gloria introduced him to Lucy and said, 'This young lady thinks there's a Hong Kong connection with my daughter's murder. She's just arrived from Hong Kong.'

'Yes. I know. Commander Ndlovu called me last night.' He drew a breath. 'Mrs Manners, I have to inform you that the men who killed your daughter and Cliff Coppen were shot dead just before dawn today, together with four of their men.'

For a long time, the old woman stared at the policeman's face and then she said, 'Are you sure it was them?'

'Yes. We have complete evidence.'

'Did Creasy kill them?'

'Yes. Together with Maxie MacDonald and Michael. There was a gun battle at Binga, down the lake.'

'I thought Michael was in Harare.'

'Yes. So did we. But he checked out of his hotel yesterday and must have travelled fast to get there.'

'Were the murderers blacks?'

'No. They were whites. Father and son.' He looked at his watch and said, 'But I'll give you all the details on the plane.'

Gloria was a little dazed. She blinked her eyes a few times and then asked, 'Plane?'

'Yes. Your plane, Mrs Manners. We are going to Bulawayo right away. I ran into your nurse at reception and asked her to pack your things. I also asked the manager to alert your crew. I'd like to be on the way as soon as possible.'

Gloria was getting her thoughts together. She asked, 'Why Bulawayo?'

The Inspector stood up and looked down at her. He said, 'Because Michael was badly wounded during that shoot-out.'

'Oh, God. Will he be all right?'

'I don't know. I happened to be at Binga when the alert came in. We got him to the hospital in Binga, but it's very small. When I left Binga, two hours ago, his condition was stable. About now, he's being flown down to the hospital in Bulawayo, which is well-equipped. Creasy and Maxie are with him. In the meantime, Commander Ndlovu is on his way from Harare to Bulawayo, together with three of the murderers' associates, who are under arrest.'

Suddenly Gloria was all business. 'OK, Inspector, let's go. I guess Miss Kwok should come with us.'

'Yes, indeed,' Gilbert said, walking around to push Gloria's wheelchair.

CHAPTER 28

It was late evening when Creasy walked into the room. The black nurse, who was also a nun, stood up from her chair beside the bed.

Creasy said, 'Would you please leave us now, Sister?'

She nodded and bustled out, closing the door behind her. Creasy sat on the edge of the bed and took Michael's hand in his and asked, 'How do you feel?'

Michael did not answer the question. He looked up into Creasy's eyes and said, 'Tell me.'

'It's not good.'

'Tell me!'

Creasy paused for a moment and then said, 'Your shoulder wound is no problem. You'll recover full use of your arm.'

'And the other wound?'

'That's bad. The bullet cut your spinal cord. You'll be paralysed from the waist down.'

There was a long silence and then Michael said, 'I guessed it. I also guessed there's no remedy at all. Not now, not ever.'

'That's it,' Creasy said. 'I had the doctor here speak to a specialist in London and got the same diagnosis. The damage is irreparable. After eighteen years of war here in this country, the doctors have a lot of experience of gunshot wounds. There can be no reprieve. You must be strong. You can leave here in about two weeks and get back to Gozo and get started on a new kind of life. It won't be easy but you're strong and you're tough . . . and you'll handle it. Juliet and I will be with you.' He squeezed Michael's hand, and then felt his own hand gripped tightly and heard Michael's strained voice.

'I don't want to handle it. I don't want to go through life like that. Every time I looked at the mean bitter woman in her wheelchair, I asked myself how anyone could live like that. OK, so she'd lived a long time before it happened, but do you think I want to go through forty or fifty years, getting meaner and more bitter as every day goes by? There's no way, Creasy.'

'It looks bad now,' Creasy said, 'but it's amazing how people get over it and make a reasonable life – even a good life. I've known many such people. At first, they can't face the thought, but later on they come to grips with it. It's hard work, but you can handle it. I know you.'

Michael was very slowly shaking his head on the pillow.

'I don't want that life, Creasy . . . I just don't want it and I'm not going to change my mind. You know what I want you to do?'

Creasy sighed. 'Michael, I'm not going to do it. Get that right out of your mind. You're not my natural son, but you're my son in every other way. Your life has to go on. Who knows? In five or ten or fifteen years, they might find a new surgical technique to reconnect the spinal cord.'

Again, Michael was slowing shaking his head.

'You don't really believe that, Creasy. They're just words.'

'Who the hell can know, Michael? They're making tremendous strides in medical and surgical techniques. There are guys I've known who died from wounds in Vietnam who'd still be alive today.'

'Just words, Creasy . . . I want you to do it.'

No words were spoken for more than a minute, while the two men looked at each other, and then Creasy said, 'I'll make you a promise. We'll get back to Gozo, and in three months from now, to the day, if you still want me to do it, then I'll arrange for you to have an accident.'

Another long silence, finally broken by Michael. 'Three months?'

'Yes.'

'To the day?'

'Yes.'

'Then it's a promise?'

'Yes.'

Michael nodded almost imperceptibly, and squeezed Creasy's hand again. 'It's a deal.'

CHAPTER 29

Creasy got back to the Churchill Arms Hotel just after 8 p.m. It was in the Hillside suburb and not far from the hospital. The receptionist gave him his key and three messages. One was from Gloria Manners, informing him that she was in her suite with Inspector Gilbert and Commander Ndlovu. The second was from Inspector Gilbert, informing him that he and Commander Ndlovu were waiting in Mrs Manners' suite. The third was from Maxie, informing him that he was waiting in the bar. Creasy went into the bar.

Maxie was nursing a large whisky. Creasy eased himself on to the stool next to him and said to the bartender, 'A cognac. Remy Martin. Straight.'

Maxie's face mirrored Creasy's own exhaustion. Neither of them had slept for forty-eight hours.

They were silent until Creasy's drink came and then Maxie asked, 'Sitrep?'

'Bad . . . he wanted me to top him.'

'How did you handle it?'

'I told him that I'd take him back to Gozo, and if he felt the same in three months, I would do it.'

'Would you?'

'Yes . . . but I think, in three months, he'll have a different frame of mind. You know how it is.'

'Yes. It's always that way. That kid had no luck. A few millimetres to the left or right and he'd be walking around in a couple of weeks.' He glanced at Creasy and asked. 'How are you taking it?'

Creasy took a sip of cognac and shrugged.

'I've seen it all before.'

'Sure. We've both seen it all before.'

A bunch of smartly-clad businessmen came into the bar and noisily ordered drinks. Maxie said, 'I phoned home and spoke to Nicole. Of course, I had to talk to Lucette as well.'

'You told her?'

'No. I just told her that Michael was wounded and that I'd let her know his condition in a few days. Of course, she wanted to fly out immediately. There were a lot of tears. She loves that man.'

'Will she love him in a wheelchair?'

Maxie thought about it for a long time and then said, 'I think so.'

'That might be important.'

'Yes. It might. Leave that side to me over the coming weeks. Then I'll make a judgement. The worst thing is if she starts off down the road and then gives up.'

Creasy looked at his friend and said, 'I'll leave it to you, Maxie. Now why don't you go and get some sleep?'

Maxie shook his head.

'No. You've got John Ndlovu and Robin Gilbert upstairs in Mrs Manners's suite. It will be at least an hour before we can get to bed. Maybe after the meeting, we come back downstairs and hang a big one on.'

'Maybe. What's the mental state of that old bitch?'

Maxie said, 'I would never have believed it, but she was in tears when she heard about the extent of Michael's wounds.'

'In tears?'

'Yes. I guess she's blaming herself.'

'Why?'

'I don't know. Maybe because she started this whole thing.'

'She should be happy. We did what we came for. Took out the men.'

'She's not happy,' Maxie said. 'By the way, she's got a Chinese woman with her. She arrived today from Hong Kong. There's some connection between what happened here and the Triads in Hong Kong.'

'The Triads are in this?'

'Yes. The files we took out of Becker's safe indicate that very strongly. It all comes down to the rhino horn. Becker was behind the poaching. The Triads were financing it. That woman up there had her family killed by them.'

Creasy finished his drink and said, 'Let's go up and get it over with.'

When Creasy knocked on the door of Gloria's suite, it was opened by John Ndlovu.

He said, 'I'm sorry to hear about your son. I spoke with the doctor on the phone. I just wish there was something we could do.'

'There is,' Creasy said, still standing in the open door. 'You can wrap up all the legal proceedings quickly and, if possible, have those proceedings take place in Bulawayo. I don't want to have to be commuting between here and Harare in the next few days.'

'That will be done,' the African answered. 'Robin Gilbert will handle it full-time.'

He stood aside and Creasy walked into the room, followed by Maxie. Gloria was in her wheelchair. Robin Gilbert was sitting on the settee next to a young Chinese woman. Creasy looked at Gloria. Anguish was stamped on her face.

She asked, 'How is he?'

'He's paralysed from the waist down, and you can understand how he is better than I can.'

'Did you talk to him?' she asked.

'Yes.'

'Did you tell him?'

'Of course.'

'How did he react?'

'With strength.'

Her voice had lost all its edge of authority and bitterness. She said, 'I can have the best specialists in the States here within forty-eight hours.'

Creasy shook his head.

'Mrs Manners, the time for waving magic wands is long gone. The doctors here are very experienced in these things.'

She lifted her head and asked almost plaintively, 'Then what *can* I do?'

'Only one thing,' Creasy answered. 'We found the people that killed your daughter and we killed them. Our deal was that if we found them, you paid half a million Swiss francs and, if we subsequently killed them, another million. We did our job. I'd be glad if you could pay that money as soon as possible. I'm going to need it.'

'Of course. You'll be paid immediately. Can I see Michael?'

'Why?'

'Don't be cruel, Creasy. You said just now that maybe I understand how he feels better than anyone. That's true. Maybe I can talk to him. Maybe I can help.'

Irritation began to well up inside Creasy's mind. Then he realised he was looking into a woman's eyes which contained compassion and sorrow.

He said, 'You can see him tomorrow morning. Just don't cry or be maudlin.'

She stiffened in her wheelchair and said, 'I know enough not to do that.'

CHAPTER 30

Michael woke and saw the sunlight streaming in through the window. He had been awake most of the night, in spite of the medication, but realised he must have slept for at least a couple of the last few hours. He turned his head. The nun sitting by his bed was white. She was reading a book.

'What are you reading?' he asked.

Her head jerked up in surprise. She had black hair under her starched white wimple.

'How do you feel?'

'Not so bad. What are you reading?'

Sheepishly, she said, 'A Mills and Boon romance . . . I know, but I quite like them.' She put the book aside, stood up and went about her duties, taking his pulse and temperature and talking to him in a soft Irish brogue. Finally, she made some notes on the clipboard at the foot of his bed, looked at her watch and said, 'The doctor will be here in about half an hour.' She picked up the phone by his bed and he heard her tell the duty matron that his condition was stable.

After she had hung up, Michael said, 'I like to read too. I'm going to be here for quite a while . . . does the hospital have a library?'

'Oh, yes. A good one. A selection of books are sent around the wards in the mornings and evenings.'

'What time in the mornings?'

'Between ten and eleven.'

'What time is it now?'

She lifted the watch hanging from her habit and said, 'Seven-thirty.'

He turned his head and looked at the bedside table. There was a jug a water and a glass.

'Can I have some water?'

She bustled over, half-filled a glass, put a soft hand behind his neck, pulled him up slightly and held the glass to his lips. Pain stabbed through his shoulder but he made no sound. He laid his head back against the pillow and closed his eyes. The nun sat down and picked up her book. Five minutes passed, then he opened his eyes and turned his head and looked at the open window and the sunlight shining through. Another five minutes passed. He turned his head and looked at the nun.

'What's your name, Sister?'

She smiled. She had a round comely face.

'Agatha. Named after the saint, of course, but I could have wished for a namesake with a prettier name.'

He managed a smile.

'A rose by any other name . . . Agatha, I have to ask a favour.'

'What is it you want?'

He gestured at her book with his good arm.

'I won't sleep again and I need something to occupy my mind. Is it possible that you could go to the library and pick out a couple of books for me?'

She thought about it and then glanced at her watch.

'I suppose I could do that. It's just down the corridor. What kind of books do you like?'

'Well, maybe you could pick four or five for me. I like westerns or detective stories. Inspector Maigret or something; or a good thriller.'

She put her book down and stood up, saying, 'I shouldn't really leave you, but it won't take more than ten minutes.' She pointed to the button dangling from a line behind his head. 'If you come over badly, just press that.'

'Don't worry, Sister Agatha, I feel OK. A good book will take my mind off things.'

As the door closed behind her, Michael closed his eyes. He lay absolutely still for two minutes, then he opened his eyes and with his right hand pulled aside the sheet. He looked down at his useless feet. He was dressed in a white shift, loosely tied at the back. He pulled the shift up and looked at his useless legs. Beside them was a piece of paper. He picked up the paper and laid it on the table next to the water-bottle. Then he rolled out of the bed, on to the floor and lay moaning for many seconds. He managed to roll over on to his stomach.

Inch by inch, he dragged himself across the carpet towards the window, using his right elbow and gasping from the pain in his left shoulder. In his mind, it seemed to take an eternity, but finally he was there. He reached up with his right hand and gripped the window-sill. His arms and hands were strong from a regular routine of exercises, but still he had to use every ounce of strength to get his right elbow on to the window-sill with his legs dragging under him and pain shooting through his body like electric shocks. He levered himself higher with his elbow, until he got his lower chest across the window-sill. He looked out. A well-ordered parkland stretched out in front of him, with trees and lawns and manicured beds of flowers. He levered himself further forward and looked down. The private rooms of the hospital were on the top floors, the fourth floor. Directly below him was a flagstoned pathway. Another minute passed while he looked down at it. Then he muttered something in Maltese and, with one last effort, pulled himself out and over.

Ruby pushed the wheelchair down the corridor, checking the numbers of the rooms, but Gloria spotted it first and pointed.

'There: Number Twelve.'

Ruby tapped on the door. There was no answer.

Gloria said, 'The matron told us he was awake. Go ahead.'

Ruby turned the handle and pushed the door open and came back behind the wheelchair and pushed it through. The bed was empty.

Through the window, they heard people shouting. Ruby ran to the window. She looked down and saw the white-clad body and people crouching over it, shouting in alarm.

'Oh, my God!'

With a hand over her mouth, she turned back to Gloria. The old woman's wheelchair was next to the bed. She was holding a piece of paper in her hand and reading it. The piece of paper fluttered from her hands and those hands came up to cover Gloria Manner's face.

Ruby walked across the room and picked up the paper and, with the sounds of her employer's sobs in her ears, she read the note.

'My Juliet and Creasy,

Do not blame the nun. I knew I would have to trick her. Creasy, I knew the promise you made to me would be the only promise you ever failed to keep. You could not have done it and I know that I would never have changed my mind. Over the past days, I have watched that woman in her wheelchair, bitter and twisted, taking out that bitterness on others.
The years were few but they were good. Better than I ever dreamed of. Creasy, those years were a gift from you. Juliet, live my life for me.

Michael'

CHAPTER 31

He walked for two hours after leaving the Land-rover. He wore long khaki trousers and a grey shirt. He carried no weapon. He walked into the southern end of Matopos, the small game sanctuary, south of Bulawayo. He was far away from the northern area where the occasional tourist appeared. There were no roads or man-made trails, just wild African country and its inhabitants. He passed herds of kudu and impala and zebra. At a distance, he saw buffalo and skirted them. There were wild dogs, hyenas and wart-hogs. He walked as though he was on auto-pilot; he had been this way before, many years ago.

It was an extraordinary landscape: rolling hills covered by huge boulders, some as big as several houses, some perched on others in a perpetual balancing act. To the north was the burial place of Cecil Rhodes, who had tricked and fought the Matabele into giving up their land. The Matopos resembled an area where God had played a game, tossing vast boulders around on the seventh day of rest.

Creasy came to the small lake just before sunset. Several times on his solitary journey, he had stopped and listened. He was confident that no human being was within miles of him. The noises of nature had only been disturbed by himself and that disturbance was negligible. As he had walked, it seemed as though the animals had taken him back into themselves. He found a flat area under a Mopani tree and, for the next half hour, gathered dry wood. All around him, the animals were coming down to drink at the lake: the skittish impala, the careful kudu, the giraffes which had to straddle their legs in order to reach the water. It was an orderly parade. Somehow, each species knew its place in that parade. An hour earlier Creasy had passed a pride of lions feasting over a kill. There were not many lions in Matopos, and so a sort of bush telegraph must have gone through the area, telling the other animals that they would be safe from the lions these coming days, until they had to kill again.

As the sun went down, Creasy lit his fire. Close behind him, he had piled up enough dry wood to keep that fire burning all night. He pulled up a log and sat on it. From one back pocket of his trousers he took a hip flask, and from the other back pocket, a wedge of biltong. As the animals departed, he chewed at the biltong and drank the water from the hip-flask.

The night noises started. The roosting birds in the surrounding trees, settling and gossiping, the myriad sounds of the insects, the grunting of a pair of mating wart-hogs. Far away, the cackle of a hyena and, still further, the coughing roar of a lion. Small black shapes dipped and swooped over the fire: bats, feeding off the insects attracted by the light.

Creasy tried to come to terms with the pain. It was so easy in company to show his strength and hide his emotions. He had walked into Matopos to try to commune with a God whom he did not understand. A God who would take Michael's life but not his. He looked around in the dying light and wondered how God could create such a paradise and yet could, so often, allow undeserved death and suffering. His whole life had been witness to that conundrum.

Here in the Matopos, it seemed that God had no part to play. Only nature. The selection of death was simple. No one pointed a finger. A lion or a leopard or a cheetah hunted only from instinct. There was no malice or forethought. It was just a meal.

The lions came about two hours later. Four of them, three females and a black-maned male. Creasy recognised the male as the animal he had seen on his way in, feeding over the kill while the females waited their turn.

Like all cats, they had come out of curiosity. Their bellies were full. They approached the warmth of the fire slowly, but without any indication of fear. They sank down on to the earth and looked across the flames at Creasy. He looked back. They were twenty metres away. The fire was dimming. He reached behind him and gently piled on more branches. One of the females rolled over, exposing her distended belly to the fire.

The male lion sat crouched, his vivid yellow eyes watching Creasy. Over the next hour, the other two females also crept a little clsoer to the fire and rolled into sleep. The black-maned male remained motionless, and so did Creasy, except for occasionally placing another branch on the fire. Another hour passed while Creasy held a deep-down debate with himself. Once in a while, he bit off a piece of biltong and drank some water. Sometimes the black-mane belched inelegantly from his recent feast. Finally, Creasy eased off the log, folded his arms, lay down and half-slept. The black-mane lowered his head to the ground and also closed his eyes.

The noises of the night continued. Just before dawn, another sound was added. The coughing grunt of a hyena. The sound came from behind Creasy. He opened his eyes.

Before he could turn to look, he noticed the black-mane had raised his head and was looking beyond the fire and Creasy. The lion pushed himself to his feet, walked around the fire and stood not more than seven metres from the prone human. The animal looked into the darkness beyond, then drew in a breath and let forth the roar that for millennia has sent fear through the heart of Africa.

Creasy heard the scurried pattering of retreating footsteps. Across the fire the three female lions had lifted their heads. They listened briefly and then slumped back to sleep. The black-mane went back around the fire and settled himself again. The fire was almost out. Creasy put no more branches on it. The faint glow of the sun was rising away to his right. He stood up and stretched, drank the last of his water and then started throwing earth over the embers. He headed back towards his Land-rover a couple of hours away. But a hundred metres away he stopped, turned and looked back. The female lions were still asleep; the black-mane was sitting upright, looking at him.

Creasy did something he had not done for many years. He stiffened and his right arm swept up swiftly in a brief salute. Then he turned and walked on.

After he had moved away through the bush, a figure of a man rose from a cluster of boulders about a hundred and fifty metres from the extinguished fire.

For the first time in hours, Maxie MacDonald moved the switch on his rifle to safety. Then, very carefully, he followed his friend's spoor out of the Matopos . . . in the same way he had followed it in.

BOOK TWO

CHAPTER 32

The funerals in Gozo have a strange ritual at the end. The men of the congregation file silently down the isle and circle the coffin. As they move away from it, they kiss their right thumbs, then lower their hands and touch the coffin with that thumb.

Father Manuel Zerafa had conducted the service. Creasy was in the front row, with an arm around Juliet. Guido was next to her and the Schembri family next to him. The church of Our Lady of Loreto, perched above the Mgarr Harbour, was full to capacity, not only in mourning for Michael but as a sign of respect to Creasy, the man the locals called simply, *Uomo*.

Creasy watched the faces of the men as they silently filed around the coffin, following their ritual. He recognised their faces but could not remember all their names. They ranged in age from the very old to boys in their teens. The line seemed to go on for an eternity, and then his head jerked up in surprise. He was looking at the face of Frank Miller, who merely glanced at him and went through the ritual. Then another suprise – Rene Callard followed. More surprises – Jens Jensen and The Owl. Maxie was the last one. Paul and Joey Schembri moved past, circled the coffin and stood waiting by the door. Guido did the same.

The church had emptied except for the immediate group, the new arrivals who were waiting by the entrance, and of course, Father Zerafa. Six young men walked in, the pall-bearers. Paul Schembri whispered something to Guido, who nodded. Paul went up to the young men, spoke to them quietly and they turned and walked out. He gestured towards the five men at the entrance and they walked down. Together with Joey, they lifted the coffin on to their shoulders and bore it out of the church, down the steps and into the hearse. Creasy followed with Juliet and the rest of the Schembri family behind him and Father Zerafa.

A long stream of cars followed the hearse to the nearby cemetery and, after the brief graveside service, Creasy turned to the new arrivals and said, 'It was a surprise to see you.'

Frank Miller shrugged.

'We heard there was going to be a good wake after the funeral.' He glanced at the others. 'We were never ones to miss a party.' None of them spoke words of condolence to either Creasy or Juliet. They were not the type to use a word when a gesture was enough.

CHAPTER 33

Lucy Kwok found it hard to believe. She stood on the patio with a glass of white wine in her hand, looking out at the magnificent view across Gozo and the sea. It was early evening. As an air hostess, she had travelled wide and seen much, but she found all this hard to understand. She had stood at the back of the church during the funeral. Although she herself was a Roman Catholic, she had never seen such richness in a church outside of the Vatican. Statues and walls gleamed with gold and precious stones. The heavy, ornate candlesticks on the altar looked as if they were made of solid silver. But, judging from the congregation, the people did not seem to be rich.

Behind her was a babble of noise, and even laughter. She turned and surveyed forty-odd people who had made their way up to the house after the brief graveside ceremony. There were two priests among them, both holding glasses. To the left, Creasy was tending a smoking barbecue, surrounded by the five men who had arrived at the church just as the funeral began. They seemed to be giving him good-natured advice and their attitudes showed anything but grief. Beside the kitchen door a table had been set up as a temporary bar, and a young Gozitan was manning it with enthusiasm.

Lucy's eyes moved back to Creasy, and her mind went back to the moment she had first met him at Bulawayo Airport, when the coffin containing Michael's body had been loaded into the Gulfstream. His presence had an immediate effect on her – that scarred impassive face and sense of not caring – until she had managed to get a look into his eyes. Her skin had prickled at the lurking hatred she had seen.

155

As soon as the plane had taken off, he had sat down opposite her. She had started to speak some words of condolence. He had held up a hand.

'Miss Kwok, that matter is over now. Commander Ndlovu explained why you came to Zimbabwe. He told me what happened to your family in Hong Kong. Of course there must be a connection, and I want you to tell me as much as you can. It seems that whoever killed my son took his orders from Hong Kong. I want to know who gave those orders.'

They had talked for the next two hours and during those two hours she sensed a growing bond. She felt that part of his character was similar to her own. They were both grieving, yet no outsider would have noticed. Finally he had observed that her eyes were becoming heavy, and had arranged a bunk for her in one of the rear cabins.

Now she glanced again at the crowd of people and saw Juliet detach herself and walk over.

'You look tired,' Juliet said. 'Don't feel you have to stay. Just slip off to your bedroom whenever you feel like it. You had a long journey.'

'That's true, but it was a journey in some luxury, and I slept most of the way and there was no time change.' She looked at the girl's face. 'You also look tired. And your journey was West to East with a six-hour time difference. I doubt you slept at all.'

'You're right,' Juliet answered. 'Sleep was impossible. I'll crash out later and probably sleep for twenty-four hours.'

The Chinese woman shook her head.

'I've had a lot of experience with jet-lag. Stay up as long as you can keep your eyes open. Don't drink too much alcohol. You'll probably wake up within six hours. After that, again, stay awake as long as you can, and after a second sleep the jet-lag will be gone.'

Juliet made a negative gesture.

'After that I'll be heading back to Denver and another bout of jet-lag.' She looked over at Creasy and the others around the barbecue. 'This must seem very strange to you. I don't suppose you have wakes in China.'

'No, we don't. It's all very peculiar. Such a rich church on what seems to be a poor island, and then a big party where everyone is laughing and joking.'

Juliet explained. 'First of all, it's not a poor island, but it is extremely Catholic. Up until a decade ago, it was not unusual for a couple to have up to fifteen children or more. The island became very over-populated. Since the main occupation was farming or fishing, there was not enough work, so the young men emigrated, mainly to America, Canada and Australia. They worked hard and sent their money back, and many returned to spend their retirement here. Despite appearances, it's a very wealthy community. As for this party, it is unusual for Gozo, where they tend to go into protracted mourning. The tradition comes from Ireland. It's to celebrate a life that has been lived and not a death that has happened. Somehow in the mercenary wars in Africa it was adopted when a mercenary was killed in action. I can tell you that by nightfall a party will be in full swing and it will go on until at least midnight.'

Lucy glanced at the girl and said, 'You are young to know so much.'

'I've never been to a wake or even to a funeral, but I've been around mercenaries and heard them talk. When a mercenary is killed in a big explosion, especially one with flames, they call it a "technicolour funeral". When a mercenary dies in an accident, they call it an 'FU funeral" . . . a fuck-up funeral. They have their own language and rituals. In the next decade or so, that will probably die out.'

'You mean the mercenaries will die out?'

The girl shook her head.

'No. There will always be mercenaries, because there will always be wars. But the young ones are a different breed.' She glanced at the Chinese woman and asked, 'How did Mrs Manners take the whole thing?'

'Badly . . . you know about Michael's suicide note?'

'Yes, Creasy told me.'

'Well,' Lucy said, 'we all flew back in her private jet, but she hardly said a word. She ate nothing during the nine-hour flight. She stayed mostly in her cabin. I think her nurse Ruby must have given her heavy sedation. When we landed in Malta she spoke a few words to Creasy and Maxie and just said goodbye to me. I guess by now she's back in the States.'

Juliet was nodding thoughtfully, then she lifted her head, took a sip of wine and said, 'Let me introduce you around.'

Lucy put a hand on her arm.

'Wait a minute. First, please tell me who everyone is. Do you know them all?'

'Oh, yes.' Juliet pointed towards the group of men around the barbecue. 'You know Creasy and Maxie. The bald Australian is Frank Miller. He's often worked with Creasy. The handsome man next to him with the slightly hooked nose and the dark hair is a Belgian called René Callard. He spent fifteen years in the French Foreign Legion. Some of the time with Creasy. Later on, he fought with Creasy in Africa. The blond guy on the other side of the fire is Jens Jensen. He's Danish and an ex-policeman. He now has a private detective agency in Copenhagen, specialising in missing persons. His partner is the small man next to him with the thick round spectacles. He's a Frenchman known as The Owl. He used to be a gangster in Marseille. Later on, he became a bodyguard to an arms dealer and then joined up with Jens about four years ago. His great love is classical music. This is one of the few occasions where I've seen him without his Walkman and earphones.'

'A diverse bunch of men.'

'Yes, and it gets more so. The man there with the scarred face, talking to the middle-aged woman, is an Italian called Guido Arrellio. He's Creasy's closest friend. They are like brothers. But you will never see them show the slightest sign of affection. Guido was also in the Foreign Legion. Both he and Creasy were kicked out when part of the Legion rebelled at the end of the war in Algeria. They went off to the Congo and fought together for many years . . . One day, about ten years ago, they ended up in Gozo for a few days' holiday. Guido fell in love with the hotel receptionist. A few weeks later, he married her and took her off to Naples where they ran a small *pensione*. She was the daughter of the woman Guido's talking to.'

'Was?'

'Yes. She was killed in a car crash a few years later. Her mother is Laura Schembri, her father is Paul – the small dark man over there, talking to the priest. The young man behind the bar is their son Joey. Joey's wife Maria is in the kitchen, making the salad. The Schembri family are very close to Creasy and me . . . I think Laura is the only woman who can get Creasy to do something he doesn't want to do – but then, there is a special bond between them. Creasy was once involved in a battle against a Mafia gang in

Italy and was badly wounded. Guido suggested that he come to Gozo to recover and stay at the Schembris' farm on the other side of the island. He stayed for about two months. During that time the Schembri's younger daughter, Nadia, returned from a failed marriage in England. She and Creasy had an affair and she became pregnant. She told nobody and Creasy went back to Italy. When he finished the job he returned to Gozo, again wounded. After recovering, he married Nadia and they had a daughter, and for the next few years lived peacefully in this house.'

She turned to look at the Chinese woman. 'But in December 1988, Nadia and her daughter caught a Pan Am flight in London to join Creasy in New York. The plane blew up over Scotland and everybody was killed.'

The girl fell silent. Lucy Kwok looked across the patio at the man tending the barbecue.

Quietly, she remarked, 'A lot of tragedy and death surrounds that man.' She turned to look at Juliet: The girl's face was a picture of sadness.

Juliet nodded and said, 'Yes. And it's not over yet.'

'It's not?'

'No, in a few days he'll be off to Hong Kong . . . and there will be more dead.'

'He told you that?'

'No. But I know that man. He won't rest until he's dealt with the people who caused Michael's suicide.' Her slim body shook briefly, but then her voice lightened as she pointed out some of the other guests. The young ones had been friends of Michael and the older ones, friends of Creasy.

It was an hour later when the phone rang. They were eating at makeshift tables. Creasy looked up at Juliet, and she got up and went into the kitchen. A minute later she called from the door.

'Creasy, it's Jim Grainger calling from Denver.'

Creasy wiped his mouth with a paper napkin. He went into the kitchen. It was fifteen minutes before he returned. As he sat down, he said to Maxie, 'Gloria Manners did not return to Denver.'

'Where did she go?'

'She went nowhere. That Gulfstream never took off. Right now, she's in a suite in the L'Imgarr Bay hotel, here in Gozo.'

'But why?' Lucy Kwok asked.

'I don't know. But she wants to talk to me.'

'Will you see her?' Maxie asked.

Creasy nodded.

'Yes, I will see her tomorrow morning.'

'Why would you want to talk to her?' Juliet asked. 'I mean, after what happened down there in Zimbabwe.'

Creasy picked up his knife and fork and said, 'I'll see her because Jim Grainger asked me to, as a personal favour. As you well know, Juliet, he's done me several favours, including looking after you in the States.'

'Yes, but —'

'There are no buts.'

CHAPTER 34

Creasy walked into the hotel lobby just after ten o'clock in the morning. He was not in a good frame of mind. The wake had gone on until the early hours and he had a headache from the drink.

As he approached reception, a short well-dressed man with a dark moustache stood up from a group of people at a table in the corner. He walked across the room and touched Creasy briefly on the shoulder. Creasy had known him for many years. He was the hotel manager, and the tap on the shoulder was a gesture of condolence.

'You have a Mrs Manners staying here,' Creasy said.

'Yes, she's in 105.'

'When did she check in?'

'Yesterday morning.'

'Has she been a problem?'

'On the contrary. She's taken all her meals in her room with her nurse, and the staff tell me that she tips well and is very kind.'

'Is she in her room now?'

The manager looked at the receptionist and said, '105 – in or out?'

'In, sir,' the girl answered. 'She hasn't left her suite since she arrived.'

Creasy said to the manager, 'I'll be in Room 105 for the next twenty minutes or so. Do you remember that hangover cure you recommended all those years ago?'

The manager grinned under his black moustache.

'Sure . . . Do you want me to send one up?'

'I'd be eternally grateful.'

Creasy walked down the corridor to the end and tapped on the door of Room 105. It opened to reveal Ruby, looking apprehensive.

'Hello, Ruby.'

'Hello, Creasy. Come on in. Can I get you a coffee or something?'

'No, thanks. Something is being sent up.'

He walked into the room and, through the french windows, saw Mrs Manners sitting in her wheelchair on the wide balcony. He walked out, pulled up a chair and sat opposite her. The hotel was perched on the cliff above the harbour. Like his own house, it had one of the most spectacular views on Gozo.

From the balcony door Ruby asked, 'Can I get you something, Mrs Manners?'

Gloria shook her head.

'Thank you, no, Ruby . . . but maybe Creasy wants something?'

'I've already ordered,' Creasy said, and Ruby disappeared back into the suite.

Creasy was puzzled. When Gloria Manners had spoken to Ruby he had noticed the change in her voice. It was as though the life had gone out of it. No abrasion. He looked at the woman. Her face had aged. The lines were deeper, and the eyes more sunken.

'I'd assumed you'd be back in Denver by now,' he said.

'I had no intention of returning to Denver before I could speak to you. I did not want to do so before Michael's funeral. I'm sorry that I had to put Jim Grainger under pressure to arrange this meeting.'

Creasy said, 'Why did you come here?'

Gloria gathered her thoughts, and then said, 'There were several reasons. The first was that I wanted to express to you my deep sorrow that I was the cause of Michael's death. First, because I hired him – second, because I gave him such a bad example of what life in a wheelchair was like.'

Creasy drew a breath and looked directly into the woman's eyes as he spoke. 'You were not the reason for Michael's death. I would have told you that on the plane coming up here, but you slept most of the time, and I understand that. I was going to write you in a few days' time. I don't want you to wallow in grief and guilt. There were two reasons for Michael's death – myself and a man in Hong Kong.'

'But I read that note!'

'That note was an excuse.'

'An excuse?'

'Yes, just that and no more. It was an excuse for a weakness. Michael's weakness.'

The woman was looking at him without comprehension. Creasy explained, 'Mrs Manners, I adopted Michael from an orphanage not more than a kilometre from here when he was seventeen years old. I trained and moulded him to be a man like me, for a special purpose. He was strong and skilled and I loved him very much. As much as a father could love a natural son. But I also moulded him into my own life style, and that was the only life style that he ever understood. When Michael was paralysed from the waist down, he knew that he could never live that life style. He also knew that he had full use of his arms and upper body. Certainly, he could have lived a fruitful life. There's a man on this island who was paralysed in the same way after a car crash. He was a young man. He built a new life. Last year he took part in the Paraplegic Olympics and won a bronze medal. Michael knew that man well – and admired him. But because of the life style that I had created for him, he couldn't see himself in that role. He couldn't see himself in any role. In that hospital in Bulawayo he asked me to kill him. I told him to wait three months – if he still felt the same way then; I would do it. The problem was that he didn't believe me.'

The old woman had been looking out to sea while she listened. Now she turned her face back to look at Creasy. She asked, 'Would you have done it?'

'Yes.'

'You could have done that?'

'Yes.'

A ferry was coming into the harbour, loaded with day-trippers. She watched it silently and then, just as she was about to speak a waiter appeared at the balcony door. He held a tray on which was a single glass containing a purple liquid. He gave the glass to Creasy, touched him on the shoulder and left. Creasy lifted the glass to his lips and drained it in one go.

He said to Gloria, 'About ten years ago I went to a wedding at another hotel and drank too much champagne. Champagne doesn't agree with me. In the morning the maître d' mixed me a drink which cured my hangover in about half an hour. That maîtred' is now the manager of this hotel.' He lifted the glass. 'That was the same concoction. I hope it works as well as the last time.'

'Would you really have killed Michael after three months, if he had asked you to?'

'Yes. But he wouldn't have asked. The mistake was mine. I should have stayed with him that night in Bulawayo, and the following nights. I thought he was stronger.'

'But that note!'

Creasy sighed. 'That note was an excuse.' He stood up. 'Mrs Manners. What was written in that note contributed probably less than one per cent to Michael's decision. He never expected you to read it . . . I regret that you did. Now, go back to Denver with peace of mind. Your daughter's killers are dead – thanks, in part, to Michael. Let him be a good memory, not a bad one.' He put the enpty glass on the table.

She said, 'Creasy, please give me ten more minutes of your time. Then you can leave and so will I.'

He saw the pleading in the woman's eyes, paused, and slowly sat down again.

She said, 'Was what you said just balm for my concience?'

'No. It was the truth. Maybe you have to live with your conscience in other areas, but not about Michael's suicide. Last night we held a wake. Some old friends of mine – and Michael's – arrived unexpectedly. Last night we buried Michael's soul. That is now in the past.'

'So easy?'

'Not easy. In the next few days I'll travel to Hong Kong and some more bodies will be buried. Then I'll sleep easier.'

She was watching him closely and, in spite of his cold and calm exterior, she could see the pain deep in his eyes. She said, 'Hong Kong is why I wanted to talk to you.'

'Hong Kong?'

'Yes. During the last two days that we were in Bulawayo you were obviously preoccupied and busy. Did you have a chance to study Commander Ndlovu's report on the Beckers?'

'No, but I have a copy. I'll be reading it over the next few days.'

'Well, I read it very carefully and then discussed it with Commander Ndlovu. Much of it was compiled from the files you found in the safe at Becker's house. Three things came out of it: first of all, Becker got his orders from someone in Hong Kong, who the police assume is the 14K Triad – but they cannot prove that. Second, it was a chance remark made by my daughter, Carole, at a cocktail party in Harare that caused her death and that of Cliff Coppen, Lucy Kwok's family in Hong Kong and, ultimately, Michael's.'

'A chance remark?'

'Yes. Perhaps she was boasting a little. The conversation had been about the black rhino. She said that her boyfriend was working with an eminent Chinese medical researcher who had proved that powdered rhino horn does not improve male potency, but actually contains a cancer-causing agent. It turns out that the man she was boasting to was an associate of Rolph Becker's who, naturally, immediately alerted him. Third, Commander Ndlovu spoke to a senior policeman in Hong Kong in the Anti-Triad Department. Although they know that 14K was behind the murder of Lucy's family, they do not have enough evidence to proceed against the leaders.'

'That's always the case,' Creasy said. 'It's why I'm going to Hong Kong.'

'You will go alone?'

'Yes.'

The old woman noticed that his face was slightly wet with perspiration. She watched as he took out a handkerchief and wiped his forehead. He looked down at the empty glass in front of him and said, 'It seems that the hangover cure is not working so well this time. If anything, I feel worse.'

'I won't keep you too much longer, Creasy. It's just that I want to ask you something. And before you say no, I want you to think about it for a day or so.'

'Ask.'

'I want to continue with the whole operation . . . all the way to Hong Kong. I won't get in your way, and I won't be issuing orders or waving my so-called magic wand. I just want to be there at the end. I don't want to return to Denver without knowing what's happening.'

Creasy started to say something.

She said, 'Please, Creasy – two more minutes. Please understand – it was my daughter who set this whole thing off. She could not have known it, of course, but it was her fault. She paid with her life and so have others. I want you to let me keep funding the operation and base myself in Hong Kong. I've had some research done and faxed to me. The Triads are very powerful, especially the 14K. You will need people to help you – and not just Maxie. You will need much more than Maxie.'

Creasy wiped his forehead again and stood up. He said, 'Mrs Manners, I don't have to think about it. The answer is no. If I need to hire a couple of guys, I can do it myself. You paid promptly and I thank you for that.' He turned to go.

She said, 'The research on the Triads is in the green folder on the table. Take it with you. Meanwhile, I'll stay here for at least seventy-two hours in the hope that you'll change your mind.'

'You can stay as long as you like, Mrs Manners. It's a free country.' He went into the sitting-room. The green folder was very bulky. He paused and then picked it up. He would look through it and send it back tomorrow.

As he drove back towards Victoria the sweating stopped and he felt his body going cold in the warm air. On impulse, he turned left and into the village of Xewkija, where his doctor lived.

As he was shown into his doctor's study, he said, 'Sorry to bother you, Stephen, but I've got a fever, and I think it might be malaria.'

The doctor gestured to a chair in front of his desk and asked, 'Where have you been lately?'

'I just got back from Zimbabwe. I spent some days in the Zambezi Valley.'

'You surprise me, Creasy. Surely a man of your experience would have taken prophylactic pills at least three weeks before your departure?'

'Naturally,' Creasy replied. 'But I only knew I was going a couple of days beforehand.'

'Okay, so we take a blood sample and I'll let you know tomorrow. In the meantime, I'll give you some medication . . . I suppose it would be a waste of time asking you to spend the next twenty-four hours in hospital?'

'Yes, it would. I'll be fine at home.'

CHAPTER 35

The fever broke on the second night. Creasy was fortunate; the infection had not been very bad. But, still, Maxie and Guido had to change the sheets on his bed half a dozen times, when they became soaked with his sweat.

His recovery was swift. When the doctor came in the morning, he was sitting up in bed, leafing through the pages in the folder that Gloria had given him.

The doctor checked him over and then said sternly, 'It wasn't so bad. But you're weaker than you think. I would normally ask my patients to spend at least five or six days in bed after such a bout of malaria. But, knowing you, I'll be happy to extract a promise of forty-eight hours. Then don't overdo anything for a few more days.'

After he had left, Maxie came in.

'How do you feel?'

'Fine.'

'The doctor said forty-eight hours. Just make sure you follow instructions for a change.'

Creasy closed the folder and asked, 'What are your plans?'

'I'm heading home tomorrow. I'm going to close the bistro for a couple of weeks and use some of Gloria Manners's money to take Nicole and Lucette on a luxury holiday. I spoke to Nicole on the phone last night. She said Lucette's really cut up about Michael.'

Guido came in, and after more inquiries about Creasy's well-being, he turned to Maxie and said, 'Laura phoned and invited us for lunch. She's making rabbit stew and, believe me, you don't want to miss that.'

'Bring some back for me,' Creasy said, 'She always makes too much, anyway.' He lifted the green folder and gave it to Maxie. 'On your way, please drop that off to Gloria Manners at the hotel and tell her that I won't be changing my mind.'

'What is it?'

'Oh, just some general information on the Hong Kong Triads. Just say goodbye for me.'

When Juliet came into the bedroom half an hour later with a cup of hot soup, Creasy was fast asleep. She stood for several minutes, looking down at his face. Then she turned around and went out, taking the soup with her.

When he awoke, it was mid-afternoon. He drank some water from the flask by the bed and pulled himself out of the bed to go to the bathroom. It was then that he realised how weak he was. He moved carefully across the flagstoned floor. As he came out, Guido was entering the bedroom, followed by Maxie. Creasy tried to walk normally and almost tripped. Guido hurried forward and put an arm under his elbow and helped him to the bed.

'How was lunch?' Creasy asked.

'In fact, it was so good there was nothing left for you.'

They both sat down at the foot of the bed, and Guido said, 'We've come to talk to you.'

'About what?'

'About Hong Kong.'

'What about it?'

'We didn't take that folder back immediately. We took it back after lunch. Meanwhile, we read the contents. We already know that the Triads are formidable. We also know that once you're over this malaria you're heading to Hong Kong to take out the head guy of the 14K. When Maxie gave Mrs Manners the folder and your message, she told him that she had offered to fund a major operation to take out that guy.'

Maxie interjected, 'She also told us that it was her daughter's indiscretion that caused her own death and those of Lucy's family. We think you should take up her offer.'

'Is it any of your business?'

Guido provided the answer. 'Yes, it is. We liked Michael very much. For me, he was as a nephew. Apart from that, you already have the nucleus of a good team.'

'And the money's good,' Maxie said.

Creasy gave them both a hard look and then said; 'If I decide to take a couple of guys with me, I'll pay them from my own pocket.'

'Like who?' Guido asked.

'Well, like Frank and Rene. They're staying on a few more days. I'll make my decision before they leave.'

Guido sighed. 'Creasy, you're an intelligent man. But sometimes you can be very stupid. Of course, Frank and Rene will go with you. But there's no way they'll accept any money from you, apart from basic expenses. They too were very fond of Michael. And of course that goes for me.'

'And me,' Maxie chimed in.

'I thought you were going off on holiday,' Creasy said.

'That's no problem,' Maxie answered. 'I'll cut it down to seven or eight days. You won't be ready to move for at least a week.'

In a determined tone of voice, Creasy said, 'There's no way that I'm going to be working for that woman any more. This time it's personal.'

'She's changed,' Maxie said. 'That's very obvious from just a brief conversation. She just wants to be in Hong Kong. She just wants to stay in her hotel and only asks that she be kept informed.'

'There's another aspect,' Guido said. 'I was talking to Frank and Rene last night. The market for mercenaries is pretty bad, these days. Frank's working as a security consultant with an airfreight company, and Rene's resting.'

'And another thing,' Maxie said. 'Jens and The Owl haven't had a good paying job since the end of last year.'

Creasy's eyes felt heavy, and he knew that within a few minutes he'd fall asleep. He looked at Guido and said, 'All this sounds suspiciously like a subtle form of blackmail.'

Guido shook his head.

'It sounds like good common sense. You'd be in total control of your own team. The fact that an old woman is sitting in a wheelchair in a hotel seems immaterial. You won't even have to see her or talk to her. Maxie can do that.'

Creasy's eyes were closed, and his voice slightly slurred. 'I'll think about it.'

Rene Callard and Frank Miller were sitting by the pool with Lucy Kwok. The two men had just come back from fishing and their catch was proudly laid out on the patio floor. Three baby tuna and two small lampuki.

Maxie looked down at the fish and remarked, 'That's all you got after four hours? They won't even cover the cost of the diesel. You'd have been better off buying them in the market.'

'They probably did,' Guido said with a grin, 'and spent the rest of the day chasing tourist girls on the beach . . . When are you guys heading out?'

'We're booked on the morning flight to Frankfurt.'

'I should postpone it,' Maxie said.

Guido said, 'There will be a job and it will pay very well. Also for Jens and The Owl.'

Maxie was looking at him. He asked, 'Are you so sure?'

Guido nodded.

'Yes. I know his mind like it was my own. When he wakes up he'll call a meeting in his bedroom. By the way, where are Jens and The Owl?'

'They went for a drink in a bar called Gleneagles,' Lucy said, 'about two hours ago.'

Guido turned to Maxie. 'You'd better phone them there. Tell them to get back here reasonably sober. After that, I suggest you call Mrs Manners and tell her not to leave Gozo until she hears from you or Creasy. It will probably be later this evening.'

CHAPTER 36

'I find it hard to take this whole culture.'

Creasy looked up from his bowl of soup. Juliet was sitting at the end of his bed.

'What culture?' he asked.

'Well, it seems to be a constant cycle of death. And you're right at the centre. It's a culture of constant vengeance. Gloria Manners's vengeance for her daughter's death, Lucy's vengeance for her family's death, and now your vengeance for Michael's death.'

He gave her a long look and said, 'For God's sake, don't come on with the Mother Theresa bit! If it wasn't for this culture you talk about, you'd either be dead or trapped as a heroin addict in some whorehouse in the Middle East or North Africa!'

'I know that, Creasy. You and Michael saved my life and gave me a home. Don't waste one second thinking that I don't thank God for that every day of my life . . . It's just that now you're planning to go off to Hong Kong . . . and there will be more killings. When will it all end?'

'It will end when a certain Tommy Mo Lau Wong is dead and buried.'

'Do you have to go?'

She saw the brief flash of irritation in his eyes as he answered.

'Yes. That man was ultimately responsible for Michael's death. The slate will be wiped clean and then maybe the circle of death, as you call it, can end.'

'You don't understand, Creasy! I want that man dead as much as you do. It's just that I don't want you dead as well. Lucy has told me something about the Triads and their power . . . Try to understand. First, I lost one family, and then I got another. Now I've lost half of that new family. I can't bear the thought of losing the other half.'

His voice softened very slightly. 'You have to bear it, Juliet. It's part of life and, if you like, the culture that you found yourself in. Maybe after this, that kind of life will change, but there can be no promises. I am what I am. But I do understand you. I remember, a few years back, your asking me to train you as I trained Michael. You were very young. The best age to be trained. I started to do that, but then it became obvious to me that, although you were enthusiastic, your heart was not really in it. I was glad when you began to take an interest in medicine.'

She was nodding thoughtfully. She said, 'I know. I'm very pleased to be at college in the States and staying with Jim . . . It's just that I worry about you.'

He gave her one of his rare smiles.

'I worry about you too, what with all those over-sexed young Americans running around the campus. However, in spite of that, I want you to fly back tomorrow. You've already missed almost a week of the semester.'

She gave him a dutiful nod and stood up, saying, 'Finish all your soup. There's plenty more, if you want it.'

'It's enough,' he said. 'Please ask Guido and Maxie to come and see me in about ten minutes.'

As she reached the door, his voice stopped her.

'Juliet, don't worry too much about me. I've been persuaded to take a high-powered team along.'

She turned and said, 'Yes; I guessed that. And I'm glad. But in a way it spreads the worry wider.'

'It does?'

'Of course. You'll be taking Guido and Maxie, Frank and Rene and Jens and The Owl . . . They're all very close to me.' She shrugged. 'But then I guess that's part of the culture.'

CHAPTER 37

They trooped into the bedroom, carrying chairs from the dining-room, and sat down in a semicircle round the bed. They were all there, including Lucy Kwok, except Juliet.

Creasy said, 'I know this is a bit of a farce. Of course I could have got up and we could have had this meeting around the dining-room table. The fact is that I promised my doctor to stay in bed for forty-eight hours, and that's what I'm going to do.' He looked at the Dane, 'Jens. As usual, I want you to handle communications and the co-ordinating of information.'

Jens pulled out a small notebook and a pen. Creasy's eyes moved to Maxie.

'Did you talk to Mrs Manners?'

'She asked me to tell you thank you, and to confirm that she will in no way interfere. She just wants to be kept informed.'

'Okay. That's part of your job.'

'Thanks a lot,' Maxie said.

'Well, you were the great persuader.' Creasy gestured at the Chinese woman. 'I tried to persuade Lucy to stay here until it's all over, but she has refused. As it happens, she might be useful in Hong Kong with the language, but she'll need protection and so might Mrs Manners. So, Lucy, you'll have to stay in the same hotel suite with her.' He looked at Callard. 'Rene, you'll provide that protection. Don't take any bullshit from the old woman.'

'I don't take bullshit from anybody,' Callard said.

'OK. Then the three of you can move from here to Hong Kong on her jet in five or six days from now.' He looked again at the Dane. 'Jens, do you think you can arrange press creditisation, because I want your cover to be a journalist?'

'It's no problem. The head of the crime bureau on the top Danish newspaper is a good friend from my days in the police. He'll fix it.'

'Good. I want you and The Owl to fly to Hong Kong in the next two or three days and check into a different hotel to Mrs Manners. You are to pretend to be tourists, but since Jens is also a reporter and happens to be in Hong Kong and planning a series of articles on the Triads, it would be quite normal for him to take time off and request an interview with Inspector Lau Ming Lan. We received good, if reluctant, co-operation from the Zimbabwe police; but only because of pressure from the US government. We will not get co-operation from the Hong Kong police. The situation is totally different. They'll probably get very pissed off if they find out that we're operating on their patch. The other thing I want you to do, Jens, is rent a house or a large apartment somewhere in Kowloon for a minimum of one month, or up to six months, if you have to. A house would be better.'

Guido remarked, 'Six months for a house in Kowloon is going to be damned expensive.'

'So be it,' Creasy answered. He looked at the Australian. 'Frank, I want you to fly up to Brussels tomorrow with Maxie, and have a meeting with Corkscrew Two to arrange weapons and their shipment to Hong Kong. I'll give you a list in the morning. Then you wait in Brussels until you hear from Jens.'

The Dane was busily making notes. Now he looked up and asked, 'In whose name do I rent the house or apartment?'

Creasy thought for a moment and then glanced at Miller and said, 'Ask Corkscrew Two's advice on that . . . he's the expert. Tell him that the house or apartment must be rented and the weapons installed within ten days.'

Lucy spoke up for the first time. 'Who is this Corkscrew Two, and how can he get weapons into Hong Kong?'

Creasy explained. 'He's the son of a man known in the business as The Corkscrew. He specialised in the smuggling of arms worldwide and was the very best. His contacts were legendary. He retired a few years ago and passed the business and contacts on to his son who, naturally, became known as Corkscrew Two. He's as good as his father was, and he'll have no trouble getting arms into Hong Kong.' He closed his eyes for a few moments, then reached out to his bedside table, shook two pills out a bottle and swallowed them. Then he looked at Guido and said, 'We're going to need two or three more guys.'

'I agree . . . but who?'

'Let's put our minds to it. They have to be top-line.'

Maxie said, 'Before I left Brussels I heard that Tom Sawyer's available.'

'He'd be perfect,' Frank said. 'Apart from anything else, he's a bloody good mortar man.'

'Yes, try to locate him when you get to Brussels. What was the last anyone heard of Do Huang?'

Maxie said, 'The last I heard, he was in Panama. He'd been doing a job for the CIA with some of the other guys in El Salvador. He's probably still in Panama City and stone-broke. He always headed straight out from operations into the nearest casino. Incidentally, I also heard that Eric Laparte was in Panama, on the same job with Do. But the news is not so good. The rumour is that he's been hitting the booze for the past few months.'

'I hope it's just a rumour,' Creasy said. 'Eric was one of the best.' he thought for a moment. 'Anyway, if Do Huang is stone-broke that's a plus. We could certainly use him.' He glanced at Lucy and explained. 'Do Huang is half-Vietnamese, half-Cantonese. He speaks Cantonese fluently, so he could be useful in an undercover role.'

Maxie said, 'As soon as I get back to Brussels I'll try to get a lead on them.'

Creasy shook his head.

'Let Frank do that. You're taking your wife and her sister on a few days' holiday, and apart from setting things up with Corkscrew Two, Frank will be twiddling his thumbs until he hears from Jens.' He looked at the Australian. 'If you locate them, give me a ring here, and in three or four days I'll go over and check them out.'

'I can go over if you like,' Guido said.

Creasy shook his head.

'No. You know Do Huang well, and he trusts you, but you don't know Eric Laparte. You won't know what to look for. Besides, he hardly trusts a single soul on this earth. But he trusts me. Anyway, you ought to spend two or three days with Laura and Paul.'

He closed his eyes again for a few seconds. When he opened

them, he said, 'That's about it.' They all stood up and started to file out. Creasy said, 'Lucy, wait a moment, please.' When the door was closed, he said, 'Apart from Rene, they'll all be out of here by tomorrow. If you like, you can move into the L'Imgarr Bay Hotel. You'll be comfortable there.'

'Who will cook for you?'

'That's no problem. Rene can rustle up some food, and I'm sure Laura will be sending over mountains of the stuff.'

She thought about it and then shook her head.

'Since I'm going to be cooped up with Mrs Manners in that hotel in Hong Kong for quite a time, I'd prefer to stay here until we leave . . . Is that all right?'

'Sure.'

CHAPTER 38

Frank Miller walked in just after nine o'clock. Corkscrew Two was at one end of the long bar, drinking his usual Perrier water with a thick slice of lemon. Frank walked to the other end of the bar. It was a large utilitarian room with plain wooden tables and sawdust on the floor. It was a sort of brokerage house, where deals were made by mercenaries and for mercenaries. A stranger walking into this bar would receive a frosty reception. But Frank was no stranger. The bartender, Wensa, himself a retired mercenary, gave him a nod of welcome and a glass of the house wine.

'Work?' he asked.

'Yes. A good one.'

'With the Man?'

'Yes. But it's behind the back teeth.'

'How is he?'

Frank thought about it and then said, 'He's had his personal ups and downs, but you know the Man, he's come through it and he's fine.'

'So why is he working?'

Frank shrugged.

'He only has to work when he wants to and he only takes on jobs that attract him . . . I guess it's in his blood, just like it's in mine.'

Wensa nodded.

'I know what you mean. Every once in a while, I get the urge as well . . . but then for me it's not possible. Tell the Man hello from me when you see him.' With a stilted walk, he moved down the bar to serve another customer. In the last days of the Biafra war, he had stepped on an AP landmine.

Frank leaned forward and glanced down the bar and Cork-screw Two nodded. They both moved to a corner table at the back. It was traditional in that bar that, when people sat at the two corner tables, nobody went near enough to hear even a whisper of conversation.

There were no preliminaries. Frank reached into an inside pocket and passed over a folded sheet of paper. Corkscrew studied it through his thick horn-rimmed spectacles. He was in his mid-forties and his sparse hair had receded halfway across his head. Otherwise, his features were without distinction. Finally, he lifted his head and looked at Frank across the paper.

'Where?' he asked.

'Hong Kong . . . and fast.'

Corkscrew Two's eyes dropped again to the paper. When he raised his eyes again he said, 'You told me it was for the Man. What's he going to do – take over China?'

Frank spoke openly, knowing that the man opposite had discretion branded on his heart. 'We're going after a Triad gang. They've got about a zillion soldiers, so we need a little fire-power.'

'How soon?'

'Not later than eight days. I'll have an address for you and a contact phone number within forty-eight hours. Your contacts will be myself or Rene Callard.'

Corkscrew Two's eyebrows lifted.

He murmured, 'With you along as well, plus Rene, it's going to be a high-class team.' He tapped the paper with his right hand. 'But looking at this list, I guess that you're going to be seven or eight.'

'About that . . . Tom Sawyer's in town and I'm meeting him in fifteen minutes. Maxie's in and so is Guido Arrellio.'

'Very high-class,' Corkscrew Two murmured again.

Frank nodded and asked, 'You don't see any problems in finding those machines and getting them to Hong Kong?'

The skeletal man shook his head.

'Finding them is no problem, but I'm going to suggest an addition. You've asked for a dozen Uzi SMGs. I have those. But I also have a new SMG which is very interesting. It came out about three years ago and it's made right here in Belgium by Fabrique Nationale. They call it the FNP90. It's very light, because most of its components are made from a special plastic which also makes it difficult for airport securities to detect it. It has a velocity to pierce body armour at one hundred and fifty metres. If you have a decent budget, I suggest that I include half a dozen.'

'Do that,' Frank said. 'The man has used that weapon and likes it . . . and our budget is open-ended.' He said the last words knowing that Corkscrew Two, despite his business, was honest to the marrow of his bones. 'Does moving those machines to Hong Kong within eight days present a problem?'

He noticed the merest smile on the face of the man opposite.

'None at all. I've been supplying arms to certain criminal gangs there and in southern China at an increasing rate for the last five years.'

Frank stood up, realising that Corkscrew Two was probably the main arms supplier to the 14K.

'Have you shipped any of those FNP90s in that direction lately?'

'None at all,' the Belgian said, also standing up. 'And I give you my word that I won't, until you let me know that your operation is over.'

They shook hands and Frank headed back to the bar. Corkscrew Two went to the telephone.

Tom Sawyer was punctual. He walked across the large room, glancing around, then moved up beside Frank and gave the bartender a nod. Again the bartender poured a glass of house wine. He passed it over and refilled Frank's glass. Frank turned to look at the man. He was big and broad and as black as ebony. His real first name was Horatio, but from childhood he had been known as Tom. He had left his native Tennessee to join the Marines, but had quit after his first stint because he could not stomach the schoolboyish discipline. They carried their glasses over to the corner table and within a few minutes Frank had filled in the American on the events of the past few days. When he had finished, Tom Sawyer said, 'It's a pity about Michael. He was a good man. How's Creasy taking it?'

'He shows nothing. But I guess he's hurting. One thing's for sure – he wants that Tommy Mo's ass. Are you in?'

Tom Sawyer asked, 'What's the rest of the team so far?'

Frank told him, and the American nodded, 'Damn right, I'm in. I don't have to ask you if the money's good?'

'It's top of the range.'

'When do I start?'

'You just started. We'll be heading for Hong Kong in three or four days. Jens and The Owl are already there. In the meantime, you can help me here. I'm trying to track down Do Huang and Eric Laparte. The rumour is they're in Panama City.'

The big black man nodded.

'The rumour's correct. That old windbag Hansson passed through here last week. He came from Panama City. Aparently Do is working on a construction site, and Eric's drinking himself to death.'

'Can you get addresses for me?'

'I can give you a contact in Panama City who can do that.'

CHAPTER 39

At about four o'clock in the morning, Lucy Kwok Ling Fong had a nightmare. In it, she was walking into her house in Hong Kong again and seeing her father, mother and brother hanging from their necks. She jerked awake in a cold sweat.

It was a very hot sultry night and, although the windows were open and the ceiling fan turned above her, her whole body was wet. She got out of bed and went into the adjoining bathroom. She was about to slip under the shower, when she realised that she did not want to sleep again until the sun came up. It had always been like that, even as a child. Whenever she had a nightmare she had never been able to sleep until she had seen the sun. She decided to go to the kitchen, make herself a coffee and then have a swim.

Five minutes later she was sitting by the pool, wrapped in a large towel, sipping at a mug of beautiful Italian coffee and waiting for sunrise. She glanced around the patio. There was a single light over the kitchen door. The pool lights had been switched off. She took off the towel and was naked. She walked down the steps into the pool and its cool water. She decided to swin ten lengths. The exercise soothed her mind. She swam in a breaststroke so as not to make much noise. After the ten lengths, she sat on the steps with water up to her waist. She could hear a dog barking in the village below, and then from the side of the pool, a voice said, 'I have a beautiful Chinese mermaid in my pool.'

Instinctively, her hands came up to cover her breasts. He was sitting in a canvas chair, with only a brightly-coloured sarong tied around his waist.

'How long have you been sitting there?' she asked.

'About ten minutes,' Creasy answered. 'I came out to have a swim and found a mermaid.'

'You couldn't sleep?'

'No. And I guess you couldn't, either.'

She shook her head.

'I had a nightmare. And when that happens I have to wait for the sun to come up before I can sleep again.'

His voice was soft but there was a harsh timbre to it.

'What was your nightmare about?'

'It was about my family.'

'Are you all right now?'

'Yes. I'm all right.'

Suddenly Lucy realised that during the conversation her hands had fallen away from her breasts. She noticed that his gaze was on them but she did not raise her hands again. She leaned back in the water, with her elbows on the upper step.

She said, 'When do you think we'll be heading for Hong Kong?'

'Frank called today. He managed to locate those two guys in Panama, so I'll be going there tomorrow to check them over. Yourself, Mrs Manners and Rene will head to Hong Kong a couple of days later.'

'So, take your swim.'

He stood up, saying, 'I've got to fetch my swimming trunks.'

'Are you shy?'

It was quite dark, but she saw the white of his teeth as he smiled.

'I guess not.'

Now she could see his body language. He dropped the sarong and she could see the body. He dived in.

He stroked her, as though soothing a kitten which had been taken from its mother. Neither had consciously seduced the other. It had been as natural as a flower spreading its petals. They swam in the semi-darkness for several minutes and then sat on the steps and talked. She related, in detail, her nightmare and then abruptly broke down in tears. He put his arms around her shoulders, and held her close until her sobbing stopped.

'I'm sorry,' she murmured. 'I've tried to be strong, but sometimes it's difficult, especially at night. I wake up feeling like an orphan . . . which is what I am. You just happen to be here with a shoulder to cry on.'

'No one is really an orphan if they have friends,' Creasy answered.

'I know. But even among friends I sometimes feel lonely.'

'You won't be lonely tonight,' he said. 'And you won't wait for the sun to come up before you sleep. You'll sleep in my bed, with your head against my shoulder. Nothing else needs to happen. If you have another nightmare, I'll be there.'

She suddenly realised that was exactly what she wanted: to be able to close her eyes and sleep and know there was somebody next to her. Somebody who could protect her against anything.

They climbed out of the pool and dried themselves and went to his bedroom. It was a huge vaulted room with a vast bed, framed by a wispy mosquito net hanging from the ceiling. In Lucy's eyes, that bed was akin to sanctuary. It was as though the net added even more protection. He opened a drawer and gave her a sarong, saying, 'I always sleep in these, ever since my Far East days.'

For a moment she hesitated, trying to decide whether to tie the sarong about her breasts or around her waist. Finally, she decided that, since he had already seen her naked, around her waist would be more appropriate and certainly more comfortable. He lifted the mosquito net and she slipped under it and on to the bed. He followed. She was facing away from him. He put an arm around her waist and pulled her close, and murmured, 'Sleep now. Nothing can harm you.'

She could not sleep.

She heard the soft sound of his breathing, near her ear. She snuggled back against him. She felt totally secure, but still she could not sleep.

After fifteen minutes, he said, 'What's the matter? Your body is tense. I told you nothing would happen. You won't wake up in the night and find me on top of you. You have to trust me.'

With total honesty, she said, 'I do trust you . . . more than anybody I've ever known. I'm not worried about that, it's just that I'm nervous. I guess I've been that way ever since my family were killed.'

He took his arm from around her and sat up and switched on the low light above the headboard. She rolled on to her back and looked up into his face. He was smiling slightly and in the dim light, the hardness of his features had given way to a shaded softness.

'There's going to be a major role reversal here,' he announced.
'How?'

'Well, you're a beautiful Oriental woman, and I spent many years in the Orient. Whenever I came out of Cambodia or Laos or Vietnam, the first thing I did after checking into a Hong Kong hotel was go to a local massage parlour. A real one, not a sex joint. On dozens of occasions, the hands and fingers of an Oriental girl eased the tension out of my body. I know the technique. So maybe now it's my turn. Roll over on to your stomach.'

She did so and he straddled her and the next moment, scarred hands and fingers were working at the muscles in her shoulders and neck. It only took her a minute to realise that he knew exactly how to find the areas of tension. He used a strength that bordered on pain, but after fifteen minutes, her whole body began to relax. Then he pulled himself from on top of her, knelt beside her and with the sides of his hands beat a tattoo down her back, like a drummer. It went on for many minutes and again came close to pain. It was as though her body was taking in thousands of electric shocks. He moved lower and did the same to her buttocks. Five minutes later, it all changed.

He began to rub her back with the palms of his hands. At first, with a lot of pressure, but then slower and softer. She felt like a kitten being stroked and she heard his voice saying, 'Now, your muscles are relaxed. Maybe you can sleep.'

There was no possibility of sleep. During the past few minutes, the gentleness of his hands had aroused her. She reached down to her sarong and pulled it off. She lay naked on her stomach and murmured, 'Some more, please . . . just a little more.'

For a moment, she thought she might have broken the spell, but then his hands were sliding over her naked bottom and down her thighs, and later still between the cheeks of her bottom as she inched her legs apart. She heard him saying gruffly, 'This is supposed to be purely therapeutic.'

'It is,' she answered, her face against the pillow. 'It's more therapeutic than you would believe . . . When was the last time you made love?'

Above her, he chuckled. 'That's not a polite question to ask a man who hasn't had the time or been in the situation to make love for months.'

She rolled over on to her back and smiled up at him and

whispered, 'Now we will reverse the roles again. How long is it since you made love to a Chinese woman?'

She watched his face as he thought about that.

He said, 'At least fifteen years.'

'Have you forgotten how it was?'

'No. Such things are never forgotten. It's a coincidence, but she was a nurse at a private hospital in Hong Kong.' He touched the scar on his shoulder and said, 'I'd been wounded in Laos. I was in bed, immobile, in that hospital for about three weeks. She looked after me. She had to give me bed-baths. She was very thorough and every day washed every part of me. I had a great embarrassment one day when I got an erection during that ritual. But she wasn't embarrassed. I was in a private room. She closed the door and locked it and she came back to me and made love to me while I lay on my back.'

'Was she beautiful?'

'Perhaps to others she was no great beauty, but she was sweet and gentle and, in my eyes, definitely beautiful.'

'Did you give her money?'

'No. I think I'm a good enough judge of character to know that she would have been insulted. It only happened once. I waited for two months after I had left the hospital, then sent her a jade bracelet, with a note of thanks for looking after me.'

As she watched his shaded face, she felt a surge of emotion. She asked, 'Do you think I'm beautiful?'

He was looking at her face. His eyes travelled down her naked body: the small high breasts, the curved waist, the wisp of jet black hair at the apex of her thighs, and the long slim legs all the way down to small highly-arched feet.

'That's a rhetorical question,' he said.

She frowned in puzzlement. 'What does "rhetorical" mean?'

'It means to ask a question, when you already know the answer.'

'But I thought you hardly noticed me.'

'I'm very good at not showing things. But for the past days I've hardly been able to keep my eyes off you.'

'I would not have guessed,' she murmured, and then patted the bed beside her. 'Lie here.'

He slid down beside her and then definitely experienced the role reversal. She gave him a kiss on the lips, at first chaste, just touching his mouth with hers, but her fingers were moving through the hairs on his chest like a flock of butterflies fluttering through grass. As the butterflies moved further down, the kiss became less chaste. Her small tongue probed between his lips and the fingers on his chest were replaced by her breast moving in gentle circles. He could feel the nipples as they became erect; he could feel his own erection, and so could the butterflies.

She eased him on to his stomach and this time, she straddled him. As she leaned forward, he felt her warm breath on his neck. Her tongue flicked gently around his neck and across his shoulders, meandering along his spine. She nipped at his skin with her teeth as she slid towards his feet and as she moved down, the soft mound between her legs brushed his buttocks. As her tongue flicked between his inner thighs, he clenched his teeth and gripped the pillow. It was akin to pain . . . but the pain of self-control was becoming unbearable. He rolled over to face her.

It had been a long time for him and he groaned with pleasure. She had, in such matters, an exquisite sense of timing. Her whole body slithered over his as she lifted her mouth and whispered 'Don't move . . . and don't be macho . . . let me do it.'

The butterflies had become a velvet vice as they gripped him and guided him into her. It was as though he was piercing an oyster made of silk . . . an oyster that was hungry and that devoured him. Her tongue was in his mouth again, soft and inquisitive. He ran a hand down her back and on to her smooth bottom, put his other hand around her neck, and in his mind began to worry that it would all be over too quickly. He felt the passion building up from his feet and tried to slow it down, but she gave him no chance. She moved her bottom to a perfect rhythm. She was kissing his ear. Again her tongue was probing, and he could hear the mounting beat of her breath and realised that she was as close to release as he was. Suddenly, she brought her legs around his waist and he could feel her feet on his buttocks, forcing him harder into her. Her body spasmed as he came with her. She burst into tears. She shed tears for her family, and for the security and warmth. He held her close to him and her sobs subsided.

CHAPTER 40

The Owl was listening to Beethoven on his Walkman and, with his right hand in the air, trying to emulate von Karajan.

He was lying on the plush settee and looking out over a very busy Hong Kong harbour. One of the two bedroom doors opened and Jens Jensen came out. He was talking, but it did not penerate The Owl's earphones. The Dane started shouting. The Owl held up a hand. The symphony was coming to an end. His hand beat the air and then with three short downward movements, he brought the symphony to a close. He switched off the Walkman, took off the earphones and looked at his friend. Jens was dressed in Bermuda shorts and a bright Hawaiian shirt, and carrying a smart black leather briefcase. He glanced at his watch and said, 'Let's go. Our appointment's in half an hour.'

The Frenchman shook his head.

'Jens, I'm not going anywhere with you dressed like that. You look like you just walked out of Disney World after having hijacked the pay-roll. We're going to meet a senior policeman at police headquarters. If you walk in looking like that, Inspector Lau is not going to take you seriously.'

He received a very disgruntled look from the Dane, who said, 'You don't understand these things. Our cover is that we're here on holiday, during which time I'm going to do some research for a newspaper article on the Triads.'

The Owl swung his feet to the ground and stood up, saying, 'You would certainly be a threat to the Triads. If they saw you dressed like that, they'd die laughing. Now, go and change into a pair of slacks and a short-sleeved shirt.'

'You're like my wife,' Jens said. 'Every morning when I

wake up, she's already laid out the clothes for me to wear that day.'

The Owl said, 'Apart from marrying you, your wife has good sense and style.'

The Dane went back into the bedroom.

They crossed the harbour on the Star ferry. It only took ten minutes and during that time, they both gazed at the metropolis in front of them.

'I feel at home here,' The Owl said. 'It's bigger and busier, but it reminds me of Marseilles.'

'It's got a lot more crooks, as well,' Jens observed.

'That's true. And it's got one more, since I arrived last night.'

'So you really see yourself as a crook?'

'I have to,' the Frenchman answered. 'Don't forget, I started off in the streets of Marseille, an urchin stealing everything I could lay my hands on. Then I worked for a whole series of villains, strong-arming protection rackets. It was only when I was hired by Leclerc to watch his back, that I more or less went straight . . . I have a feel for this city and I'll be useful to Creasy because, as sure as the Pope is a Catholic, if I'd been born Chinese, I'd be a Triad. I know their minds.'

The Dane glanced at him. They had been the closest friends now for three years, ever since Creasy had borrowed The Owl from the arms dealer Leclerc in Marseille, to watch Jens's back. It had been a lasting arrangement. After helping Creasy to crush the drug-dealing and white-slave trafficking Blue Ring, Jens had left the police force and opened his own detective agency in Copenhagen. The Owl had come in as an open partner and rented a small flat in the same district as Jens's home. He was a regular fixture. Jens's wife enjoyed his quiet company and their eight-year-old daughter Lisa considered him her favourite uncle. The business had thrived. They specialised in locating missing persons and had tracked them down all over Europe. It was, in a way, bounty money, but when they found a person who genuinely wanted to remain missing and had committed no crime, they sometimes took a moral stand and quietly left that person where he or she was. Although Jens was competent with a hand gun or a rifle, he was no expert. He relied more on his brains and his IBM, and although The Owl looked exactly like an owl, he was deadly with a throwing knife, a pistol, a rifle or a submachine-gun.

They were ushered into Inspector Lau's office by a young constable. The Inspector was in his mid-forties, slim and dressed in a civilian suit and tie.

Jens handed over the letter from the newspaper. Inspector Lau read it, and then looked up and said, 'The Triads operate in most European cities with a Chinese population but, to the best of my knowledge, they don't operate in Copenhagen. Are your readers really going to be interested?'

'Definitely,' Jens answered. 'We have a small Chinese population, but it's growing and, for sure, the Triads will become interested sometime in the future.'

'What do you know about the Triads at this point?' the policeman asked.

'Quite a bit,' Jens answered. 'I know of their origins and how their good intentions were perverted to crime. What I would like to know is something about their size, their influence and their power in Hong Kong today. For my articles, I've decided to concentrate on one particular Triad – the 14K.'

'Why that one?'

'Because they're the biggest and they have branches not only in America but also in several cities in Europe.'

Inspector Lau nodded thoughtfully and then asked him, 'Mr Jensen, were you ever a policeman?'

The Owl glanced at his friend and saw the brief, startled expression.

'Yes . . . How did you know?'

The Inspector took a file from the top left-hand corner of his desk and opened it. He read out: 'Jens Jensen. Born 15 April 1959 in Aarhus, Denmark. Educated at Katedralskolen in Aarhus and the University of Copenhagen, majoring in social sciences. Joined the police in September 1982. After serving for three years in the Vice and Prostitution Department, was transferred to missing persons. Resigned from the police in June 1990 and opened a private detective agency called Jensen and Associates, together with a partner called Marc Benoit, a French citizen.' The Inspector looked up and gestured at The Owl. 'I assume, this gentleman.' There were several other pages in the file, but the Inspector closed it and laid it in front of him and looked up at Jens.

'I'm impressed,' the Dane said. 'How did you get that?'

'It was circumscribed, Mr Jensen. You have to understand that I have taken a personal, almost obsessive, interest in 14K Triad since they murdered my boss, Colin Chapman. He was a man close to me, and for the past two weeks I have been doing everything to find evidence against them and their leader. I know that Miss Lucy Kwok Ling Fong flew to Zimbabwe to try to meet up with a man called Creasy, who was working on a case which was linked to that of the murder of her family here by the 14K. As you well know, this man Creasy is a mercenary. My late boss already had an Interpol file on the man. You may know that Interpol keep files on all known mercenaries. I have been in communication with Commander John Ndlovu, of the Zimbabwe Police, and so I know that Mr Creasy eliminated the killers, in that case. I checked further on Mr Creasy's activities, and discovered that three years ago he and a group of other mercenaries wiped out a criminal group in Italy, France and Tunisia. The computer threw up the name Jens Jensen, a Danish policeman who had taken unpaid leave and was thought to have been involved in that operation.' The Inspector smiled and spread his hands. 'And so, Mr Jensen, when you phoned me yesterday to ask for an appointment to discuss your article on the Hong Kong Triads, a little bell went ding-a-ling in my head and I reached for my files.'

Jens said, 'I think you're a good policeman, Mr Lau, and I think I have to come clean.'

'That is not necessary, Mr Jensen. I think I've worked it out. You are staying in a double suite at the Regent Hotel, which is not the cheapest abode in the world. So you were definitely not hired by Lucy Kwok, because she does not have that kind of money. I found I had a rapport on the telephone with Commander John Ndlovu. He told me all about Mrs Gloria Manners and her private jet, so I guessed that she is your employer, together with Mr Creasy and the man called Maxie MacDonald. I deduced that you and your partner, Mr Benoit, are the advance guard. You are on a recce, building up a dossier on the 14K, and the others will follow.' He tapped the file to his left. 'If I understand Mr Creasy, he will not be coming just with Maxie MacDonald, even though the two of them appear to be formidable. They are not enough to go against the 14K and so I deduce that while you are here, compiling your dossier, Mr Creasy is building a team.' He flipped open the file on his left and riffled through the pages. 'That team will almost certainly include an Australian mercenary called Miller and an ex-Foreign Legionnaire, a Belgian by the name of Rene Callard. They also worked with Mr Creasy and you on that operation three years ago.'

Jens glanced at The Owl, who simply shrugged. He had a bored expression on his face, but the Dane knew that he was taking everything in and analysing it with a razor-sharp mind. Jens looked back at the Chinese Inspector and also shrugged. Inspector Lau's face assumed a stern expression.

He said, 'I suppose that in the next few days. Mr Creasy will arrive with a group of mercenaries and, of course, try to smuggle some arms into Hong Kong or acquire them locally. That, of course, is illegal and will not be tolerated. It's also illegal for a Danish private detective to arrange an interview with a Hong Kong police officer under false pretences.'

Again Jens glanced at The Owl, who this time shifted uneasily on his chair.

'Are you going to arrest us?' Jens asked.

Inspector Lau shook his head.

'No, not this time. But I'm giving you an official warning and I want you to pass that warning on to your friend Mr Creasy. If you or he have or find any evidence which may link the 14K with the murder of Lucy Kwok's family, then you must contact me immediately. But Mr Jensen – it must be firm evidence. Thank you for your visit.'

The two men stood up and mumbled their thanks and turned to go. Inspector's Lau's voice stopped them.

'I think you have forgotten something, Mr Jensen.'

Jens turned in surprise. The Inspector was pointing at a small square yellow envelope which had suddenly appeared on the desk. Jens studied it with puzzled eyes.

The Inspector said; 'You must have brought it with you.'

The Owl was the first to understand. He said, 'Of course,' reached down, picked up the envelope and slipped it into his jacket pocket.

The Owl kept the envelope in his pocket until they were sitting on the ferry. Then he passed it over to the Dane. It was flat and its contents were hard. Jens opened it and pulled out a black computer disk. Both men looked at it in silence.

Then The Owl asked, 'What do you think is on it?'

'I don't know,' Jens replied. 'But one thing's for sure . . . it's not *Swan Lake*.'

CHAPTER 41

Do Huang was building a wall. He was a short man, but very stocky for an Oriental. The Panamanian sun was hot and he sweated, bare-chested, as he lifted the breeze-blocks and set them into the mortar. He was also hung over. He had been given his meagre pay, the evening before, and spent a large part of it on a decent Chinese meal in Panama City and a bottle of wine and, later on, too many brandies. But there was no respite from the job. The foreman was a Mexican who liked to throw his weight about, and also a formidable clock-watcher. He treated the labourers like dirt and especially Do Huang, whom he referred to sneeringly as 'the Chink'. Do Huang would have gladly cut the man down, but work was hard to come by in Panama, or anywhere else, for that matter.

Do Huang's work assignment had been laid down at fifty square metres and, apart from a half-hour break for a sandwich and a glass of water, he had worked throughout the day. He had about fifteen minutes more work, when the Suzuki jeep pulled up near the building site. He turned and gave it a brief glance, and then turned again as he saw the driver getting out. He straightened up and watched as Creasy approached and gave him the customary kiss.

Creasy said, 'What the fuck are you doing lifting bricks?'

Do Huang was a little shamefaced. He said, 'It's the only work around at the moment.'

'No, it's not,' Creasy said. 'I have a job in Hong Kong. It's against the Triads – the 14K.'

Do Huang's face split with a smile of pleasure. He said, 'Then, if you're here and it's against the Triads, it must pay very well.'

Creasy told him the terms and Do Huang was impressed. He looked down at the grey breeze-blocks at his feet and his smile widened. It faded again as the foreman approached, shouting, 'Come on, Chink! What the fuck do you think this is, a social gathering? And who is this man? Does he have authorisation to be here?'

Do Huang glanced at Creasy and saw the look on his face and held up a hand. He said to the foreman, 'He's a friend from far away. He'll stay with me for only a minute and then wait for me, while I finish my day's work.'

The foreman looked at Creasy and said, 'I want you off this site in fifteen minutes and you had better not come back.'

Creasy said, 'I assure you, I will never return.'

'It better be that way,' the Mexican muttered.

Do Huang turned back to Creasy and said, 'That one is a prime asshole. Who else is in on the job?'

Creasy went through the list of names and Do Huang said, 'Sounds all right to me. How did you find me?'

'Tom Sawyer tracked you down.'

'When is the job?'

'Now.'

Do Huang thought for a moment, then said, 'Maybe you'll give me a lift to what they call the guest house, where I stay, and I'll pack my bag and come with you.' He pointed at the breeze-blocks at his feet and said, 'Now, wait for me in the jeep. I'll be finished with this job in ten minutes.'

So Huang settled the last breeze-block in its place and scraped off the mortar, and then walked across to the wicker chair where the foreman sat under a sunshade, inspecting his domain. The Mexican was large, but flabby, and when Do Huang lifted a foot and placed it on the armrest of his chair and pushed it back, the Mexican let out a roar of rage. He struggled to his feet and charged like a bull.

Do Huang hardly seemed to hit him, but every time one of his hands or feet flicked out, they obviously hit a nerve and the Mexican crashed down. The sub-foreman came running to help, but Do Huang simply swivelled on the ball of his left foot and his left hand stabbed out with straightened fingers and the man doubled up and then pulled away. The whole thing lasted about two minutes. Creasy watched as Do Huang looked down at the semi-conscious Mexican and said, in a voice loud enough for the whole workforce to hear, 'Think twice, before you next abuse one of the human beings who does a good day's work for you.'

Do Huang got in the jeep.

'Where did you say we're going?'

'I didn't. But I'm trying to locate Eric Laparte. I have a rough idea where he lives.'

'Don't say you want him on the team?'

'Why not?'

The Vietnamese shrugged.

'When I last saw him, months ago, he was drinking himself to death.'

Creasy said, 'We'll see just how dead he is by now. Do you know where he is?'

'A few years back he bought an old planter's house, north of here. He was living with a woman and the last I heard she had left him. Couldn't take his boozing.'

'Do you know where that house is?'

'Sure.'

Do Huang spotted the small road on the right. Creasy turned into it. They bumped along for about five hundred metres and then the house came into view. It was a typical, dilapidated planter's house with a tin roof and a wide veranda all around it. As they parked the jeep, a dog came round the corner, barking. It was black with a white stomach and paws and a sheen on its coat. It was well-fed, perhaps a little too well-fed. She was a cross-breed, probably a stray, and aggressively suspicious.

A voice came from a long dirty white hammock on the veranda: 'Slinky, *tais toi!*'

The dog sank on to its haunches, growling softly. Eric Laparte swung his long legs out of the hammock, stretched out of his sleep and focussed his eyes on Creasy and Do.

'*Mon Dieu,*' he said. 'I thought you were dead.'

Creasy moved forward and Do followed. The man was over two metres tall and dressed only in faded khaki shorts. They could see the ribs in his thin body. He had a grey beard and lank, grey hair hanging almost to his shoulders. Above the beard, his face was as gaunt as a skull and his dark eyes were sunk deep into his head. He greeted them with the customary kiss and said, 'I can't offer you a drink. I don't have any in the house.'

Creasy glanced at Do and said, 'That's strange. I heard you were a lush.'

'I was,' the Frenchman admitted, 'but I quit three weeks ago.' He pointed at the wall surrounding the overgrown garden. 'I threw half a bottle of tequila over that wall.'

'Why?'

'Because I realised I wasn't just killing myself, I was also killing another creature.'

'Who?'

Laparte pointed at the black dog.

'Slinky. I'd been on a two-day tequila binge and passed out, more or less in a coma. I must have been gone for two or three days. I woke up with Slinky licking my face and whimpering . . . it wasn't food she wanted . . . she just wanted me to come back to life.'

'And you haven't drunk since?'

The Frenchman shook his head.

'No. I was on the road to death. I've given that up.'

'Can you still fire a gun?'

'You bet.'

'How about a demonstration?' Creasy said.

Laparte turned on his heel and walked into the house. The dog remained, watching Creasy and Do with studied suspicion. Two minutes later, the Frenchman emerged, carrying a pistol in one hand and a magazine in the other. He switched off the safety and loaded the magazine. Holding the pistol in his right hand, he looked at Creasy and asked, 'What's the target?'

Creasy pointed to an oleander tree fifteen metres away. 'The flowers of that tree.'

All of a sudden there was a blur of movement and the garden echoed to the sounds of gunshots. One after the other they watched the flowers shatter and fall from the tree. Creasy dropped his gaze to his watch. Six seconds had passed. He turned to look at Do, who was still staring at the fallen flowers, then he walked forward and punched the Frenchman on his shoulder saying, 'You may have been a lush, Eric, but not any more. I want you for a job – a big one.'

*

Two hours later, they were standing outside a plush dogs' home and Eric Laparte was arguing with Creasy. Slinky was at his feet.

'I just don't like the people,' Laparte said. 'They are not *sympathique*.'

Creasy rolled his eyes in exasperation.

'For Chrissakes, Eric. She'll be pampered here. The fucking kennels are even air-conditioned! I'll give them money to feed the bitch fillet steak every day – with a béarnaise sauce, if you want.'

The Frenchman shook his head.

'They are not *sympathique*. I can tell that Slinky does not like them.'

Creasy became angry. He leaned closer to the Frenchman and said, 'All those tequilas over all those months have bent your brain. The job pays half a million Swiss and will probably last less than a month – and you're worrying about a fucking dog?'

Finally, Eric Laparte gave in and, after some negotiation, he handed the dog over to the woman who had emerged from the garden, saying, 'If I come back and find she's not in shape, I'll have your ass.'

Neither Creasy nor Do Huang was surprised at the Frenchman's attitude. Most of the hard men they had known had a sentimental streak, especially when it came to animals or children.

CHAPTER 42

For half an hour, the Dane sat in front of the small screen of his IBM laptop computer, tapping through the files. The Owl stood behind him, watching over his shoulder.

Finally, Jens turned in his chair and said, 'That disk contains the entire police files on the 14K Triads since 1948. It's totally comprehensive. It even has computer images of the walled villa in Sai Kung which Tommy Mo uses.'

'But why?' The Owl asked. 'After piling shit all over us, why would Inspector Lau give you that disk?'

Jens stood up and stretched. He looked out the window across the harbour. Apart from his family, he had three passions: his computer, ferryboats, and a desire to track down the best brewed beer in the world. He said, 'To understand Inspector Lau, you would have to be a policeman or an ex-policeman. Then you would understand the frustrations of policemen in all civilised countries, when they know who a criminal is and what crimes he has committed, but can do nothing about it. Inspector Lau's boss was murdered by the 14K, but he cannot prove it. Tommy Mo has a complete screen around him. He never gets his hands dirty. That villa and the other properties are all owned by front companies. The Triads operate here almost with impunity. All the police ever catch are the small fry. They never get near the fat cats at the top. That's why Inspector Lau gave us that disk . . . It's invaluable for the operation.'

The Owl shrugged a little sceptically.

'Do you think he informed his boss?'

'Yes. Not just about the disk, but also everything else. And, if my guess is correct, the Commissioner told him something like "do what you have to . . . but I know nothing about it".'

'Do you really think so?'

The Dane nodded.

'Yes. In fact, I can see the whole pattern. They know all about us. They have worked out that Creasy will be arriving soon with the rest of the team and that he'll have arranged the necessary weapons. It would have been very easy for Inspector Lau to have arrested the two of us and deported us by now. The same thing applies to Creasy and the others when they arrive. The fact that he didn't touch us indicates that they're turning a blind eye. I think that Inspector Lau and his Commissioner would be as happy to see Tommy Mo dead as we would. Especially if we take out some of his hierarchy along with him.' He gestured at the computer. 'That disk contains the names of that hierarchy and every important 14K member. It details their methods and their mentalities. I'm going to reduce it to a twenty-page report for Creasy and the others.'

The phone rang. It was Frank Miller. He had arrived with Tom Sawyer half an hour earlier. They were staying at the nearby Hyatt Hotel. They arranged to meet for a drink in the bar of that hotel at seven o'clock in the evening.

'How do you like Hong Kong?' the Australian asked.

'I love it,' the Dane enthused. 'The local San Miguel beer is not at all bad, and from my hotel window I can see a dozen ferries.'

CHAPTER 43

They were twelve. They were all men, and they were all Chinese. They sat at a round table, and as they ate dish after dish, their eyes watched each other like starving hawks. They had just started the tenth dish, lemon chicken with bamboo shoots, when one of the men gave the very slightest of groans. The others immediately all pointed their fingers at him and burst out laughing. A moment later, the tablecloth beside the man was lifted up and a young girl crawled out.

It was a game Tommy Mo liked to play with his henchmen. The girl would be under the table before the men sat down and then, one by one, she would perform fellatio on them. The idea was that no one should show any sign on his face of what was happening. The first one to do so would normally have to pay the bill, but in this case they were dining at Tommy Mo's sumptuous villa in Sai Kung, and so the man was spared the expense. Before the meal, which had been more of a feast, they had conducted a Triad Lodge meeting with all its ceremony and paraphernalia. The building itself was in the grounds of the villa. It was square-shaped with four gates. Each gate was guarded by mythical generals known as the 'four great faithful ones'. Their emblems were on the wall beside the gates.

The ceremony had been held to initiate a new member into the Triad Lodge. It was an important coup because he was a very wealthy Hong Kong businessman who had several companies listed on the Hong Kong Stock Exchange. He also had considerable influence in Beijing. He would in no way be involved in the more violent aspects of the 14K, but would be a hidden asset. His benefits would derive from the 14K's widespread intelligence network and its ability to apply violence against a competitor when necessary.

The initiation had gone well. He had been coached for many weeks about the form of handshakes, the ceremonial robes worn by the office bearers and the significance of the red wooden cask filled with rice. He was word perfect in the thirty-six oaths taken with the ritual drinking of a mixture of blood and wine. The blood had come from the middle finger of his left hand and from that moment, if any 14K member asked him where he lived, he would reply, 'in the third house on the left.'

Next to the cask of rice was the red club for punishing those members who erred from the rules and the sword of Loyalty and Righteousness. Next to that, a symbolic abacus on which the Triads calculated the money owed to them by the Manchus in the form of reparations when they helped in their overthrow. Finally, there was a rosary and a white bloodstained shroud, in memory of the massacred monks of Shao Lin monastery in Fukien province where, legend had it, the Triads were founded.

The Initiate was the one at the table who had groaned. The other eleven were all high officials of the 14K. They all wore traditional robes, and the mood was generally relaxed. Tommy Mo himself was a little tense, however. The past week had brought some setbacks. Three soldiers of the 14K in London had been killed in a restaurant by members of another Triad group. So far, he did not know which one, and that irritated him. The 14K had also lost money in an investment in a real estate company whose chairman had absconded to Canada with several million dollars. The Vancouver branch of the Triad were looking for him, so far without success. Then there was the black rhino horn powder. News had come from Zimbabwe of Rolph Becker's violent death. Tommy Mo would have to find somebody else in that country or in Zambia to continue the logistics of the rhino poachers.

Fifteen miles away, in a strongly guarded warehouse in Kowloon, Tommy Mo had five and a half tons of black rhino horn powder worth, at current market prices, sixty thousand US dollars per kilo. He had been building up that stock for the past ten years, buying up any powder which came on the market. Just like international dealers who try to corner the markets in silver or gold or any other precious metals, Tommy Mo prided himself on the fact that he had cornered a commodity which had more value per gram than any of the precious metals. He knew that there were less than four hundred black rhinos still alive in the wild, and once they were eliminated the value of his stock would multiply at least tenfold, if not more.

Yet there was something even more worrying on Tommy Mo's mind. The 14K had managed to infiltrate three of its members into the police force, and one of them was already a sergeant. Although not in the Anti-Triad Department, he had developed friends within it, and had been asked carefully to find out any information that might come in from the Zimbabwe police. He had been informed that afternoon that the deaths of Becker and his son were highly organised, involving top mercenaries. A certain Mrs Manners had hired them. She was the mother of the dead woman. He also knew that Lucy Kwok Ling Fong had flown to Zimbabwe, so it was almost certain that a connection had been made between the deaths of her family and the death of Carole Manners. If this American woman was looking for ultimate vengeance, then she might finance an attack on the head of the 14K.

At first, the thought had caused Tommy Mo amusement. The very thought of a bunch of *gweilo* mercenaries trying to attack him on his own territory was nothing more than a joke. However, a strange lurking feeling would not go away. In his position, he should be well above becoming a target for anybody. He inspired fear and should never know that feeling himself. He brushed aside the thought. Within twenty-four hours he would have a copy of the police dossier in front of him.

He decided to get his mind off the subject. He smiled at the new initiate at the table and said, 'Why don't you phone that agency you use and have them send out half a dozen *gweilo* women. We'll have some fun.'

One of the diners who had drunk too much rice wine let out a high giggle and pointed across the table saying, 'You'd better get a *gweilo* boy for Hon Pang.'

There was a sudden silence and all eyes turned to Tommy Mo. Slowly he stood up, his face impassive. He walked around the table until he stood behind the man who had made the remark. Then, in a soft whisper which was heard by everybody, he said, 'Your mistake was not to insult Hon Pang, but to drink too much wine on such an occasion. You have made too many mistakes in the past days. I entrusted you with the killing of the policeman Colin Chapman and the woman Lucy Kwok Lin Fong. Your incompetence allowed her to escape and she remains a threat to us. I will give you one last favour. You can choose which way to die.'

The new initiate, the wealthy Hong Kong businessman, watched in silence.

The man stared at the table in front of him and then said, 'By the sword of Loyalty and Righteousness.'

Tommy Mo nodded.

'You have saved a small part of your face.' He pointed across the table at the man who had been insulted and said, 'Hon Pang, you have the honour.'

They went back to the meeting hall and the initiate watched the ritual. He had to turn away as he saw the sword slash down on the prone man's neck and the blood gush out.

CHAPTER 44

Creasy flew in from Bangkok. The others would be arriving during the next twenty-four hours from various Asian destinations, and checking into different hotels. He would base himself in the safehouse.

Before taking off, he had spoken to Jens on the phone and had been informed that a safehouse had been located and rented in Kowloon. Mrs Manners had arrived with Lucy and Rene, and they were in the Peninsula Hotel. The news related from Rene via Jens was that Mrs Manners was presenting no problems. Corkscrew Two had been in touch, and the weapons were on their way. The Hong Kong police were pretending not to co-operate, but had supplied vital information. Jens had faxed Creasy his twenty-page analysis on the 14K, and Creasy had studied it carefully, trying to get a feeling for his enemy.

Creasy tried to look into the mind of Tommy Mo. Within a few minutes, one fact became obvious. If Tommy Mo was deeply intelligent and knew that assassins were on their way, he would simply melt into the background, move without an entourage into his milieu. In the most densely populated area on earth, Creasy would never be able to find him. Meanwhile, Tommy Mo could send his soldiers out after Creasy and his team. But from all his experience of such people, Creasy knew that Tommy Mo would and could not disappear. There were two reasons: first, to disappear would cause a loss of face among his followers, and such a loss of face to a Chinese could ultimately be fatal. Second, like most bullies, Tommy Mo would be a coward. The thought of hiding out on his own would not be an option. He would want his power around him, a kowtowing gun-toting sychophantic entourage. He would retreat to his Sai Kung stronghold, not realising that to barricade himself inside his villa with a small army was total false security. It was a military tactic at least a century out of date. It was vital that Tommy Mo ran to his villa.

Creasy's thoughts turned to his team, and the thoughts gave him satisfaction. The team was balanced between intellect and skills; above all, it was massively experienced. They might not be the youngest bunch of guys engaged in warfare, but they knew the difference between a pep talk and a bullet in the head. There would not have to be any pep talks or orders – just a request or a suggestion. The best kind of team.

He felt the aircraft tilt as they began the descent to Hong Kong. Assuming that Tommy Mo retreated to his villa, Creasy would divided his forces. He would lead one unit, and Guido the other. Guido – literally a brother in arms. They shared an almost telepathic understanding. He considered how he would dispose the rest of the men between them. As the minutes passed, it all fell into place.

Next Creasy's thoughts turned to Lucy, causing disquiet in his mind. She was his kind of woman. She had a mystery and a sensuousness. She had a good mind. She held a tragedy. It was a combination designed to reach out and grab him.

As the plane lined up for its landing over the harbour, he thought of Michael. Creasy looked out the window at the skyline of Hong Kong island. It was very different from his last visit, fifteen years before. The buildings were taller and even more clustered. Among the millions of people was a man who had caused his son's death. A kind of pantomime villain who dressed in gaudy outfits for irrelevant rituals, but who dealt out death – be it to humans or the black rhino. A macabre joker.

As the plane's wheels screeched on to the runway, silent words went through Creasy's mind.

'I've arrived, Joker.'

CHAPTER 45

The Commissioner of Police surveyed Inspector Lau Ming Lan through his thick spectacles and commented, 'You should have asked my permission.'

Inspector Lau looked back through his own thick spectacles and answered, 'You would not have given me permission.'

The Commissioner's voice remained stern. 'I should bring you up before the disciplinary board.'

Inspector Lau shrugged.

'Do so. For the last ten years, I've worked in what we now call the Anti-Organised Crime Department, but which we all know by its previous name, the Anti-Triad Department. We all know what they are and who they are, but we can do nothing. I have wasted ten years of my life. A few weeks ago, my boss was murdered by the 14K. I know who was responsible . . . and so do you . . . but we are powerless to do a thing about it. Tommy Mo walks around with impunity and laughs at us. We pick up small fries from the 14K, but you and I both know we have no chance of getting the top men. It's an insult to my work and to Colin Chapman's work and to every single man who works in our department.'

The Commissioner looked down at the one-page report in front of him and said, 'So why did you give me this?'

Inspector Lau carefully considered his answer and then replied, 'I belong to a disciplined force. By giving that Dane our computer disk on the 14K, I broke the law. In a sense, that report is a confessional.'

'You broke the law and your discipline.'

'Definitely. It came from frustration. You've seen the report from Commander John Ndlovu in Zimbabwe. He suspects that the woman Gloria Manners is financing a team of mercenaries to come to Hong Kong, a team aimed at the 14K.

'By law, we cannot co-operate with that team but instead, as my report suggests, the Hong Kong Police Force suddenly becomes blind in certain directions over the coming days. I suspect that Tommy Mo, through his infiltration of our force, has also read that report from the Zimbabwe police. We know that yesterday he moved into the Sai Kung villa, together with Hung Mun and between forty and fifty of his top fighters. My guess is that he'll wait there and see what happens.'

Again, the Commissioner looked down at the single sheet of paper. He remarked, 'You suggest that these men will arrive under false passports and that we instruct the Immigration Department not to be too critical of passports over the next few days.' He looked up, his expression still severe. 'You have by your very clever investigation discovered that these men have a safehouse in Braga Circuit, and that within days they'll launch an attack on the villa in Sai Kung. A violent attack. You suspect that they will be buying or importing illegal weapons. These are all illegal acts under our laws, and yet you have the temerity to suggest that we turn a blind eye.'

The two Chinese men looked at each other through their thick spectacles for a long silent moment, and then Inspector Lau said, 'We must have laws. As a policeman, I understand that. But even policemen have emotions. Colin Chapman was not a *gweilo*. He was one of us. He was your friend and mine. He knew more about our culture than you or I will ever know. But we do know that he was murdered on the direct orders of Tommy Mo. Sometimes, justice comes in strange forms. I have broken discipline and you have every right to apply sanctions on me ... I accept your decision.'

The Commissioner looked down again at the single piece of paper, then, slowly and very deliberately, he tore it up, dropped it into the waste-basket beside his desk and said, 'I never saw that piece of paper. But if the Governor sends me to jail for a thousand years, you will share my cell.'

Inspector Lau stood up and said, 'When this man, Creasy, reads the contents of that disk, he might well decide that the risk is not worth the money – no matter how much he and the others are getting paid. One thing is for sure. The odds are totally on Tommy

Mo's side. He has ears and eyes everywhere. Even in our own force – maybe even in my own department. By giving that disk to the Dane and by asking your permission to turn a blind eye, we may have eased the odds very slightly . . . but only very slightly. I don't think those people have more than a two per cent chance of getting anywhere near Tommy Mo. But even a two per cent chance is better than nothing. It's certainly better than we've had over the past ten years.'

The Commissioner also stood up and said, 'I will issue the necessary instructions. For the next few days, passports will not be overly scrutinised at the airport. Concurrently, the police presence in the Sai Kung peninsula will be very busy elsewhere.'

Inspector Lau moved to the door. As he reached out to open it, the Commissioner's voice stopped him. 'Have you considered what Tommy Mo's reaction might be?'

'Yes. He will attack.'

'How and where?'

'At the woman, Gloria Manners. She is funding the campaign against him.'

'How will he attack?'

'She is staying in the Presidential Suite at the Peninsula Hotel, together with Lucy Kwok Ling Fong. He will try to infiltrate. They have a double target. They missed Lucy Kwok the first time and, for sure, they'll try again.'

'Presumably, this man Creasy will have them protected.'

'Of course.'

'But do you doubt that the 14K can penetrate that hotel?'

'If they can, I'm sure this Creasy has made enough provision.'

CHAPTER 46

'She has arrived.'

'Who?'

'The woman, Gloria Manners.'

'Where is she?'

'In a suite in the Peninsula Hotel.'

'She's alone?'

Hung Mun shook his head. 'She came by private jet, together with Lucy Kwok.'

'She came just with Lucy Kwok?'

'No. There was a man with them. According to his passport, he's a Belgian called Rene Callard. They cleared customs together and were met by the manager personally. An hour later, the private jet took off. Its flight plan was to Bangkok.'

'Do we have anybody at the Peninsula Hotel?'

Hung Mun shook his head.

'We have people in every hotel in Hong Kong except that one . . . The loyalties of the staff there stay with the Kadoorie family.'

'So be it . . . but we have our men at immigration. Has Creasy arrived or this Maxie MacDonald?'

'The immigration computers show no such names.'

'False passports?'

'Maybe . . . so, in the meantime, you stay here in Sai Kung.'

Tommy Mo looked down at the piece of paper and remarked, 'If we kill this old woman, everything ends.'

Hung Mun shook his head.

'I think not. I think this man Creasy is coming, and her death will not stop him. I think, also, she will be protected. She's in the fifth floor Presidential Suite, and to get to her will be difficult.'

'You said we have to attack. So how do we do that?'

'We have to get Lucy Kwok. She will be the hand in our negotiation.'

'How do we get Lucy Kwok? If she's with this old woman, she has the same protection.'

'We have to get her out of the hotel.'

'How do we do that?'

'We have to watch that hotel and all other hotels in the area. We have our people in all the other hotels. We must mobilise the 14K.'

CHAPTER 47

The customs officer studied the packing list and then the airway-bill. Finally, he looked at the large steel container which measured twelve feet by six. He turned to the airfreight forwarder next to him, who happened to be a cousin, and asked, with a slight edge of sarcasm in his voice, 'Why would anyone ship furniture by air, at such a cost?'

The cousin shrugged.

'The customer is very rich and impatient.' He was not at all concerned. He had met his cousin the night before at a Dim Sum restaurant and, after paying for a good meal, he had passed over the envelope containing the two gold sovereigns.

The customs officer looked again at the airway-bill, and this time he smiled. 'It's very heavy furnitre,' he said. 'It weighs more than a coupld of tons.'

'Solid mahogany,' came the reply.

Ten minutes later, the airfreight forwarder drove out of the airport customs area behind a truck carrying the container. He stopped very briefly at a side-street near Nathan Road. The passenger door opened and Corkscrew Two slid into the car.

'Any problems?' he asked.

The Chinese man pointed at the truck ahead.

'No problems, sir. They're in there.'

Creasy and Frank Miller had just finished lunch in the safehouse when the doorbell rang. The two men exchanged glances and then Frank stood up, wiping his face with a napkin, and went down the corridor to the door.

Creasy also stood up and moved to the corridor, and watched as Frank pressed a button and spoke into the intercom. A voice came back, simply saying, 'Corkscrew Two.'

Half an hour later, the three of them were unloading the carefully packed weapons and checking them one by one. Apart from the two RPG7s, there were four Uzi submachine-guns and six FNP9 lightweight submachine guns, which, because of their mostly plastic construction, looked almost frail, but which were one of the most modern and effective short-range weapons ever devised. Then they unloaded a variety of pistols ranging from Colt 1911s, all the way down to lightweight Berettas, together with spare magazines and boxes of ammunition and soft chamois shoulder-holsters. Then the boxes of grenades, both fragmentation and phosphorescent. Two boxes of flares followed, one 2-inch mortar and a steel box of mortar bombs and, finally, a variety of clothing comprising black trousers and long-sleeved shirts, black socks, black boots, black webbing and chest pouches and black balaclavas.

The others arrived one by one about an hour after dark. After Jens and The Owl had been introduced to Eric Laparte and Do Huang, Creasy led them all into the dining-room and they sat down for their first full-scale strategy meeting. Creasy was at the head of the table. He looked at the faces around him and said to Jens and The Owl, 'We are what we are and we're not ashamed of that. You will not know the words I'm going to speak, but for the rest of us, they are a Bible. They come from a prayer written by a French paratrooper who died with honour in 1942. His name was Andre Zirnheld and his courage was legendary. His words were thus:

> "Give me, God, what you still have,
> Give me what no one asks for;
> I do not ask for wealth
> Nor for success, nor even health –
> People ask you so often, God, for all that,
> You cannot have any left.
> Give me, God, what you still have;
> Give me what people refuse to accept from you.

I want insecurity and disquietude,
I want turmoil and brawl,
And if you should give them to me, my God,
Once and for all
Let me be sure to have them always,
For I will not always have the courage
To ask you for them."

When he ended the prayer, the silence was intense. Jens Jensen broke the silence.

'We need that prayer. The information I have is daunting. Not all of us will leave this place alive.'

Eric Laparte lifted his head. He looked as though he had had a facelift that had gone wrong. He said, 'That's part of the prayer. Without the risk, there is no purpose . . . without a purpose, we have no blood . . . without blood, we are nothing. Sometimes we keep it and sometimes we lose it.' He looked at the faces around the table. 'Maybe for some of us, the time has come. Maybe that time has been overdue . . . How many wars? How many wounds? We have a just cause.'

There was a combined murmur of agreement and then came the briefing from the Dane.

His laptop computer appeared and, for an hour, he talked without interruption and then Creasy took over. He explained that for the coming days they would mount a major surveillance on the villa in Sai Kung. They needed to find a way to get in. A frontal attack would be suicidal. He then went through the composition of the two teams. Creasy himself would lead Tom Sawyer, Frank Miller and The Owl in one team, and Guido would lead Maxie, Eric Laparte and Do in the other. Creasy and Guido would be the ones to infiltrate the villa, before the operation started. The teams had been selected for their various skills. Maxie and Frank Miller would handle the RPG7 rocket launchers. Eric Laparte and Do would handle the 2-inch mortars. The would all have SMG's, pistols and grenades. Creasy immediately came up with an argument from Jens Jensen.

'What about me? the Dane demanded.

'You'll handle communications and the base,' Creasy answered.

'So, I'm not capable of being in the field?'

Creasy sighed. 'You well know that somebody has to co-ordinate the operation. That's your job. You're damn good at it and we'll all feel secure with you at the centre – that's a bigger contribution than any of us have to make.'

Before the Dane could answer, there were murmurs of approval from the others and Guido said, 'Jens, it is a question of security in our minds. The most important thing in a fire-fight is knowing what the rest of the team is doing. We'll all be carrying mobile phones and once the action starts we need to have total confidence in the co-ordination. I know from experience that you're the best man for the job and it's the most important job on the team.'

There were more murmurs of assent from around the table. The Dane was mollified, but still he had another argument. He glanced at The Owl and then back at Creasy and said, 'The Owl is not a mercenary. He has never fought a war. Perhaps he should be guarding Gloria instead of Rene.'

Creasy was beaten to an answer. The Owl looked at Jens and said, 'I've fought in plenty of wars in the backstreets of Marseille and that's a lot more dangerous than the Congo or Vietnam. I thank you for your concern, Jens, but I'm going to be at the front end on this thing.'

The Dane said, 'Will you go into action with your Walkman on your belt and Chopin in your ears?'

'No. Wagner is more appropriate. I'll be listening to *Götterdämmerung*.'

CHAPTER 48

Lucy Kwok was surprised. He had told her that, once she arrived in Hong Kong, she was never to leave the hotel and the presence of Rene Callard. But half an hour earlier, he had phoned Rene and then spoken to Gloria and then to her. He had simply said, 'In exactly half an hour, leave your hotel, cross Nathan Road to the Sheraton Hotel and go to Room 54. Don't worry. A couple of our guys will be covering you.'

She did as instructed and, in spite of herself, was nervous. She knew that she was a prime target. As she crossed the busy road, her eyes darted back and forth. It was futile. She would not have recognised a Triad member if she saw one. She turned at the entrance to the hotel and studied the street, trying to spot her cover. It was no use. Nathan Road was busy twenty-four hours a day and teeming with people. She crossed the vast lobby to the lifts. Two minutes later, she was knocking on the door of Room 54. It opened and Creasy stood there with one of his rare smiles.

He said, 'I thought it was time that we had a brief hour of leisure.'

Two minutes later they were making love on the huge bed. It amazed her that such a violent man could make love so gently. He seemed to know every spot of her body which wanted to be stroked and kissed. For such an obvious man of action, he was infinitely patient, building up desire until every nerve wanted him inside her. Even then, he was gentle, and she realised that on the few occasions they had made love, he had learned exactly what to do with her.

Afterwards, as they lay in each other's arms, he talked about the operation. At that moment, Maxie MacDonald and Guido were watching the villa. In four hours, they would be relieved by Tom Sawyer and Do Huang, and four hours later, by Eric Laparte and The Owl. The surveillance would continue, twenty-four hours a day for at least four days, and then they would make their final plan for the assault. In the meantime, another two men had been added to the team. They were Tony Cope, an ex-British Naval Officer who had spent time in the elite Special Boat Service, and Damon Broad, also ex-Navy. They were in Manila, chartering a fast cruiser and within three days would be taking a holiday cruise in Hong Kong waters, not a million miles from Tommy Mo's villa in Sai Kung.

Finally, Creasy clambered off the bed and went to the mini-bar and took out half a bottle of Moët et Chandon champagne. He poured her a glass.

'You're not having any?' she asked.

He smiled.

'It may not have seemed like it for the last hour, but actually, I'm working.'

She drained half the glass, smiled up at him and said, 'You do your work very well . . . that was beautiful.'

Most of her mind and body was relaxed, but there was an edge of tension. She had decided not to talk about it until the operation was over, but suddenly she felt the total necessity of hearing some answers. She asked the first question.

'What are your feelings for me?'

His answer came after a pause. 'My feelings for you are very strong.'

'Do you love me?'

'I'm not very good with words or expressing myself. I never have been and never will be. You mean a great deal to me.'

'What does that mean?'

He thought about it with obvious care, and then said, 'I've always felt that I'm a twilight man.'

'In what way?'

'Well, ever since I was seventeen years old, I've been a soldier, and I've been in battles many times in different parts of the world. Understand that a foreign legionnaire or a mercenary is always the last line of defence. The French Foreign Legion never won a war. They were totally expendable. You get paid your money and you take the risk. So we were, and are, all twilight men. We always think of ourselves as being in the twilight of our lives. Because the night can come at any time. It makes it hard to fall in love – but of course, it does happen.'

'Did you love your wife?'

'Yes.'

'Did you tell her?'

'Yes. But it took a long time and I think she knew it before I did.'

'Have you ever loved anybody else . . . I mean, a woman?'

'Yes. One other. She's also dead – maybe I carry that curse with me, which is why I shie away from that word.'

'Did you tell her?'

'Yes. And a few minutes later she was dead.'

'How?'

'Blown up in a car bomb, in London.'

She put down the glass of champagne and lay back on the bed and looked at the ceiling. She said, 'Being in love with you sounds like a dangerous occupation.'

He stroked her raven hair.

'I thought you'd have realised that by now.'

CHAPTER 49

Rene Callard looked like a slightly ageing playboy, but when it came to work, he was as intricate as a watchmaker.

The Presidential Suite lived up to its name. It had three bedrooms, its own kitchen, a vast lounge and an adjoining dining-room. The whole apartment was embellished with antique Chinese furniture and artifacts. Rene went over it inch by inch, checking for any bugs. Then he spoke to the hotel's general manager, who sent up the security manager. Rene sat the small but intelligent-looking Chinese across the dining-room table with a notepad and pen in front of him, and they went through the procedures. He wanted eight by ten photographs of the room maids assigned to the Suite and the entire Penthouse floor, together with their names. Each floor had its own service area and kitchen, and so he wanted photographs and names of all the staff working on that floor. He wanted to see every single one of them personally. During Mrs Manners's stay at the hotel, no other staff were to be allowed on to the top floor. He also wanted details of all the guests who came and went to the various other suites on the floor, their nationalities and their professions.

In effect, it was necessary that Mrs Manners's security be rated on the same level as a Head of State, except for one important exception. There should be no security guards at all on the penthouse floor. Rene wanted to be the only one with a gun. He would know the face of anyone who had a legitimate reason to be on that floor. If a member of the staff became sick and had to be replaced, he must be informed immediately. If any member of staff needed to enter the room, they were to phone first and, once they had rung the doorbell, they should move back and away to the right by not less than five metres and never, under any circumstances, have a hand in a pocket or be wearing any other garment except the standard hotel uniform.

The security manager was impressed. Many Heads of State had stayed in the hotel since it was built in the late nineteen-twenties and they were used to an army of security men, all assuming that sheer numbers would protect their charges. But this quietly spoken Belgian was on his own, and his preparations were precise.

'Are you expecting trouble?'

Rene shrugged.

'I'm expecting everything from a leaking tap to World War Three.'

Finally, he said, 'If either Mrs Manners or Miss Lucy Kwok leave the Suite, you or your deputy will be informed five minutes beforehand. Do you understand why?'

The Chinese smiled.

'I think so. If I or my security staff spot either of the two ladies moving around the hotel, or entering or leaving it, then we know that, unless we've been pre-advised, there could be the possibility of impersonation.'

The Belgian nodded. He was also impressed.

'I'm sure Mrs Manners will be both grateful and generous. Thank you for your time.'

After he had ushered out the security manager, Rene sat down with Gloria and Lucy and took them through the routine. They listened solemnly and then Gloria remarked, 'It sounds like we're living in a gilded prison.'

'That's exactly right, Mrs Manners,' Rene said. 'And this evening we'll be joined by Jens Jensen and his computer. He tapped the tiny mobile phone in front of him. 'All of us have one of these and when the action starts, we keep in touch that way. Please make no outgoing phone calls using the hotel system. It's probably secure . . . but we can't be sure.'

'When will the action start?' Gloria asked.

'I'm not sure,' he replied. 'But my gut feeling is that things will begin to happen in the next forty-eight hours.'

Gloria asked. 'Do you feel bad about being stuck here with us and not being in the front-line?'

'Believe me, Mrs Manners . . . I am in the front line. So are both of you.'

CHAPTER 50

An eagle would not have spotted it. The hide had been built by Maxie MacDonald, and it blended into the countryside as cream into coffee. Tom Sawyer and Eric Laparte were concealed inside. Tom held very powerful binoculars and Eric held a notebook and a felt-tipped pen. The 14K villa and compound was situated about a kilometre away below them. The hide was comfortable. They lay on sleeping bags and they had a cooler beside them, containing soft drinks and foil-wrapped sandwiches. They would be there for another three hours before Maxie and The Owl replaced them.

The surveillance had started two days earlier, and already the notebook was showing a pattern. A black Mercedes was a frequent visitor, as was a truck containing live fish and a pump pushing oxygen through the tank. Another refrigerated truck also called frequently. Tommy Mo had at least fifty people inside that compound; they all had to eat. There were other casual visitors, almost always arriving in a Mercedes or a BMW, but there had been no pattern to their movements.

Suddenly, Tom Sawyer raised the binoculars and glanced at his watch. 'Log it,' he said. 'The garbage truck is arriving.'

The Frenchman also glanced at his watch and made a note in the log-book. They watched as the garbage truck pulled up in front of the massive metal gates. The gates were opened and the truck went through. The two men were high enough to see inside the compound and the routine was normal. The truck passed around to the staff compound at the back, its rear lifted up, and three servants threw in black garbage bags. Ten minutes later, the garbage truck emerged through the gates and drove away towards Sai Kung village.

Eric Laparte flicked through the pages of the log-book and said, 'They're efficient. Seven p.m. on both nights, give or take fifteen minutes.'

Tom Sawyer was studying the villa compound through his binoculars. He said, 'They make the mistake of routine. The supply trucks come at different times during the day, but the garbage truck always comes at the same time.'

CHAPTER 51

There was no moon. Creasy and Guido were sitting on their haunches among the rocks, looking out across the black sea. They had been squatting there for half an hour without saying a word. Their friendship was of the kind that did not need many words. In fact, the enveloping silence itself gave them comfort.

They both saw it. The briefest flash of light from the sea. Guido reached down and picked up the rubber-encased torch beside him, pointed it and pressed the button twice.

Ten minutes later, they were scrambling aboard the silenced black rubber dinghy which had come in almost unseen. They were greeted without words, just a hand on their shoulders, from the sole occupant.

Half an hour later, they were sitting in the comfortable saloon of the MV *Tempest*, in deep discussion with Tony Cope and Damon Broad. Creasy and Guido drank mineral water. The two ex-Navy men were drinking pink gins and Creasy felt no need to admonish them; the British Navy had won most of their battles half-drunk. They all studied the chart on the table. It took about half an hour while Creasy pointed out the location of the villa and the possible embarkation sites. He then looked up at Tony Cope and said, 'Brief me on the vessel.'

Tony Cope was a quintessential naval officer. Rank was everything. And since Creasy was his superior, he gave him the deference required and his tone of voice was respectful.

'The *Tempest* is sixty-five feet over all, with a semi-planing hull. Twin turbo-charged diesels, with a total horsepower of nine hundred. Top speed: twenty-eight knots. Optimum speed: twenty-three. Normal range at optimum is four hundred and fifty sea miles, but we've bolted on deck tanks, which double that. We are provisioned for a dozen people for thirty days.'

Creasy glanced at Guido with a slight smile and then he himself assumed an officer's tone. 'You got the machinery?'

Tony Cope nodded.

'Yes. We cleared immigration and customs at fourteen hundred hours yesterday. At sixteen hundred hours, the gentleman who calls himself Corkscrew Two asked permission to come aboard. He gave the correct passwords. A few minutes later, a truck arrived alongside with some cases of spare parts for our engines. They had been correctly passed through customs. Inside those cases were two heavy machine-guns. We took a small harbour cruise and Mr Corkscrew Two assembled the weapons and bolted them to the deck, fore and aft. They are now concealed by two upturned dinghys.' He glanced at Damon Broad and for the first time smiled and said, 'That man is quite a character. When he finished his work on the heavy MG's, he said, and I quote, "That's it. In a couple of hours, I'm off home. Doesn't the Royal Navy have a tradition of hospitality?" He then drank most of a bottle of Pusser's rum and strolled down the gangplank as though he'd just had a glass of water.'

'He's like that,' Creasy said. 'Never drinks on the job, but when he's finished large bars have to restock their cellars.'

The Police Commissioner was working late and, like every head of every police force world-wide, he had a million problems. But his main problem, on this night, was the 14K and his maverick Inspector Lau Ming Lan. There had been a message on the Commissioner's Ansafone an hour and a half earlier, requesting a private meeting at nine-thirty. The Commissioner had mixed feelings about Inspector Lau and the 14K.

There was a glint of unusual excitement in Inspector Lau's eyes as he walked in the door. He sat down and said, 'There are at least ten of them.'

'Ten of who?'

'Creasy's little army.'

'How do you know?'

The Inspector reached into his pocket and pulled out a small mobile phone, measuring no more than three inches by two. He laid it on the Commissioner's desk and said, 'That's the latest model from Sony. It's being marketed by Hong Kong Telecom.'

223

The Commissioner picked it up, looked at it and said, 'It's amazing . . . but what about it?'

Inspector Lau pointed at it.

'I assumed that this man Creasy would need communication between his people. We have excellent cellular communication in Hong Kong. I had the phone company submit reports to me on every mobile phone rented or purchased in the last seven days and by whom. The report showed that two days ago Mrs Gloria Manners rented ten of those mobile phones through the Peninsula Hotel.'

The Commissioner was impressed but he tried not to show it. He started to make a speech about law and order, but Inspector Lau was talking on enthusiastically.

'And there's more. I twisted a few arms at Hong Kong Telecom, and so now I know the frequencies used by those phones. I can listen in to every conversation – I've already started to do so. And there's another advantage. Because of our radio listening beacons – to try to combat the smuggling to China – we're able to pinpoint transmissions. The frequencies of the mobile phones of Creasy's team have been programmed into our computer. Every call will be logged and the computer will show the area from which it's made. We're already getting results.'

'Like what?'

Inspector Lau pulled a page of a computer readout from his pocket, studied it and said, 'Of course, one location is the Peninsula Hotel. Incidentally, Mrs Manners and the people with her are no longer making outside calls on the hotel telephone system.' He looked back at the paper. 'Another location is between Kadoorie Avenue and Braga Circuit, another comes from about two miles off the coast of Sai Kung.'

The Commissioner raised his eyes.

'Yes,' Inspector Lau confirmed, 'they have a boat. It's a large and fast cabin cruiser, called the MV *Tempest*. It arrived from Manila yesterday and cleared immigration and customs routinely. It has a crew of two . . . both British. A couple of hours after it arrived, spare parts were delivered on board in two large cases.'

The Commissioner sighed theatrically, stood up and started to pace back and forth across his spacious office. Then he made his speech. It was stern and to the point and covered all legal and police principles.

Inspector Lau listened with humility, his head bowed. He looked up when the Commissioner had finished and said quietly, 'I have discovered another location from which one of those mobile phones is transmitting.'

'Where?'

'Less than one kilometre from Tommy Mo's villa in Sai Kung,' he said. 'At this moment that villa is under observation.'

The Commissioner sighed and said, 'Okay, proceed, but cautiously. And from now on I don't want to hear or know anything more about it . . . Away with you.'

At the door, Inspector Lau turned and said apologetically, 'There is one last thing, Commissioner.'

The Commissioner was looking down at his desk. He looked up grimly.

'Are you sure it's one last thing?'

'On the sacred memory of my beloved grandmother, I make that promise.'

'What do you finally want?'

'I have been trying to read Tommy Mo's mind and put myself in his place. The only real thing he knows is that Gloria Manners and Lucy Kwok Ling Fong are in the Presidential Suite of the Peninsula Hotel. For sure, he will not try to attack them there. They will be perfectly protected. But he will try to get one or both of them out.'

'How?'

'I have no idea, but knowing Tommy Mo's power and his cunning, he will certainly try.'

'So?'

'So, there are four entrances to the Peninsula Hotel, including the service entrance. I want twenty-four hour surveillance on all those entrances, starting tonight.'

The Commissioner sighed yet again. 'That means forty-two men on eight-hour shifts, in two-man teams.'

'Exactly.'

The Commissioner thought for about ten seconds and then said, 'Five days and that's all . . . Don't you realise how stretched we are when it comes to manpower?'

'Yes, Sir. But I want to choose those men myself and have them directly under my command. Also, apart from the four normal unmarked police cars they would use, I want an extra two, in case of emergency.'

Again the two Chinese looked at each other through thick spectacles. Then the Commissioner turned to the console of his computer and started to punch buttons. He said, 'I'm sending a signal to the Heads of Personnel and Transport, instructing them to be under your personal command for the next five days.'

'Thank you, Sir.'

CHAPTER 52

'Is he sure?'

Hung Mun nodded.

'He's a good man. We obtained a photograph of Lucy Kwok and circulated it around the hotels to our people. One of them works at the Sheraton Hotel as a room boy. He swears that he saw the woman in the corridor there last night. She went into Room 54 and stayed about an hour.'

Tommy Mo nodded in satisfaction and said, 'Naturally, you found out who was occupying Room 54.'

Hung Mun answered, 'The room is registered in the name of a Mr James Johnson for one week, as of two days ago. But apparently he almost never uses the room. I guess that he's staying somewhere else and just uses the place as a love-nest.'

Tommy Mo smiled.

'And that means that Lucy Kwok is his lover.'

'We must assume so.'

'Let us do that, Hung Mun, and let us assume that Lucy Kwok will visit him there again. We must have one of the teams on hand. Arrange that we have rooms booked on the same floor and our watchers covering every entrance.'

Hung Mun asked, 'If she goes back there, do we break into the room and grab them both?'

'No ... We must be more subtle. She must be taken as she comes out of the room and before she reaches the street. It must be very quiet and with no fuss. I don't want the police involved. Meanwhile, try to get a description of this man, Johnson. He may be one of the men working for the Manners woman.'

Hung Mun stood up, bowed respectfully and left.

CHAPTER 53

They were gathered at the safehouse in Braga Circuit. It was the final strategy meeting before the assault on Tommy Mo's villa the next day.

They sat around the large oval dining room table. On the wall, in front of Creasy, was an enlarged ordnance map of the Sai Kung peninsula, showing every building, road and track and the contours of every hill and valley. Various arrows, crosses and circles had been superimposed with felt-tipped pens in a variety of colours. Beside the map was a diagram of the villa and its surrounding compound. Creasy was flicking through the pages of a notebook, the surveillance log of the various watchers over the past few days.

He looked up at Tom Sawyer across the table and said, 'You got it exactly right, Tom. The way in for Guido and myself is in the back of the rubbish truck.' He turned to Do Huang. 'We'll hijack it shortly after it leaves the town, and Do will drive it. The routine is that they open the gates to let it in and then close the gates as soon as it's inside the compound. It drives down the side-road past the villa to the service building behind. Guido and I come out there. Guido will cover me with an SMG and grenades while I head straight for the villa, and then he'll follow me to the villa.' He turned to Eric. 'You're the mortar-man. From your position, you'll not be able to see over the wall, but Tom will have a view from higher up the hill. The moment we cross the gap between the service building and the villa, you open up with your mortar and range in between the two buildings and try to keep the fighters from getting to us, while we deal with Tommy Mo and his people in the villa.' He glanced at Maxie. 'Meanwhile, Maxie and Frank

228

will move in with the RPG7s and breach the wall on each side. The moment that happens, the mortar fire has to end. Both teams enter the compound through the breaches.' He stood up and walked around the table to the map and pointed. 'The beach is here, about eight hundred metres away. There will be two large Avon dinghies waiting, one for each section. The motor launch will be a hundred metres off-shore, covering our embarkation with two heavy machine-guns. We head straight for the Philippines.'

Guido was studying the map. He asked, 'Substitution?'

Creasy nodded and glanced around the table.

'If I get hit, Guido takes command. If Guido gets hit, Maxie takes command. If Maxie gets hit, Frank takes over.' He pointed at the tiny mobile phone on the table, with its earplug attachment. 'We've tested those things and they work damn well. We'll have a conference patch and be able to talk to each other and listen to each other – but let's keep the talking to a minimum, especially when the action starts.'

Creasy moved back around the table and sat down. He glanced at Eric Laparte and said, 'The mortar barrage is vital. You have to be dropping those bombs between those two buildings within seconds of Guido and me exiting that rubbish truck.'

For the next hour, they discussed the strategy and their movements until Creasy and Guido were satisfied.

CHAPTER 54

They had finished dinner and were watching television when Rene's mobile phone rang. He picked it up, moved across the suite to the windows and spoke into it quietly.

Lucy called out 'Is that Creasy?' When Rene nodded, she said, 'When you've finished, can I speak to him?'

Rene had been speaking in French. He continued speaking into the phone and then said to her, 'Yes, but he needs to talk to Jens first.'

Jens pushed himself up and walked over. The phone conversation turned to English. Above the noise of the television, Lucy could hear one part of the conversation. It was obvious that Creasy was briefing Jens on their final dispositions for the attack on the villa the next morning. After five minutes, the Dane beckoned to her. She walked across and took the phone, moved further away and spoke quietly into it.

'How are you?'

'I'm fine. How are you coping?'

'Well, we're just sitting and waiting . . . I don't think I'll sleep tonight.'

'You must try.'

'I will, but I think it's hopeless . . . I'm frightened.'

The tiny receiver next to her ear still managed to carry the deep resonance of his voice.

'Lucy, you have nothing to be frightened about. Rene has got that place buttoned up.'

'I'm not frightened for myself, Creasy. I'm frightened for you . . . the twilight man.'

His laugh was soft. 'Don't worry. This twilight man always sees the sun in the morning.'

'But I still worry . . . Are you going to bed now?'

'No. I have to make a couple of calls at midnight to tie up the last details.'

There was a sudden urgency in her voice. 'It's only ten o'clock now. Can I see you?'

There was a pause, then he said, 'Lucy, I can't come to you and you can't come here.'

'What about the place we met last time . . . Do you still have the room?'

'Yes, but I would need to have some cover on you when you move from one hotel to the other.'

'Can't you arrange cover?'

He sighed and said, 'Lucy, I know what's going through your mind. It happens all the time with women who are involved with men about to go into battle. You think you have a premonition that we might never see each other again. But Lucy, there are no such things as premonitions. It's just a matter of apprehension.'

'Creasy, I'm Chinese. We have premonitions but no apprehensions . . . I would just like to spend an hour with you, and if you have cover for me, then surely there's no danger. This is the busiest place in Hong Kong.'

There was another silence, then he said, 'There's always danger.'

She almost whispered into the phone. 'Please . . . just this time . . . Do it for me.'

Again, he hesitated. Then she heard him talking to somebody in the room. His voice came back. 'OK. Maxie and Frank have agreed to give you cover . . . But be careful, Lucy. I'll see you in half an hour. Put Rene back on the phone.'

She called to Rene and handed him the phone. He listened and then said, 'OK. Will do. I'll arrange things at this end.'

He went to the hotel phone and called the security manager and informed him that Miss Lucy Kwok would be leaving the hotel in half an hour and returning approximately one hour later.

She passed the time by making sure that Gloria was comfortable in bed and about to fall asleep. Rene opened the door for her, checked the corridor and, as she passed through the door, said, 'Be careful. If anyone approaches you, just run.'

She gave him a smile and said, 'Don't worry, Rene. I can run very fast.'

It went very smoothly. She dodged the traffic across Nathan Road, knowing that Maxie and Frank were close to her. But she never set eyes on them. A few minutes later, she was knocking on the door of Room 54. And a few minutes after that, the phone was ringing in the villa in Sai King.

An hour later she gave Creasy a last kiss and ran her hand down his naked chest. From the moment she had entered the room they had hardly spoken a word, simply held each other and made soft slow love.

She dressed quickly as Creasy picked up his mobile phone and started slotting the last pieces of the puzzle into place.

He cupped the phone and said to her, 'Maxie will be waiting in the lobby. I'll see you in a few days.'

She went to the door, turned and gave him a last look. Then she moved out into the corridor and towards the lifts. It was a long corridor and she was close to the lifts when two doors on each side of her opened. It was over in seconds. A hand around her mouth and another around her waist. She could make no sound. She realised that there were four or five of them. She tried to bite the hand across her mouth and was stunned by a blow to her head.

CHAPTER 55

Inspector Lau was the first to receive the information.

He set up a mini-operations centre in his own office, together with a young constable who was a protégé as well as an electronics wizard. The constable had arranged a loudspeaker link to the banks of mobile phones, and every conversation between the mobile phones of Creasy's team were channeled through that loudspeaker. Another loudspeaker relayed the special police network set-up between the police surveillance teams and headquarters. It was ten minutes past eleven when the first message came through the police loudspeaker. It came from the police car which had been keeping a watch on the Nathan Road entrance of the Peninsula Hotel.

A woman had been seen coming out of the entrance at eight minutes past eleven. She resembled Lucy Kwok Ling Fong. They had observed her crossing Nathan Road and entering the Sheraton Hotel. In the meantime, Inspector Lau had listened to the conversation between Creasy and Lucy Kwok and Rene Callard, and knew that Creasy and Lucy were having an assignation somewhere nearby.

There had been no other communication for an hour, and then one of the speakers came to life. It was Creasy calling Callard, telling him that Lucy was on the way back and should be with him in five minutes and asking Maxie and Frank to copy, which they did. Three minutes later Maxie's voice was coming through the loud speaker. He was telling Creasy that Lucy had not come out of the lift.

Seven minutes passed, and then Creasy was issuing instructions, and from those instructions Inspector Lau realised that

Lucy Kwok had been snatched by the 14K between Creasy's room and the lift. Definitely snatched by the 14K.

The constable turned on his swivel chair to look at his Inspector.

Inspector Lau shrugged and said, 'We don't interfere.'

The constable thought for a moment and then remarked, 'If the 14K have her, they will almost certainly take her to the *Black Swan* at Hebe Haven. They've done that kind of thing before.'

Creasy's voice came through the loudspeaker: 'If they've got her, they are probably taking her to the Sai Kung villa.'

A series of clicks came through the loudspeaker in Inspector Lau's office. A voice said: 'I've been listening in. I'm a hundred metres overlooking the road to the 14K villa. No vehicle has passed in the last twenty minutes.'

The constable was looking at his computer screen. He turned and said, 'Voice recognition . . . that's the Frenchman, Eric Laparte.'

Inspector Lau was looking at the loudspeaker as though it was the holy grail. He turned to his constable and said, 'This is better than any game invented by Nintendo . . . And definitely more exciting.'

Creasy's voice came over the loudspeaker: 'Eric, move down to the road. Try to get to a bend, where a car would have to slow down. If a large black car – probably a Mercedes – comes by, use your SMG and blast its tyres. What's Tom's location?'

'Two hundred metres further down the road.'

'Link up. Put Tom on the other side of the road.'

'Will do.'

In Inspector's Lau's office, the constable said, 'It's almost certainly the *Black Swan*.'

Inspector Lau leaned forward, cupped his hands to his face and thought with great speed, imagining the scenario in the suite at the Peninsula Hotel. He could almost see the Dane, Jens Jensen, crouched over his laptop computer, punching in the files that showed the known and suspected safehouses of the 14K. There were half a dozen scattered around the Colony. One of them was a luxuriously converted twenty-metre fishing junk, which the 14K used in their legitimate business to entertain visiting customers. It was spacious and contained a fully-stocked bar, two huge cabins with four-poster beds, and a saloon and a galley which could cater for up to ten customers. It had a permanent crew of four, all members of the 14K. It was berthed at the marina at the Hebe

Haven Bay. Its location and description were contained on the disk that he had given Jens Jensen. Inspector Lau's mind was moving into high gear. His fingers itched to reach for the phone and call his counterpart in the Marine Police, but he resisted the temptation.

He began to struggle with his conscience. The Commissioner would definitely not approve, but he could not help himself. He decided that the odds were still enormously in Tommy Mo's favour. He put down the microphone and picked up another phone on his desk and punched in a number. Seconds later, he heard the Dane's voice answering.

Inspector Law said, 'You will recognise the voice of the man who gave you the disk.'

'I do.'

'Right now, you're looking at your computer screen and you've just put up the file. "14K . . . Safehouses".'

There was a pause and the Dane's voice said, 'You're right . . . How do you know this number?'

'It doesn't matter. Just be confident that your network has not been compromised by anybody else but me and my personal assistant. We have surveillance on the car containing Lucy Kwok. It is heading for the *Black Swan*. There will be no police action.'

He hung up before the Dane could answer, and then sat back again and looked at the loudspeaker which would relay, in detail, the coming events. The call came three minutes later. It was from the Dane to Creasy, at the safehouse. Inspector Lau marvelled at the brevity of their conversation, and would continue to marvel throughout the night.

The Dane said: 'We have location of our woman.'

'Where and how?'

'Heading towards a converted luxury fishing junk in the marina at Hebe Haven. Information from the man who gave me the disk.'

There came a thirty second pause and Inspector Lau could imagine Creasy in the safehouse at Braga Circuit, studying the map.

Then Eric Laparte's voice came over the airwaves: 'We're eight kilometres from Hebe Haven marina. We can get there in about twelve to fourteen minutes.'

Another thirty seconds silence and then Creasy's voice: 'You go, but leave Tom on the road, just in case it's a diversion.'

The constable turned from the screens and looked at his boss. He said, 'At last, Lau Sinsan. At last . . . after all these years . . . at last.'

The Inspector held up his hand again, as another voice came through the speaker.

'I've been copying . . . I can be off Hebe Haven in twenty minutes.'

The constable's head jerked back to his screen. He studied it for a few seconds and then said, 'It came from the sea. It must be Tony Cope from the MV *Tempest*.'

The Inspector was nodding in satisfaction.

'Yes. Ex-Royal Navy, ex-Special Boat Service. They're waiting to take Creasy's team off to the Philippines after the assault on the villa.'

The constable reached for the thermos flask of black coffee, but his ears were locked on to the loudspeaker.

Creasy's voice: 'Move to one nautical mile from the Hebe Haven Bay to the North, and if any vessel comes out, track it on your radar. Have your Oppo ready with a dinghy to pick me up at map reference B/14.'

The crisp English voice snapped back: 'Understood.'

Jens Jensen's voice echoed around Inspector Lau's office. He was obviously reading from his computer screen. 'The converted junk, *Black Swan*, is twenty metres overall and twelve metres on the beam. She only draws two metres . . . the significant thing is that her poop deck is three and a half metres above water-level. She has twin G. M. one hundred and fifty HP diesels, which give a maximum speed of twelve knots. Her normal crew is four.'

The curt, English voice came straight back: 'I copy.'

Next, Creasy's voice came through the speaker: 'Listen, SBS. I need a way to get on to that junk.'

Inspector Lau and his constable were looking at the speaker, mesmerised. They heard the English voice say with light-hearted enthusiasm: 'I worked that out five minutes ago.'

Then there was another voice on the speaker. It was Eric Laparte talking to Creasy: 'I was too late. A back junk is just moving off its moorings. It's heading for the entrance of the bay.'

Creasy's voice came, asking: 'Are we copied at sea?'

The crisp, English voice came through the speaker: 'You're copied at sea. We are two nautical miles from the entrance to Hebe Haven. We'll pick up that junk the moment it leaves the shore, and track it from a distance of one nautical mile.'

Creasy's voice: 'Are you showing navigational lights?'

The English voice sounded pained: 'Are you joking?'

CHAPTER 56

Lucy Kwok lay on the vast bed in the state room and listened to the throbbing of the engines.

She had literally been kicked into the cabin. Both her wrists and her ankles were manacled with very modern handcuffs, and her lips were bleeding from a back-handed smack in the mouth from one of the 14K fighters. She felt no pain, only humiliation and guilt. She lay on the bare mattress of the bed and thought of the risks that were being taken by the people trying to help her. Guilt built up like a guillotine above her head. She felt the movement of the boat as it passed out into the open sea. She brought her fear and that guilt under control and made a resolve that, no matter what, she would not give way to any threats, or any abuse, or any pain.

CHAPTER 57

Inspector Lau looked at the two silent loudspeakers. He glanced at his constable and then at his watch. The hour hand was approaching midnight.

'What do you think?' he asked the constable.

The constable leaned back in his chair, away from the computer screen. He liked Inspector Lau. The man always involved him and always asked his opinion. The constable felt as though he was part of a team and not just a subordinate. He said, 'The 14K know what's coming. They know that Mrs Manners in the Peninsula Hotel is the paymaster. It's logical that they'll negotiate with her. They look on the mercenaries she has employed in the same way as they regard their own fighters. They will not believe that those mercenaries have a mind of their own.' He tapped the screen of his computer. 'But we know differently. Mrs Manners has fired a bullet at them and they cannot realise that it will never be stopped.' He pointed up at one of the loudspeakers. 'I listened to the conversation between Creasy and his team. I heard their voices. They are all bullets. They have all been fired.'

Inspector Lau said, 'I think that sometime soon you'll become a sergeant, and shortly after a Master Sergeant . . . your work during these past two days has been exceptional. What do you think will happen next?'

The constable reflected for a moment and then said, 'You already know.'

'Tell me.'

The constable said, 'Tommy Mo sits in his villa in Sai Kung, knowing that he holds an ace in his sleeve. Within the hour, one of his people will contact Mrs Manners and tell her that, unless she pulls off her mercenaries, he will deliver the head of Lucy Kwok Ling Fong on a silver platter to her suite in the Peninsula Hotel.'

'And if she agrees?'

'If she agrees, Tommy Mo, being the man he is, will scent an advantage and, being a Triad . . . and Chinese, he will press for a bonus.'

Inspector Lau nodded in satisfaction.

'How much?'

'Some millions . . . in US dollars.'

'So what do I do?'

'You need to listen to those negotiations.'

'How?'

'You have to tap in to the switchboard of the Peninsula Hotel.'

'How do I do that?'

The constable said, 'Inspector, you know exactly how you do that. You have to get a court order, authorising the Hong Kong telephone company to tap in to the switchboard of the Peninsula Hotel.'

Inspector Lau glanced at his watch. It was 12.30 a.m.

'You realise what I have to do to get that court order?'

Yet again, the constable smiled.

'You have to get our beloved Commissioner out of bed and, in turn, he has to get the Government Prosecutor out of bed . . . who in turn has to get the on-duty judge out of bed, who, we know, has a phone and fax at his home. And then, under the new regulations, he must fax the senior duty-policeman, who at this time is Chief Superintendent George Ellis, authorising him to allow a phone-tap on the required lines.'

Inspector Lau sighed. 'Thank you for reminding me.' He looked at the phone on his desk. 'The Commissioner will not be pleased.'

The constable stood up, stretched and said, 'Inspector, you make your phone-call and I'll set up the technology and a third speaker.'

Inspector Lau studied the phone in front of him. As he tried to make a decision, he heard the crisp English voice coming from the loudspeaker: 'I have a radar reading and the profile fits the vessel under surveillance. It's heading for the Ninepins.'

With another sigh, Inspector Lau reached for the phone.

CHAPTER 58

'It's because you're in love with her,' Guido said.

'That has nothing to do with it,' Creasy answered angrily.

It was a very rare occasion; the two close friends were arguing. They were in the darkened garden of the safehouse, redistributing their team in the light of events. Creasy said that he would go alone to meet up with Tony Cope and Damon Broad on the MV *Tempest* and then, together with Tony Cope, would make an assault on the *Black Swan*.

Guido was arguing that either himself or another member of the team should accompany Creasy. It had been decided that the attempt to rescue Lucy Kwok would take place just before dawn and, if successful, the attack on the 14K villa in Sai Kung would follow almost immediately.

Creasy had decided that he would go alone to the launch, and that Guido and Do Huang would hijack the rubbish truck, and the other two teams would remain unchanged. But Guido knew Creasy's mind as well as his own. He knew, and all the others knew, that Lucy was in love with Creasy and that maybe her love was reciprocated. Consequently, Creasy did not want anyone to think that he was favouring her.

Guido's voice hardened. 'Creasy, you have to lead the team on the villa assault. It's your team, not mine. Lucy has to be a secondary consideration. I'll do everything I can to get her out. But it has to be me. I know how you feel – but it has to be me.'

In the dim light, Creasy looked into his friend's eyes, and knew that he was right.

'All right,' he said. 'But don't forget that Tony Cope's an ex-

Special Boat Serviceman. He's more of an expert at this sort of thing than any of us.'

They turned back into the house. The others were all alseep upstairs, or pretending to be. He had only woken Guido when the news had come through about Lucy's abduction. There was no point in disturbing the others until nearer the time. He glanced at his watch and wondered if, and when, Tommy Mo would be in touch with Gloria. If she had heard nothing by 2 a.m., then Guido would move off and meet Damon Broad and be ferried out to the *Tempest*. Creasy would then assemble the rest of the team at 4 a.m., and head out to Sai Kung.

Guido went into the kitchen and returned with a pot of coffee and two cups. Then he produced a packet of cards, and the two old friends did what they had done so often before. They played gin-rummy and drank coffee while they waited.

CHAPTER 59

The *Black Swan* belied its name. With its wide beam and huge stern, it looked nothing except cumbersome. It was anchored in among the small group of Ninepin Islands, about two miles from the South-East tip of the New Territories.

Two men in black clothing patrolled the decks, submachine-guns slung over their shoulders. Below, in the saloon, five other men were drinking whisky. The eighth man was in the back cabin, abusing Lucy Kwok Ling Fong.

As soon as they had left Hebe Haven, the men had stripped her and tied her wrists and ankles to the large four-poster. The others had left, leaving just the leader, who Lucy had guessed to be a Chui Chau from the way he spoke Cantonese and from the dark complexion of his skin. She also guessed that he would be in his mid-fifties and a senior fighter for the 14K.

He looked down at her naked body and said, 'This can take as long as you wish. You will tell me everything about the American woman and the people she has hired. How many they are, their names, what weapons they have and what they plan to do.'

She had looked up into his small cruel eyes and realised he could well be the leader of the fighters who had killed her family. Her terror turned to rage and the words hissed out of her, in the most traditional and deepest insult a Chinese woman can hurl at a Chinese man.

'I wouldn't give you the steam off my piss!'

As she spoke, her head craned up, and she spat in his face.

He jumped backwards. She could not see his eyes, because he was wiping her spit from his face with the back of his hand, but when he had lowered his hand, she had seen the venom flowing out of them. He had stood very still for almost a minute, just looking at her. Then he went to a cupboard and returned with a short length of rubber hosepipe.

'My orders,' he had said, 'are to get information from you, but without leaving a mark on your body. I don't know why my boss is being so soft-hearted, but I promise you, I can give you a mountain of pain, without leaving a mark.'

It had continued for an hour. He knew exactly how to use the rubber hose. One by one, her nerve endings screamed out with pain but within half an hour, she had stopped screaming and resolved not to make a single sound, no matter what.

After the hour, he had stood back and smiled at her ravaged face.

'You're brave, Kwok Ling Fong. You can accept much pain.' He looked at his watch and she guessed that he had a time-scale. He had a sneering smile on his face.

'You are brave in your body, but we'll now find out how brave you are in your mind and your dignity. If you don't give me the information I want, now, I'll call one of my men in and he'll rape you. He will not be gentle. If, after that, you refuse to talk, I'll call the next man in, and he'll do the same, and it will continue until you talk. We are eight men on this boat . . . when the last one finishes, the first one will be ready to begin again. None of us will be gentle . . . you will be raped in every orifice of your body.'

She tried to spit at him again, but her mouth was dry. He laughed and went to the cabin door, opened it and called a name. A man came in and stood at the foot of the bed, looking down at her naked body. She listened as the leader gave his instructions and saw the lust creep into the man's eyes as he reached to unbuckle his belt.

CHAPTER 60

The phone-call came at 2.45 a.m. and, apart from reaching Gloria at the Peninsula Hotel, it also came through the newly-installed third loudspeaker in Inspector Lau's office. The voice was surprisingly educated; the English, perfect. The constable and Inspector Lau looked at each other in surprise. The message also contained no obvious threat.

The conversation opened: 'Mrs Manners, I'm very sorry to disturb you at such an hour, but it happens that I very recently met a young Chinese lady of your acquaintance.'

'Who are you?'

'My name is not important. It's just that I felt that you may wish to help her.'

'Of course, you're talking about Lucy Kwok. Where is she?'

'Well, I didn't really catch her name but she did tell me that you were investing rather a lot of money in Hong Kong with some of your associates. It would definitely help her if you stopped investing that money with those associates and sent them packing.'

'Where is she?'

'I don't know. I'm acting on behalf of some business associates. They feel that if you immediately drop your present project and invest five million US dollars with them . . . then the young lady I mentioned will be much happier than she is now.'

'This is obviously a ransom demand.'

'Certainly not, Mrs Manners. It is simply a suggestion to make a rather urgent alternative investment, which will be reflected in the condition that your young friend finds herself in at the moment. I'm afraid the time-frame is very small. We need your answer within four hours, and the investment will have to be made by noon today.'

'You expect me to find five million bucks within eight hours?'

'We have every confidence in your ability to do so. You'll be contacted this morning. Please give this proposal your very careful consideration.' The line went dead.

In the hotel suite, Gloria had been writing down the conversation. She had followed Creasy's instructions exactly. She handed the notepad to Jens, who was standing beside her with Rene. The Dane picked up his mobile phone, dialled Creasy's number and read him the transcript.

Across the harbour, Inspector Lau had also jotted down the conversation, even though it was being automatically recorded. He looked up at the constable and said, 'That was the voice of a lawyer. He's Chinese, but educated in England . . . the accent is obvious. I'll track that bastard down, even though he never made an open threat in the conversation.'

'But it was obvious,' the constable said. 'Either five million dollars by tomorrow and the mercenaries sent away, or Lucy Kwok Ling Fong loses her head.'

The Inspector lifted a hand for silence. Voices were coming through one of the other speakers. It was Jens Jensen, speaking to Creasy and relaying the conversation. Then Creasy was talking to Gloria and telling her that in four hours' time, she must agree to their demands and ask for details of how the money was to be delivered. By noon that day, it would be over, one way or another. She should demand proof that Lucy was alive unharmed. Without that proof, she would not pay the money.

'Should I have the money transferred?' she asked.

'Can you do it in such a short time?'

'Yes, I can.'

'Then do it,' Creasy said. 'Just in case. But I think in the next five hours Lucy will either be rescued or dead.'

There was a silence from the speaker and then Gloria's voice came again: 'Creasy. Maybe I should go along with them. Pay the money and call this whole thing off . . . The only thing that matters now is to save Lucy's life.'

Craesy's voice came out of the speaker in a flat monotone: 'Mrs

Manners. They'll kill her anyway. It's out of your hands now. Just follow my instructions. Now pass me to Rene.'

Another pause, and then Creasy was giving Rene instructions. Until further notice, he was not to open the door of the suite to anybody. Rene and Jens were to cover te door, with submachine-guns from different defended positions.

Rene's voice said: 'Don't worry on this end, Creasy. Good luck to you and the guys.' Then the connection was broken.

The constable turned from his computer screen to Inspector Lau and said, 'It's going to be an interesting morning.'

CHAPTER 61

It was just after three o'clock in the morning when the door opened to Inspector Lau's office. It was the Commissioner of Police.

Inspector Lau immediately stood up to attention and so did the constable. The Hong Kong Police is a very disciplined force. The Commissioner was dressed in very casual clothes: a pair of jeans and a T-shirt, and a demin jacket. He glanced around the room and his eyes alighted on the three loudspeakers on the wall. He was about to ask a question, when voices came out of one of the loudspeakers.

It was Guido, talking to Tony Cope: 'Rendezvous. Three-thirty hours at B/14. Confirmed.'

'I copy.'

The Commissioner looked at Inspector Lau, who decided to go on to the attack.

'What are you doing here, Sir? At this time of the night?'

The Commissioner glanced at the constable and then back at the Inspector. He said, 'That's a brilliant question. You ring me up in the middle of the night to arrange a phone-tap on the Peninsula Hotel, and tell me in your usual succinct way to have a good night's sleep . . . How the hell can I sleep? I came to see what's happening. Not to be a boss . . . and not to interfere. But my guts tell me that something is happening tonight and I want to witness it.' He gestured at the row of loudspeakers. 'And, I guess, to listen. Who set that up?'

Inspector Lau was still standing. He gestured at the constable and said, 'Constable Wang Mung Ho. He's been a computer buff from the moment he left his mother's womb.' He pointed at the right-hand speaker. 'We are patched into Creasy's mercenary team on their mobile phones on that speaker.' He pointed at the middle loudspeaker. 'That carries our own police telecommunications.' He pointed at the left-hand speaker. 'That carries any phone-call made to or from the Presidential Suite of the Peninsula Hotel.' He pointed at the computer screen in front of the Constable and said, 'Constable Wang has, over the last two days, been able to set up graphs on his computer to identify voices and also to identify the origins of transmissions.'

The Commissioner walked up behind the constable and looked at his screen. As he stood there, a voice came through the right-hand speaker.

It was the voice of Damon Broad saying: 'Rendezvous on the beach in three minutes. Flash your torch twice after two minutes.'

Another voice said: 'I copy.'

A third voice came through the speaker, saying: 'We are lying one nautical mile off the Ninepins. I have the *Black Swan* on radar. We are on silent mode.'

The Commissioner looked down at the constable and said, 'What was that?'

The constable turned his head and explained. 'That was Damon Broad, communicating with Guido Arrellio. In three minutes, he'll pick Guido up from the beach in a silenced dinghy and take him out to the MV *Tempest*. The other voice was Tony Cope, who's commanding the *Tempest*. Guido and Tony Cope will attack the *Black Swan* just before dawn.'

The Commissioner drew a breath to say something, but was interrupted by the sound of another dialogue from the speaker.

It was Jens Jensen, talking to Creasy: 'Dawn is at six hundred zero seven hours and the garbage truck moves out of Sai Kung village, at six forty-five. Its speed is reduced to less than ten miles an hour at map reference E/12.'

'I'll be there,' the voice came back.

The speaker went silent and the constable looked up at his Commissioner and explained, 'That was Creasy talking to the Dane, Jens Jensen. The Dane is at the Peninsula, co-ordinating communications between the team. The Dane is also a computer expert.' The constable glanced at his watch. 'In half an hour, the team will move towards Sai Kung and infiltrate close to the villa.'

From behind him, the Commissioner heard Inspector Lau say,

'The 14K have demanded five million US dollars from the American woman Gloria Manners by noon today, against the release of Lucy Kwok. They will call her again at six a.m. She will play for time.'

The Commissioner stood there with his hands folded, looking at the computer screen. Then he looked at the three loudspeakers on the wall. Then he looked back at the constable and said, 'You've done a very good job, constable.'

The constable twisted in his chair, and looked up at his Commissioner.

'Thank you, Sir.'

The right-hand loudspeaker came to life. It was Creasy talking to Eric: 'Are you back in position?'

'Affirmative.'

'Any movement?'

'Negative.'

'I wake the team up in twenty minutes. We'll be in position in one hour.'

'Info on the woman?'

'Guido's on his way.'

The Commissioner settled himself into a chair while Inspector Lau switched on the coffee percolator. Constable Ho was tapping the keys of his computer. He turned and said to the Commissioner, 'Guido will board the MV *Tempest*, in about forty-five minutes. From past transcripts, we know that Creasy and Do Huang will hijack the garbage truck as it leaves Sai Kung villa, at about six forty-five a.m.'

The Commissioner glanced at his watch. He looked up at the row of loudspeakers and said, 'Inspector Lau. Are we sure that Tommy Mo and his chief henchmen are in that villa?'

'We are sure, Sir.'

CHAPTER 62

Guido had left his car a kilometre from the shore and scrambled down the low coastline to the beach, holding an illuminated compass in his left hand. He held a black canvas bag containing clothes and his weapons, and weapons for Tony Cope. He waited on the rocky foreshore, listening for the sound of an outboard engine. He waited for two minutes and heard nothing. He pulled a torch from his canvas bag, and flicked it on twice. From the sea came an answering flash. It was remarkably close.

Two minutes later, the black shape of the dinghy slid on to the beach. Guido dropped the bag over the prow and saw the dim outline of Damon Broad at the helm. As the dinghy reversed off the beach, Guido said, 'I heard nothing.'

'That's the idea,' Damon said. 'We extended the exhaust below the water-line and encased the motors on all the dinghies.'

As they sped across the silent unruffled water towards the Ninepins, Guido said, 'Give me a sitrep.'

Damon Broad said, 'The *Black Swan* is anchored in among the Ninepins. Tony did a recce about an hour ago. You thoughtfully provided us with night-glasses. There were two look-outs on deck, but they're amateurs. They sat on the wheelhouse roof, which meant they could see far out to sea, but could not observe the waters immediately below them. Since there's only a new moon covered by cloud, they could see nothing far out to sea. Tony's worked out the assault.'

'Anything else?'

There was a long pause and then Damon said, 'Tony approached to within three hundred metres of that junk and drifted at the same distance past it, for about an hour. For the first half of that hour, he heard intermittent screams . . . Then they stopped.'

They continued the forty-minute passage in silence, until Damon Broad said quietly, 'I wish I could assault that junk with you.'

Guido's voice was quiet and almost caressing. 'Don't worry, Damon . . . When I get on to that junk, I'll do what you want to do.'

CHAPTER 63

The Commissioner sat and drank coffee and, for the next hour, watched the row of loudspeakers. Not a sound came from them. By nature, he was an efficient, but impatient man. Finally, his impatience broke through. He said to the constable, 'Has your communication set-up gone down?'

Wang shook his head.

'No, Sir. Any minute now, things will start to happen.'

Another five minutes passed and then voices began to come through the speakers, and the constable started interpreting who the voices belonged to and where they were coming from. First, it was Guido talking to Creasy; telling him that he was aboard the *Tempest* and about to move on the *Black Swan*. Creasy adviced back that the team were preparing to move out of the safehouse and head to Sai Kung. Every transmission was cryptic in the extreme, and without Constable Ho's explanation, the Commissioner would have been confused.

Then, at 6 a.m., another loudspeaker carried the transcript between Gloria Manners and the smooth talking go-between. She told him that she agreed to the terms of the investment and that the money was being transferred to Hong Kong and would be available before noon. He informed her that payment must be made in gold sovereigns and that she could exchange her dollars for sovereigns at the Hang Seng Bank, which always kept a large stock. He would call back in two hours, to give her the details of the exchange of the sovereigns and her Chinese friend.

Ten minutes later, Creasy was talking to Guido, reporting that he and Do Huang were in position outside Sai Kung village, waiting to hijack the garbage truck. Ten seconds later, Jens

Jensen was reminding the team that first light was in twenty-three minutes.

The Commissioner tore his gaze from the row of loudspeakers, looked at Inspector Lau and said, 'Your friends are well-organised, but my money is still on Tommy Mo.'

'How much, Sir?'

'Inspector, you know that gambling for money is illegal in Hong Kong . . . dinner at the Sung Wah restaurant.'

'You're on, Sir.'

CHAPTER 64

Guido and Tony Cope went through the 'buddy' routine. They stood facing each other, dressed in black and fully-armed. Their faces were blackened, and they wore black knitted skull-caps. They checked each others submachine-guns, ensuring first that they were on safety, and then that the magazines and spare magazines were primed. They then went through the same procedure with the pistols that they carried in holsters on their right sides, and the grenades attached to the webbing on their chests. Damon Broad looked on. He had never seen the procedure before, but the logic of it was obvious.

Earlier, Tony Cope had explained the method of boarding the *Black Swan*. It was a method that the Special Boat Service had adopted from the centuries-old pirates who, up until the present day, were the scourge of the straits of Malacca. Those pirates would come up at night behind a vessel in fast boats. They would have long bamboo poles with cloth-covered hooks on the end, and latch on to the stern rail, and then storm up those poles.

Tony Cope had explained that, although they did not have bamboo poles, they had two very long boat-hooks which he had adapted. They would approach to within two hundred metres of the *Black Swan* with silenced engine and then row in under the stern. If the look-outs were still sitting on the *Black Swan's* wheelhouse, they would see nothing.

There was a very slight northerly breeze. As they attacked the *Black Swan*, Damon Broad would bring in the *Tempest* towards the north, switch off the engine and drift down towards them. At the first sound of gunfire, he would man the heavy machine-gun on the stern and cover the decks of the *Black Swan*, by which time, the look-outs would be dead and Guido and Tony would be below-deck, cleaning up. The plan had the perfection of simplicity and Guido offered no argument. They completed their checks and climbed down into the dinghy.

It took fifteen minutes to approach the *Black Swan*. Tony Cope steered with a luminous compass in his left hand. Guido sat in the prow and watched the little stalagmite islands loom into shape. Then, in their midst, he saw the dark ominous shape of the *Black Swan*. Tony cut the engine and they both crouched down. It was not even necessary to use the oars. Over the next ten minutes, a gentle breeze carried them under the stern of the junk.

Tony rose with one of the long padded boat-hooks in his hands, reached up and gently hooked it over the stern-rail. Guido went first, pulling himself up hand over hand until he gripped the rail. he lifted his head and heard the two look-outs talking on top of the wheelhouse. They were just shadows, about eight metres away. Quietly, he pulled himself aboard. He felt, rather than saw, Tony beside him. He touched Tony on the shoulder and pointed to the two shadows and then touched his chest and pointed at the open door of the wheelhouse, moved forward on his rubber-soled boots and ducked through the entrance.

Guido looked down the hatch into the saloon and saw four men sitting around the table, playing mah-jong and laughing and drinking. There was a bottle of almost empty Black Label whisky on the table. He flicked off the safety of his FNP90. Then he slowly started down the companionway. He had almost reached the bottom before one of the men looked up and saw him.

It was the last thing he saw. In a two-second burst, Guido sprayed bullets across the table. Two of them died immediately. The other two scrabbled on the deck, screaming in agony. As Guido changed a magazine, he heard Tony Cope's SMG open up on the top deck. Guido switched to single shot, and put a bullet through the heads of the two wounded men. Shouts came from his left. A bulkhead door opened and a man came through, holding a pistol. A one-second burst and the man was punched back through the door. Guido ran and jumped over the body and his eyes took in the tableau: Lucy – tied to the bed on her stomach and the naked man scrambling off her body. The naked man hit the floor, rolled over and held up his hands. Guido emptied the rest of the magazine into him.

CHAPTER 65

The garbage truck came slowly around the tight corner. The driver hit the brakes as soon as he saw the obstacle in front of him. It was a small tree, its branches lying right across the road. The truck came to a halt and the driver said to his assistant, 'Pull that out of the way.'

The other man cursed from under a rice wine hangover. He opened the cab and jumped down. As he approached the tree, the driver heard a voice on his right. He turned and saw the dark muzzle of a pistol pointing between his eyes. Behind it was a blackened Caucasian face, under a black skull-cap.

Twenty seconds later, the driver and his assistant were lying in he roadside ditch, handcuffed together, both by their ankles and their wrists. The garbage truck was trundling away down the road.

In Inspector Lau's office, the voices came through the speaker, again, very cryptically. First, it was Do Huang talking to Maxie MacDonald. Wang identified the voices for the Commissioner and his Inspector.

'We have possession of the vehicle.'

Timescale?'

'Between ten and twelve minutes.'

'We're ready.'

Then Guido's voice: 'I'm coming ashore.'

The sun had risen. Eric Laparte, with Maxie beside him, holding the first of the bombs, was a hundred metres away to the east of the compound in a clump of bushes with his mortar set up. Above them on the hill, Tom Sawyer was looking through binoculars at the compound. All was quiet. Two men were squatting in front of the villa, half-asleep in the early sunlight.

Tom took the binoculars from his eyes, looked to his right and saw the garbage truck approaching. He unclipped the small mobile phone from his belt, punched the buttons and said, 'About two minutes.'

His voice carried into Inspector Lau's office, into the suite at the Peninsula Hotel, into Creasy's ear, and into the earplugs of the rest of the team.

Do Huang reached the gates and hit the horn of the truck impatiently.

Tom watched as the two men in front of the villa roused themselves and went to the gate. A minute later, the garbage truck was passing through the gates and moving down the road beside the villa. Tom spoke into the mobile phone: 'Mortar . . . about sixty seconds.'

He watched as the garbage truck pulled up in front of the service building. He heard the sound of its horn again, and saw the two men carrying out black garbage bags. The automated back of the truck lifted, and as Do Huang came out of the cab, Creasy came out of the back.

The war started.

Do Huang shot the two men with the garbage bags, and then ducked behind the truck, facing the service building. Creasy ran towards the villa. The two half-awake guards at the front of the villa grabbed their submachine-guns and ran towards the truck. Creasy lifted his SMG and, while still running, emptied his magazine at them. They spun away into the dust.

Eric waited until Do Huang had backed away from the garbage truck towards the villa. The moment he was clear of the intervening space, Tom lifted his phone and said: 'Mortar.'

Two seconds later, Maxie dropped the first bomb down the mortar tube. Tom heard the crumps of the detonations and then watched the result. He signalled: 'Back ten metres.' Eric adjusted the mortar and then Maxie was dropping the bombs down the barrel. Six mortars were in the air as the 14K fighters spilled out of the service building. The bombs dropped among them at three-second intervals, killing them instantly.

Tom dropped the binoculars, picked up his SMG and ran down

the hill. He came up beside Frank, who had the barrel of the RPG7 over his shoulder. He watched as the rocket took off slowly, gathered speed and smashed into the wall. Seconds later, he heard an explosion on the other side of the compound, which had to be Maxie's rocket, also breaching the wall. He saw the shape of The Owl beside him, racing for the breach, and raced after him.

Creasy reached the front of the villa. He could hear shouts from inside. He did not try to open the door; he just lifted his submachine gun and blasted away at the lock. Do Huang was behind him, facing out, his SMG held high and ready.

Creasy went through the door in a crouch. There were two figures in the passageway on his left. He fired a full magazine and, a second later, had replaced it. Beyond the hallway was a large room with ornate furniture and, beyond that, another passage. Quickly, he glanced over his shoulder. Do Huang was walking backwards, guarding his back.

Creasy shouted, 'Do! Stay right there. Be careful on your trigger. It could be one or more of ours coming through that door.'

Then he turned and ran down the passage. From outside the building he could hear the stuttering of small-arms fire on both sides, and he knew that both teams were inside the compound. Creasy had seen photographs of Tommy Mo and his top people, and for the next three minutes, he hunted them down from bedroom to bedroom. Some died in their beds, some died rushing out of their rooms, some died with their hands in the air. Creasy had no mercy. At the end of the corridor, he paused at a massive mahogany door. He heard running steps behind him and Do's voice calling: 'Maxie's guarding the door.'

From behind the heavy door, they could hear a voice screaming out in Chinese.

Do said, 'That's got to be him.'

Creasy said, 'Back off. You fire at the lock and I'll go through in a roll. Come right after me.' They moved back about five metres and Do raised his SMG and fired a magazine into the lock. The door was half-ajar. Creasy ran forward, hit the door with his shoulder and rolled into the room.

Tommy Mo was in the far corner, wearing a pair of white underpants and holding a pistol with both hands. He managed to get off one shot, which winged Creasy. Then Creasy was firing his SMG and sending death across the room.

In the compound between the two buildings, the battle raged on. Eric Laparte lay dead, cut down as he tried to storm the service building. Tom Sawyer had taken a bullet in his left shoulder, but he leaned against the corner of the villa and with his right hand sent a deadly fire as the 14K fighters poured out of the building. Frank Miller was at the other corner, lobbing grenades.

They began to pull out. Maxie ran across the compound and crouched beside Tom Sawyer. 'Can you walk?'

'Yes,' he answered.

They headed for the breach in the wall. From the front of the villa, Creasy and Do emerged. They headed for the same breach. The Owl stood over the body of Eric Laparte and knew immediately that he was dead. They also moved out, firing a last burst at the service building. He stayed at the breach while the others went past him, and watched as the last of the fighters gathered. He lobbed two grenades, and then started running.

About twenty 14K fighters had survived the assault. They gathered themselves and their weapons and gave chase. As they came down the path towards the sea, they saw their tormentors ahead, and they saw the elegant motor vessel waiting off-shore. They ran faster. From the hill on the right, a submachine-gun opened up, and from the launch, a heavy machine-gun began to cut them down.

The surviving fighters of the 14K forgot their oaths of initiation and dived into the bushes and rocks, watching as the two black dinghies moved out from the shore to the launch. They heard the roar of engines and saw the launch head South-East, leaving nothing but the triangle of a white-topped wake.

CHAPTER 66

They listened to the last transmission beween Creasy and Jens Jensen. The MV *Tempest* had just crossed the twelve-mile territorial line on its way to Manila.

The Commissioner turned to Inspector Lau and murmured, 'So, he took casualties.'

'I'm sure they expected to,' Lau said. 'But one dead and two wounded is not bad.'

The Commissioner held up his hand and they both looked at the speaker and listened.

Creasy was saying: 'We definitely got our target and many others. Are Mrs Manners and Rene copying this conversation?'

The voices came through the speaker: 'We are.'

'OK. Listen carefully. Our ETA in Manila is about twelve hundred hours tomorrow. We need doctors and ambulances waiting, and three private rooms booked in the American hospital. It would also be useful to have an official from the US Embassy on hand, to help with any formalities. Mrs Manners – call Jim Grainger. I'm sure he can arrange that.'

'Understood,' Gloria said. 'Don't worry about anything in Manila. I'll be waiting for you.'

Jens's voice cut in: 'Ten minutes ago, I phoned and booked us into the Manila Hotel. The phone number is 482738. We'll be in that hotel from three o'clock this afternoon. If you need anything else, get a phone patch through your VHF.'

'Will do.'

The speaker went dead and as Inspector Lau turned to the Commissioner, one of the phones on his desk rang. He picked it up, listened for a moment and then passed it to the Commissioner, saying, 'It's the situation room.'

'About time,' the Commissioner said. He put the phone to his ear and at the end of three minutes said, 'Have Sai Kung station fax me a preliminary report within the hour, and I want a full report on my desk by the middle of the afternoon. Send a full team, including forensics.' He listened again and then said, 'You may be right. I'll wait for the full report.' He put the phone down and said to the Inspector, 'A Marine Police launch noticed smoke coming from the Ninepins area. They found a large burnt-out junk, and two dead bodies with gunshot wounds floating nearby. There were other dead bodies on board, but they don't yet know how many, because the wreck's still smouldering and in danger of sinking. They're trying to beach it right now. Meanwhile, the Sai Kung station reported heavy gunfire from the direction of the 14K villa compound. The first radio reports are coming in now. There are bodies everywhere. Apparently, your friends used mortar bombs and rockets to breach the walls.'

'Tommy Mo?' Lau asked.

Both he and the constable watched the Commissioner's face closely. They saw a slight smile.

'Tommy Mo is very dead. So is the entire top strata of the 14K and at least twenty of their fighters. They found one dead *gweilo*. They are still searching the place. The helicopter passed over the area fifteen minutes ago, and reported seeing a string of dead bodies near the coast.'

The Commissioner stood up and stretched his tired frame. He looked first at Inspector Lau and then at Constable Ho and said, 'You both did well. Obviously the 14K will now fracture into many pieces and be much easier to deal with.'

The other men stood too, and Lau asked, 'How will you handle it, Sir?'

'Handle what?'

The Inspector gestured out the window in the direction of the New Territories.

'Well, what happened out at Sai Kung this morning and at the Ninepins.'

Very seriously, the Commissioner answered, 'I think my report to the Governor will show that we had a larger than normal, inter-Triad war.'

'What about the dead *gweilo*?' the constable asked.

'By the time I've made two phone-calls from my office, there will not be a dead *gweilo*. Just a bunch of dead Triads.' He walked out of the office with a jaunty step.

CHAPTER 67

For the first twenty-five miles, Tony Cope had driven the MV *Tempest* on full throttle. Fortunately, the wind had only been Force One from the North-West, and the vessel rode smoothly through negligible swell. The autopilot was on, and he sat watching the radar screen. For the last fifteen minutes he had noted several blips moving rapidly in the direction of the Ninepins, to their rear. They would be Marine Police launches. Damon Broad was below in the fo'c'sle. In four hours, he would take over the watch. Creasy came up the companionway.

'Are you OK?' Tony asked.

'Yes, I was lucky. I just lost a few millimetres off my waist.'

'And the others?'

'Maxie got the bullet out of Tom Sawyer's shoulder. He should be all right. It's lucky we had a full-scale medical kit on board.'

'Those were my orders,' Tony Cope answered. 'How's the lady?'

'Traumatized,' Creasy answered. 'She wouldn't let me near her. Guido's with her. He's given her enough sedation to make her sleep, and he'll keep her asleep until we reach Manila.'

'Then what?'

Creasy stretched his tired body.

'Then Mrs Gloria Manners takes over. I've no doubt she'll hire the best psychologists and take a very personal interest.'

'She sounds like a formidable woman.'

Creasy thought about that, then said, 'I think she may be now. It's not often that you see people change, but I think she has changed.' He glanced at Tony and said, 'By the way you'll be getting a bonus.'

'A bonus?'

'Yes. You were hired to ferry this boat to Honk Kong and back and to pick us up from the beach, not to storm a junk with eight armed men aboard.'

'How much?'

'The same as the rest of the guys . . . five hundred thousand Swiss.'

For a couple of minutes the boat cruised on with only the sound of the engines in their ears. Then Tony Cope said, 'I'll split it with Damon.'

Creasy glanced at him and murmured, 'I thought you'd say that.'

Tony Cope smiled. 'It will clear both our mortgages.'

Creasy stretched again and said, 'Yeah, I guess that's what life is all about.'

EPILOGUE

'He's gone walkabout,' Guido said.

Both Jim Grainger and Juliet looked nonplussed. Guido explained. 'It's an Australian expression that comes from the Aboriginals. Whenever they get overstressed they go into the outback and just roam around for days or weeks or months.'

Juliet asked, 'He left, just like that?'

Guido nodded. He had arrived in Denver after a long flight from Manila. He looked at the young woman and said, 'He asked me to come and talk to you. To explain. It was not something he could talk about on the phone or even put into a letter. He could not do that because he would not know what to say.'

'And you do know what to say?' she asked.

'Definitely. I've known Creasy for about twenty-five years. I know what to tell you, even though he never spoke to me about it. After we arrived in Manila and all the paperwork was sorted out, he packed an overnight bag and asked me to drive him to the airport. He stood in the departure lounge, looking at the departure board, then he turned around and shook my hand and asked me to come and talk to you and to explain. Then he went off to buy a ticket . . . to where, I don't know.'

'Has he done this before?' Grainger asked.

Guido nodded, with a half-smile of recollection.

'Yes. It's not unusual. He holds his emotions tight inside. When he's been badly hurt he wants nobody to see that pain, so he goes amongst strangers. Maybe he drinks a bit too much. Maybe he looks into his soul. Maybe he chases women . . . I don't know . . . nobody knows.'

'Was he badly hurt?' Juliet asked.

265

'No, just a flesh wound.'

'I don't mean that.'

The Italian looked at her for several seconds, then said, 'He lost a son who he loved, and maybe he lost a woman who he might have loved.'

'What's her condition?' Grainger asked.

'Not good. Physically she's OK, but her mind is badly affected. Gloria Manners stayed on in Manila and is looking after her and getting her the best treatment possible. The prognosis of the psychologists is uncertain. She may come through, and if she does – who knows? She may get back with Creasy. I guess it's just a question of waiting. Waiting to see what happens to her and waiting to see when Creasy comes back from his walkabout.'

'Do you think he will come back?' Juliet asked.

'Yes,' Guido answered.

'When?'

'I guess it will be on the night of a full moon. That's the nature of a man like Creasy.'